THE HOUSE
OF PLAIN
TRUTH

Praise for

THE HOUSE OF PLAIN TRUTH

"Emotionally honest, *The House of Plain Truth* is ripe with secrets and sacrifice. Teeming with family drama and lush descriptions that leapt off the page and rooted me in place. Hemans's writing is lyrical and her characters stayed with me long after the book was over."

—SADEQA JOHNSON, author of *The House of Eve*

"*The House of Plain Truth* is a rich and layered novel. It's not only a compelling family mystery and a moving story of generational healing and reconciliation, but also a profound portrait of the emotional aftermath of voluntary and forced migration. An extraordinary achievement."

—MAISY CARD, author of *These Ghosts Are Family*

"Hemans's great triumph is how her prose witnesses history with dignified tenderness and with a clarity that never gets in the reader's way or prescribes what we should feel about the plain truth."

—CELESTE MOHAMMED, author of *Pleasantview*

"A luminous tale. Very few Caribbean writers today render ordinary Caribbean people with the extraordinary acuity of Hemans. *The House of Plain Truth* stands out not only for its keen and rich development of the inner lives of its characters, but also for its thematic echoing of a family's past and present grief, as it attempts to right its future."

—LAUREN FRANCIS-SHARMA, author of *Book of the Little Axe*

"In prose that pulses with the tempo, climate, and luxuriant beauty of Jamaica, Donna Hemans chronicles the tragic consequences of intergenerational migration and estrangement, colonial brutality, and the chaos of revolution on one family. *The House of Plain Truth* is a heart-wrenching novel of loss and grief with profound resonance in today's migratory world."

—AIMEE LIU, author of *Glorious Boy*

"A literary exploration of grief, family schisms, and belonging . . . The novel's sedate pacing, which evokes rocking-chair musings on mortality and responsibility, brings a welcome reprieve from stories laden with plot twists and action for the sake of it. Hemans's thoughtful family tale is a balm for readers."

—*Kirkus Reviews*

Praise for
TEA BY THE SEA

"*Tea by the Sea* is a powder keg of a novel, where secrets and lies explode into truth and consequences, all told with spellbinding, shattering power. Hemans doesn't just fulfill the promise of her debut, she soars past it."

—MARLON JAMES, author of *Black Leopard, Red Wolf*

"An insightful and illuminating prism of a novel, deftly examining familial identity and personal transformation. Hemans turns the kaleidoscope, catching light at different angles, to show us how one person's act of honor and responsibility can also be an act of unspeakable betrayal."

—CAROLYN PARKHURST, author of *The Dogs of Babel*

Also by Donna Hemans

Tea by the Sea

River Woman

THE HOUSE OF PLAIN TRUTH

A Novel

Donna Hemans

ZIBBY BOOKS

NEW YORK

Library of Congress Control Number: 2023934636
Paperback ISBN: 978-1-958506-07-3
Hardcover ISBN: 979-8-9862418-1-4
eBook ISBN: 979-8-9862596-3-5

Book design by Neuwirth & Associates
Cover design by Graça Tito
www.zibbymedia.com

Printed in the United States of America
10 9 8 7 6 5 4 3 2 1

To those who came before me,
without whom none of this would be possible.

"The thing about memory is this: it's who we are. We define ourselves by memories, however shape-shifting they may be."

—Connie May Fowler, "The Edge of the World"

"Sugarcane has always been for us an aggressive plant, foreign and invasive, linked to slavery, exploitation, and power; the palm tree, on the contrary, assumes its undemanding and indigenous freshness in its free, tall, and slender trunk, swaying rhythmically in the breeze."

—Reinaldo Arenas, *Necesidad de Libertad* (Need of Freedom)

PART I

YOU ARE MY MEMORY

January 1993

1.

Pearline knows well the uncertainty of an elder's memory. Knows too well that Rupert is at the age where the past and the present come at him like windswept waves, churning and frothing, then settling into a lick against the sand. Pearline stands by her father's makeshift bed on the veranda, uncertain what the morning will bring, whether he will remember her name or fall back into his memory of a long-ago time. Now that she is back in Mount Pleasant, she has made it her role to take him outside so he can look out at the small forest of fruit trees—breadfruit, pear, guava, soursop, naseberry, cherry, coconut—which he planted over the years. The abundant fruit has fed the family well. Beyond the trees are expansive green pastures dotted with cattle. Without her glasses, Pearline can barely make out the cows, and she guesses that if her father can see that far, the cows would be meaningless specks to him. The cattle are no longer his; her sisters sold his animals a while back and leased a portion of the land to a man who comes every few days to tend to the cows.

Pearline looks down at Rupert, her back to the rail, her palms flat against the wood. "Tell me the names of your children," she says. Each morning now she makes the same request, eager to catch the moments when he does remember something of the present. She is never sure if he hears her and simply doesn't care to answer or if his mind has wandered and he's unable to give an immediate response. His mouth moves, but she doesn't expect him to speak. She has learned through her years nursing elderly patients to fill the air with words, to let her voice spread like an oversized soap bubble enlarging with each breath, not louder but increasingly present, a voice that reminds her patients that they haven't been forgotten.

As if on cue, her sisters Hermina and Aileen step out on the veranda, and Pearline looks up, her gaze sweeping and quick. Hermina has pulled her hair back. Her round face, fully exposed, looks younger and fresher, as if she just washed it. Pearline touches her own face, rubbing a hand over her cheeks and around her mouth, over the splotches of dry spots that have cropped up again the last few days, feeling her own full cheeks and chin.

"The first girl name Annie," Rupert whispers and takes a deep breath. His voice is raspy.

Pearline, who thought the moment had passed, glances quickly at Aileen, who's wiping her hands on an apron, imitating their mother's age-old habit. Pearline arches her eyebrows, watching surprise bloom on both her sisters' faces. Aileen mouths, "Oh my," and turns back to face Rupert. Pearline wants to grasp her sisters' hands, hold on tight the way beauty contestants do as they await the crowning moment. Instead, she grasps the railing with its thick, uneven layers of paint and holds her body still so as not to disrupt her father.

Slowly, Rupert lists his children, unaware, it seems, that the women who stand around him are them. "Aileen. Pearline. Hermina." He can't lift his hands to count. But at the very end he manages to name all his children, including four names he hasn't uttered in nearly sixty years: Annie, Gerardo, Arturo, and David. "Arturo dead long time now. Just a boy."

Pearline weeps and lifts first her right arm, then the left, to catch her tears with the collar of her dress. She turns to Aileen and Hermina. "Mama must be turning over in her grave now. Long time she wait to hear him say their names. Long time she wait for him to remember we aren't his only children."

Hermina wipes away a tear and, turning to face the veranda, says, "Is about time. Nobody should hold all that anger in their heart for so long."

Rupert keeps his eyes on a coconut tree frond that dips and rises, each movement revealing the dull green husks of young coconuts, the brown husks of others that have already aged and dried, and a sliver of blue sky visible between the leaves. Or so it seems.

"Funny what we remember," Aileen says. "Reach this big age and all you can remember are the things from the early, early part of your life. You live this long and all you achieve mean nothing to you. Not a damn thing."

Aileen stresses the last, and Pearline thinks it's meant for her—the sister who went to America, the sister who didn't always come home for one work-related reason or another. She's trying hard not to let the hints her sisters drop build up and settle too deeply inside her. She's trying not to let her suspicious nature get in the way of this momentous moment that may never be repeated.

"He must be hungry," Pearline says.

Aileen and Hermina head back inside the house, one behind the other. Soon, one will bring him porridge, mint tea or hot chocolate, and a slice of bread that Pearline or her sisters will dip into the drink before feeding it to him soggy and dripping.

For the moment, Pearline looks out on what her father sees. Her mind churns around what she would have missed had she not come home to Jamaica and this little country house when she did. How close she had come to missing this moment when her father finally acknowledged his long-lost children. Her life had been full, kept busy with this and that. She had been too busy making a life in Brooklyn, too busy trying not to fulfill her family's legacy of failure. Three night shifts here, five day shifts there. She had been a nurse who sometimes doubled as a home health aide. She was also a mother and grandmother and church sister, busying herself to someday return home with everything, with a fulfilled life. She had come home to give up busyness.

Rupert named his children, and now Pearline begins to think that some people refuse to be forgotten. They, these siblings of hers who have lived only in her family's collective memory of a moment on a wharf in Santiago de Cuba, want to be heard. That moment, which marks the last time the living members of her family were together, is stamped in her memory. She replays it now as she has done over the years: Rupert wears his best suit and hat—he is never without his hat—and her mother, Irene, wears a starched white dress, her belly big with the baby she would name Hermina. Pearline is four and Aileen seven. Those are the two girls who return in 1933 to Jamaica. Their oldest sister, Annie, is already a married woman who chooses to stay behind in Cuba. And David and Gerardo, soon-to-be men, are staying behind too. Irene extracts a promise from Annie to take care of the boys. The goodbyes are loud and long and the voices like a cacophony of birds—English and Haitian creole, spoken by the people who are leaving, and Spanish from those overseeing the departures. Annie leans over, whispers, "On a clear day, you can see Cuba from there." Pearline believes her, and she and Aileen look out at the blue sea for a glimpse of the distant island, Jamaica. And then they are gone, the last two baby girls in the family, repatriated at the government's expense to an island they'd never known. Hermina was nearly born on the ship, but Irene makes it to shore before the baby comes.

There isn't room on the ship even for a song. A single whistle, maybe, but not a song. Rupert wants no disturbance, no outward signs of displeasure or anxiety or disappointment. A ship's passage paid for by the government isn't the way he wants to return home. He wants to come home like the men who went to Panama—the Colón man with his gold chain and pocket watch. So he finds fault in everything—the waves that rock the boat; the men who report from deck on the land visible in the distance; the clouds that roll behind, threatening rain; Pearline and Aileen, nervous and fidgeting, looking forward. From where they stand, there is no looking back. Even if they could have looked back, Rupert would have ordered them not to. From the moment he stepped onto the ship, he turned his back on Cuba and his children left behind on the wharf . . . until now—this moment when he calls the forbidden names.

Pearline wipes away fresh tears and turns again to her father and her older sister, returning to the veranda with a yellow plastic tray holding a bowl of porridge. The slice of hard dough bread sits in the porridge, already softening to mush.

"Breakfast," Pearline says, and slides into the chair by her father's side before Aileen can do so. She's playing her role well: dutiful daughter and returned resident.

"Just a little." Pearline spoons up a bit of porridge and cuts into the soggy bread. She barely looks up when Aileen steps back inside, though she hears Aileen giggle and say, "Mek she stay. She have a lot to mek up for."

Rupert barely opens his mouth, acting like a stubborn child refusing to cooperate. His stubbornness, though, isn't a product of old age, but it is the shape around which her entire childhood had grown.

He reaches for Pearline's hand, but he is too weak to tug on it. His lips move as if to speak, and she leans in close, her ear against his mouth to catch his words. He struggles to find his voice, or perhaps he is simply swallowing the small spoonful of porridge she managed to slip into his mouth. Pearline pats his hand and leans toward the tray at her side to spoon more porridge. But he reaches for her hand again.

"Rest little bit," Pearline says. "Look like you don't want the porridge. I going to bring you little tea."

Again, Rupert opens his mouth, and this time he utters one clear word after another. "Find them for me," he whispers.

"What you say, Papa?" Pearline leans in even closer, her ear almost touching his lips.

"Find them for me." Rupert's words are low, barely audible.

"Who?"

"You know." Rupert runs his tongue over his chapped lips and shifts his head again in Pearline's direction. "You are my memory now."

His voice is a ragged whisper, but the request is simple and clear. Her nursing instinct kicks in. Aphasia comes to mind, or some other condition linked to the functioning of his brain and his ability to combine words that make sense. She makes a note to ask Hermina and Aileen whether they observed any stroke symptoms but also keeps him talking to determine if his wandering mind has simply tricked him into thinking he is a young man living in a long-ago time. "Who you mean, Papa?"

Pearline watches his lips move, working to form another word. Spit collects in the corners of his mouth, and his lips are chapped. Pearline releases his fingers and stands up. "Ah going to get you some water."

Rupert drinks a few spoonfuls of the tepid water, and Pearline wipes away what dribbles down his chin. A lizard darts across the rail, and the movement catches Rupert's eye. He shifts his head, the motion deliberate and jerky, and settles his eyes on the little girl in the distance shaking guavas from a tree. Rupert lifts his right hand, his index finger shaking, but never quite points directly at the girl, who is simply a flash of red and yellow in a dress.

"Arturo." The word is barely audible, and Pearline isn't convinced that's what he says. He lowers his hand slow and steady, lifts it, and points again at the child. "Arturo. *Ven acá.*"

"That's Claudia," Pearline says. "You know Yvonne. She was

here taking care of you. That's her daughter. Long time now Arturo dead." Pearline catches herself. She knows she's rambling on about distant family relations Rupert won't remember. Besides, will it matter whether he thinks the figure in the distance is his long-dead son or her cousin Yvonne's little girl? "Take another sip," she says instead.

Rupert clamps his mouth, and Pearline sees no need to force him. She puts the cup on the floor and stands to watch Claudia collecting guavas in the skirt of her dress. When her skirt is full, Claudia runs around the side of the house to the kitchen with the weight of the guavas pulling her dress tight against her neck. A button pops. Pearline steps down on the gravel driveway, peering closely for the button, hoping it's a bright color distinct from the gray and white stones. Having delivered the fruit to Hermina and Aileen, Claudia comes back out, her steps slow and deliberate now, her lips pressed around the yellow skin of a guava. She looks up at Rupert, changes direction, and climbs the stairs. She stops chewing long enough to count each wooden stair out loud. At the top of the stairs, she turns left toward the old man, circles the makeshift bed, and leans forward to see if he is awake.

Pearline walks back and forth on the gravel, wearing out a short path the length of the veranda. She hears Claudia say her own name, imitating what the adults in her life do when they stand before the old man. "My name is Claudia."

Again, Claudia leans toward Rupert. "What you say?"

From the far end of the veranda, Pearline sees her father try to lift his hand. She can't tell exactly, but it appears he's again trying to say something. Always a nurse, she hurries back toward him. His breath is shallow, coming in quick spurts. He reaches out, grabs at the air. It seems he's trying to touch Claudia, to pull her close. His fingers brush her skin, and Claudia, holding the guava close to his mouth, bends toward him.

"No." Pearline's voice is harsher than she wants.

Rupert's lips move. "Arturo," he says and reaches for Claudia's hand. Something about the girl aggravates him or reminds him of his son, the one who never became a man. Rupert is alert, more alert than he has been in the week Pearline has been home, and she is torn between letting his memory unfold and sending Claudia away. She wants to hear what he has to say, why Arturo's name is the one he utters now.

"Arturo, go inside now." His voice is still ragged and weak, not as commanding as he seems to want it to be.

"Claudia," the girl says again, tapping her chest and biting into the guava.

Pearline sees that her father is becoming agitated by the girl's presence—too much so. His breath comes faster. The artery in his neck pulses strong. As Pearline turns to send Claudia away, Rupert opens his mouth, hiccups, and takes a big gasping breath.

"No, Papa." Pearline leans in, grabbing his wrist to feel his pulse. She shifts to Claudia. "Go call your aunties. Go. Go." Without meaning to, Pearline's voice is harsh again. She's clinical. She searches Rupert's wrist and ankles for veins thrumming with blood, presses her hand against his chest to feel for his beating heart. Pearline knows what this is. Just as quickly, she is the dutiful daughter, emotional rather than clinical, just a daughter trying to remember her father's last words and chiding herself for waiting so long to come back home. He had spoken just now, and she thinks his heart gave out in response to whatever had aggravated him so.

"Sister Pearl say to come." Claudia's little voice is loud, filling up the house, blowing back to the veranda.

Pearline blocks out the patter of footsteps on the floor, the birds cawing in the trees, and Hermina asking, "What happen?" Pearline banks the last thing Rupert said: *Arturo. Go inside now.* She catalogs his effort, the urgency he tried but failed to convey. Even at the very end, Rupert was shielding his son, perhaps making amends for something he had failed to do at an earlier time. And she sears in her memory the words Rupert whispered before his last command: *Find them for me. You are my memory now.*

A cloud moves across the sun, momentarily dimming the light. Hermina and Aileen stop midstride. Pearline looks up briefly at the sky, her mind racing to pull meaning out of everything—her father's last request, the dimming of the light, her recent and sudden decision to move back home. The cloud moves on, and sunlight again paints the veranda.

"Papa gone home," Pearline says. "He lived a good, long life."

2.

It's late afternoon when the caravan of cars turns off the main road and the passengers trek past the house, past the semicircle of citrus plants and another half circle of croton plants to the small family cemetery in the clearing out back. The croton plants' variegated leaves flutter above the open pit where the pallbearers and funeral home attendants will lower Rupert's casket. Red dirt is banked around the hole, and looking at it now, Pearline feels the tears she has been holding back welling up. She steps away from the gravediggers— sweat-stained and tired—who stand to the side, waiting to finish their task; away from the mourners who crowd in, leaving only a small space for family; away even from those reaching out to pat her arm or attempting to draw her into an embrace. Instead of stopping, Pearline waves tentatively, brushes her fingers against a woman's open and sweaty palm, pats another woman on her shoulder, and keeps walking.

"That the second daughter," Pearline hears a woman say. "She live a foreign now."

Aileen and Hermina remain up front, flanked on either side by their children, grandchildren, and husbands. Aileen, taller, thinner, holds her head down. Hermina, in distinct contrast,

is shorter, squat, and holds her back straight, head up, exposing every tear, every sputter. Pearline stays back, too tearful to
watch the final lowering of the casket or sing the mournful
hymns. Near Pearline, someone starts singing, "Soon and very
soon, we are going to see the king. No more crying now, we
are going to see the king . . ." She busies herself with Claudia,
brushing lint from the child's hair and dress and using her
fingers to tame the short strands of hair that have coiled into
little knots at her nape.

The crowd picks up the song, singing louder and louder,
bodies swaying as gently as leaves in the breeze. Every now
and then someone claps, trying to maintain the beat, but that
peters out quickly, and the moment remains solemn. Under
the canopy of trees, it feels as if each song rises and stops, settles above and around the group, shutting out the rest of the
living world.

As soon as that song ends, another begins, one running so
smoothly into the other that it feels practiced, feels as if this
entire group of people simply goes from funeral to funeral like
a choir hired to mourn the dead. Now that Pearline is here in
the yard of her childhood home, away from the church and no
longer standing near the altar with her back to the full congre-
gation, she can look around and take stock of who has come,
the faces from the past that she remembers, the members of
the community whose lives she knows nothing about, Aileen's
and Hermina's friends and coworkers whom she may never see
again. Once, she could recite everyone's story, point to a house,
and say, "Mattie mother build that house after the hurricane of '51," point to a child and say, "Lenny granddaughter,"

or hear a cock crowing and know the neighbor's yard where the sound originated. The names don't come as easily now, and the faces, weathered by years and circumstances, make it hard for Pearline to figure out who's who. But this game, matching faces and names and attempting to tag both to long-ago events, helps take her mind off the funereal hymns, the finality of the burial.

Pearline waits for the ping of dirt hitting the casket and steps back even farther outside the canopy, behind the row of croton plants this time. She doesn't want to see the final closure of the grave, doesn't want to hear the dirt raining down on the casket, doesn't want to hear the shovels mixing and scooping concrete. She's stood through this portion of a burial only once—for her mother. That time, she was near the place where her sisters now stand, just behind her father, who knelt next to the hole in the ground and watched the final sealing off of a life. Pearline and Hermina had knelt with him too, their arms draped around his back. Aileen stood behind him, ready to hold him back if necessary. Even now, Pearline feels the contractions of his midsection, his muscle and bone convulsing beneath her fingers, the untamed emotion wracking his body. It had frightened her then, that unfiltered display she had never seen in him. Her father, so stoic and stubborn in his daily life, came apart at his wife's graveside. The sound of shovels mixing concrete stayed with Pearline too, and from there on out, each time she hears that sound, she remembers her father kneeling in the dirt, crying, talking through his tears as if his wife were sitting on the other side hearing him out.

He had held up a hand too, momentarily stopping the

gravediggers from filling in the hole. "Mi just wan' say one last thing." He choked out the words, and the men stopped their movements, waiting for the grieving husband to say his final goodbye. Sound fell away. The immediate surroundings were so quiet, it felt as though life itself were gone and the three of them had been transported elsewhere. Her father leaned forward, not dipping his head toward the casket that was already settled in the hole but jutting his head as if he saw Irene sitting directly across from him on the other side of the grave. His eyes didn't waver from that single place. Pearline moved her hand from his back to his arm, uncertain if he would topple forward onto the casket, ready to grab at him if he leaned too far forward. They sat like that for what seemed like a long while, the solemn hymns rising up around them, until at last Irene's siblings stepped forward and slowly began dribbling dirt onto the casket.

This time Pearline can't get far enough away. Each hymn seems louder, and she thinks of the hymns as vines wrapping themselves around her body, not comforting but choking and causing her grief to spill without control. It's Claudia who comforts Pearline, wiping her cheeks and making small circles on her back. Pearline cries for her father, for her daughter Josette and the granddaughters she left behind in New York, for Claudia, who has taken her granddaughters' place. She cries for this new life of hers as a returned resident who gave up her life in America and came back home just in time for her father's last week alive. Only two weeks old, this new life she's carving out is already shifting. Mostly, Pearline cries because she knows her daughter will never mourn her as Pearline mourns her father now or as her father once mourned her mother. And what, she asks herself, is the meaning of this life if she isn't mourned or remembered at the very end?

"You come back just in time, eh?" The woman who speaks wraps an arm around Pearline's shoulders.

Except for Pearline's nieces and nephews and grandnieces and grandnephews, still lingering inside, the woman is the last of the mourners to leave. Pearline scratches around her memory for a name, gives up, and just nods. She knows the face—perhaps a friend of her parents, a neighbor, or a distant relative? They're walking toward the remnants of the gate in the dwindling sunlight. The shadows are long, not yet eerie, and Pearline wants this part of the evening to come to an end, to wrap up all the talk about the old times and simply sit with her own memories.

"Your father used to worry that unu would just sell the place. All o' you have unu own life all the same. Unu own house and thing." The woman stops and looks back through the dimming light at the house.

"Walk good," Pearline says, cutting off what the woman would have said next.

It's not a stranger's place to tell her and her sisters what to do with the house and land. She knows what her parents wanted, what she wants. Selling isn't an option she has considered. She faces the house and, in the low evening light, looks at it as a stranger does. The house seems smaller now to her adult eyes. Once, the house had been beautiful, but its beauty has faded with age and neglect and a patchwork of hasty fixes. Zinc sheets, held in place by concrete blocks, cover some shingles on the roof. There are at least two places on the veranda ceiling where the replacement wood isn't the exact width or length of the original wood, and along the side of the house is a combination of old window shutters and newer wood louvers. She wants them all to be the same, either shutters or louvers, but not both. The cut-stone walls need a fresh coat of paint, white, of course, but she thinks it would be good to add some color, paint it a light yellow or white with blue tint. She has never been good at choosing colors from a color wheel. The myriad shades paralyze her. When her husband, Ronnie, was alive, she would go to her closet or Josette's, pick a fabric with a color closest to what she liked, and send her husband to match that shade. After his death, she left it up to Josette to choose between duck-egg blue, robin-egg blue, aqua, and cyan. With neither of them here now, she may have to settle for whatever color her sisters choose.

The coconut trees look limp, diseased, nothing like Rupert had dreamed. Whenever he talked about his dream, he pointed to the great house on the hill above their property that survived revolts and hurricanes and multiple owners over the last two or three centuries, and the coconut and palm trees that line the driveway to this day. He said coconut trees represent freedom, unlike cane. But every coconut tree he planted quailed, dying from a disease he couldn't name, quashing one part of his dream over and over again.

Pearline hesitates for a moment, kicks up dust with her

feet, and steps on a shame o' lady growing along the driveway. She watches the leaves fold in, the plant's reflexive response to threats, and walks on, head down, looking for more of the ground-hugging plants. To the left, Pearline's young grand-nieces and grandnephews play a game with Claudia, but from a distance, she can't tell what it is other than a game that involves running and screaming. The laughter makes Pearline think again of her own daughter and grandchildren thousands of miles away, far removed from this moment.

"Whew," Aileen says and falls back into a chair. "This is the part that always get to me. People come and act like they haven't seen food in a week."

"It's over," Hermina says. "I tell Paul and my children, when I die, none of this. Bury me the next day so you don't have to plan a repast and all o' this. No nine night. Just put me in the ground. And I telling you both now, I don't even want a eulogy. Anything good anybody have to say 'bout me, let them say it now when I can still hear."

"That won't matter," Aileen says. She rakes her fingers through her hair, disturbing the now limp curls, exposing the coils underneath the straight, pressed ends. "They'll still come and sing every night for a whole week."

Pearline laughs uneasily. They're caught, she knows, between the old ways and the new, the long-standing traditions of nine nights and gatherings at the dead yard in the days leading up to a funeral. "You know as bad as it is, I missed this part in America. Too many times, all the family had was a viewing at a funeral home, two, three hours at most. Yes, people come by from time to time, but not the weeklong mourning. When

Ronnie died, same thing. Yes, people came by and talked, brought food. But we didn't have the all-night set up. No sah. And the viewings at funeral homes, not the same at all. It feel so . . . What the word I looking for?" She waves her hand, settles on "It's not intimate."

"I know what you mean," Hermina says. "It lacks the cultural context. That sound so academic. But is true. Nothing like sitting down on your veranda and watching people come sit and mourn with you all time o' day and night."

"Go to foreign and adopt the foreign ways." Aileen doesn't look at Pearline as she speaks.

Pearline waits for more, waits for whatever feelings Aileen harbors to surface, because those words feel like an indirect accusation, a quiet upbraiding of some American way of doing things that Pearline carried back home to Jamaica. Even Claudia, as young as she is, picks up on it too, saying things like "She smell o' foreign" and watching Pearline spread mosquito repellent on her arms and legs rather than sit inside away from the mosquitoes swarming outside on the veranda. It worries her a little how her years away have changed her speech and attitude and set her apart from her sisters. Sometimes she feels herself trying too hard with whatever she says or does, trying too hard to sprinkle patois in her speech and ending with a feeling that she's performing Jamaicanness.

But all Aileen says is "Night goin' catch us on the road. And unu know I don't like to be on the road in the dark."

"Room here for anybody who wan' stay." Pearline spreads her hands.

Aileen nods. "Just want to spread out in my own bed and

not have a soul bother me in the morning. Once the young people finish cleanup inside, I gone."

They're quiet for a while, the silence on the veranda like a blanket, warm and comforting. On the other side of the house, Hermina's and Aileen's children and grandchildren chuckle, telling stories of their own. Josette is the only one missing, and Pearline swallows hard when she remembers that. Theirs is an age-old battle, a daughter blaming her mother for not doing enough to save her father. No matter how much Pearline reminds herself about forgiving and forgetting, she still hears her daughter's voice, the accusation built into her distinctly Brooklyn accent, her accent a mashup of several Caribbean island accents and an American one: "You're a nurse. How come you didn't know?" And indeed, had Pearline not worked a double shift, had she come home that night for more than two hours of sleep, she would have heard her husband's slurred speech, possibly seen the left side of his face drooping. But she woke and hurried out again for the second job as a home health aide for an elderly man who wanted to die at home. In one night, she lost two to death—a patient and a husband. She also lost her daughter, who had always been her daddy's girl and had morphed into a teenager who thought her father was next to an angel and her mother Cinderella's stepmother reincarnated. Sometimes Pearline thinks her daughter also blames her for the death of the baby brother whose heart failed in the hours after his birth. It's an old story, but it feels like a present and raw one, especially now when they should be together, mother and daughter comforting each other, and Josette with her cousins cleaning up and building their own bonds.

Indeed, Pearline had worked—and worked hard. For at the back of her mind was a single driving factor: She would not carry forward her family's legacy of failure to another generation. Her father had tried and failed; he migrated to Cuba with the belief that he would make his fortune there. But he came back to Jamaica with next to nothing, just enough, he said, to buy this property on which they've lived some sixty years now. Once he returned, most everything he touched thereafter failed. Pearline couldn't repeat her father's mistake. And didn't. But at what cost?

"All the same," Pearline says, breaking the silence. She stops immediately because she hadn't meant to speak out loud. She sounds like her mother, who used that phrase to wave off conversations.

"All the same what?" Aileen asks.

"Nothing," Pearline says. "Lost my train of thought."

Somewhere inside are Hermina's and Aileen's husbands, likely asleep with their heads thrown against the back of a sofa. Pearline is ready for the day to end, to wind down her emotions and let something else in. Times like these she misses her husband's presence—a fleeting touch on her shoulder, an arm dropping around her waist, him pulling her against his body and the two of them moving slowly to a song playing in the background, both of them belting out the words, one voice hopelessly out of tune, the other a bit more in tune. Always, always, she dropped her head into the crook of his shoulder, and they sang—usually a song from the early days of their love—from beginning to end, and at the end both laughed, surprised they remembered the words. It's been years now since she has danced like that, felt the breadth of a man's chest against her own and the longing in her loins. All that is behind her now, and that isn't the kind of memory she wants to let back in. Not now.

"You know, my first real memory of this house is of Papa whacking cane stalks." Now that Pearline is back for good, memories like these float like bugs to a lamp light. "He got up early one morning, probably the day after we moved in here, and chopped down every bit of cane."

"Don't remember that at all," Aileen says.

"You never remember anything. And Hermina, you weren't born yet, or maybe it was just after you were born." Pearline remembers distinctly her father swinging his arms like a crazed man, the thup, thup of the machete hitting the stalks, the ping of the metal against stone, and her mother gripping her two children tight and yelling at Rupert to stop. He cleared the entire area, transforming the swath of land behind the house. "After Cuba, he never wanted to work in a cane field again."

"Yeah, he always used to say that," Aileen says. "He couldn't stomach the smell of burning cane either."

"Come to think of it, I never saw him eating cane," Hermina says.

Another burst of laughter rises up from inside. Pearline can't hear what the younger ones are talking about, but she's happy they've stayed to clean up, happy that she can end her day like this instead of washing pots and pans and wiping up spills.

Hermina starts to say something else, pauses, stands up, and shakes out her legs. She stretches, and her dress rides up, exposing a slip and her thighs, soft and dimpled now. She's thickened in middle age into a plumper, fuller version of Irene. Pearline looks down on her own legs and thighs, plump, too, with no hint of defined muscles. Give it six months, she tells herself, of handwashing clothes, sweeping and mopping floors, gardening, eating meals cooked from scratch. She'll be at the more comfortable weight her doctor wanted to see.

"Monday we have to start look 'bout the will and what to do with the place," Hermina says at last.

"What you mean by 'do with the place'?" Pearline leans forward to catch her sisters' eyes.

Aileen and Hermina look at each other, and Pearline senses something, suspects a previous conversation and the two of them anticipating this response from her. They have a code now, a shared way of communicating that makes her feel left out, and she thinks again of that chasm that opened up because of her American life. She is outside their *us girls*.

"What you planning?" Pearline asks again.

"One huff and puff and the whole house will fall down." Hermina looks directly at her now. "You know how stubborn Papa was. Nothing could move him."

"I have my own piece of property," Aileen says. "Can't take on the headache of managing another one. And to tell you the truth, we could all use the money if we sell."

"Stone walls," Pearline says. "This house not going anywhere."

"Stone or not," Aileen says, "this house too old. The upkeep will take every penny you have. Better you tear it down and build something new. Better yet, sell the land and use the money to buy something in Discovery Bay next to Hermina or down the road there in Cardiff Hall. And who is to tell how long you going to stay? When hard life lick you and you pack up and gone back to America, it's me and Hermina who still going to have this headache."

Pearline hasn't given much thought to the ease with which she can move between two countries and how this may bother her sisters. Aileen means to say Pearline can be American when it suits her and Jamaican when it doesn't. She can return for a complicated medical procedure that might not be available in Jamaica. She can easily seek refuge elsewhere if a natural disaster levels the island. Coming from Aileen—a simple statement of fact—it sounds bitter and harsh. Pearline hasn't flaunted the duality of her life, hasn't made a habit of showing off her American life. She starts to refute Aileen's claim, starts to explain that she intends to give up her permanent visa, but Hermina moves to the railing, talking as she moves and keeping her back to Pearline.

"It's not the house so much. It's the cattle and the crops and whole business of managing them and selling things. It not easy, and the last thing I want to do in my old age is manage this place and be running round trying to sell a little of this crop and a little of that one and worrying 'bout drought killing everything you plant and hurricane mashing up everything. Plus who coming to tief what they don't plant. All it has ever been is a headache. Headache for Mama. Headache for Papa. Why you think it going to be any better for us?"

"So you want to sell it?"

"Of course. What we going to do with all this property?"

Hermina turns around, a glint of light hitting her face and glasses. "Just about everything Papa plant here die."

"Not everything." Pearline is thinking of the callaloo plants with big green leaves, the quarts of peas they shelled and sieved as girls, crocus bags full of pimento seeds, coconut ready for the market, bunches of banana and plantain. The guava trees. Yes, sometimes the crops failed. "Every other Jamaican running down property, looking for dead lef'. Except you two, who want to sell the only thing your parents pass down to you. Anyway, we can't sell it. You know it's not what Papa wanted. Or Mama, even."

"The dead don't have a say in it." Aileen waves her hand, punctuating her dismissive words.

Pearline closes her eyes, presses her fingers over her eyes to stanch the tears she feels coming. Her father's dream was to have the rambling and needy house always surrounded by rows of coconut trees, cattle, and produce of every kind. It's the dream of most every migrant worker who left the island at one time or another to toil in distant lands: return home with something and build an even bigger life. Her dream is simpler, closer to her mother's: maintain the house as a refuge to which her wandering family can always return. It's why she came back to Jamaica.

"Papa . . ." she begins again. "You know the two of them wanted this land to be here for family. Ours. The one place we can always come back to. We can't sell it."

Aileen leans forward. "All this time you in America, it's the two of us managing all of it. Running 'bout the place to doctor and tax office, and leasing the land, and running off squatters from the bottom piece, fixing roof when hurricane come. All this time you in America, we running things. I'm tired, and I will do anything to get rid of this headache. Anything."

"You forget the well and the water pump," Hermina adds. "Not to mention—"

"All right, all right. I get it," Pearline says. "The house old."

"Miss America vex." Aileen chuckles.

"Miss America?" Pearline doesn't laugh. She breathes deeply, a practiced response. It takes her back to her childhood days, Aileen older and bossy, a needler who stopped only when her verbal jabs brought tears. She's much too old for it, but she feels it again, the burning need to cry, to let all the emotion wound up inside trickle away. "Too tired to talk about all this now," she says instead. "Let it stay till next week when the dust settle."

"Yes," Aileen says.

Even after the last cars leave and the last of the sunlight disappears, Pearline stays on the veranda in a low-slung chair with a burning mosquito coil on the floor near her feet. This is exactly as she imagined the second half of her life: a settled woman sitting quietly and contemplatively, watching the evening close like a hibiscus bloom with no urgent mission demanding her time. Except there is Claudia, who Pearline jokes has come with the house and who must be fed and dressed. Claudia comes out into the yard with a rope. Not mindful of the dark, Claudia skips down the stairs and starts twirling the rope, which grazes the stones on the driveway, the gravel slipping and sliding beneath her feet.

3.

A FLOCK OF JABBERING CROWS SETS UP IN THE BARE branches of a dying breadfruit tree. Their caws, loud and raucous, are a grating intrusion on Pearline's new morning ritual: standing on the veranda as her father once stood, palms on the railing, trying to read the sky. The morning fog slowly burns off, and the clouds shift as if a puppeteer were pulling a string for the big reveal. Here, in Mount Pleasant, the hillside town of her childhood, Pearline no longer has access to all-news radio and the weather reports that come every twenty-two minutes. As far as she can tell, each day of the last two weeks that she has been back—a full-time resident of Jamaica—the weather forecasts have been wrong, or specific to Kingston and Montego Bay, leaving out a wide swath of the hilly countryside. She tries to determine whether the dark clouds mean rain is imminent or whether the clouds will burn off with the emerging sun. What she wants is a dry day, without the pelting tropical rain turning the dirt around her father's burial site into a bed of oozing mud. There's more work to do there, and she wants it done right and soon.

It's Pearline's first full moment of quiet after the funeral. Except for Claudia, the house is empty, and, for a moment, she is thankful that Aileen and Hermina have stopped dropping by every morning like they did when she first arrived. None of the relatives who came from abroad for the funeral wanted to stay in her family's old house, opting instead for all-inclusive hotels along the coast that exude an opulence the old house couldn't even try to muster. Instead of old-world colonial charm, the house threatens with every passing year to separate from its foundation and crumple into a heap of dust and stone. The window shutters creak with every bit of breeze, the floorboards dip, and the lighting and plumbing have a mind of their own. She loves the house despite its faults. Loves it mostly because it is the one place she's known to which she could always return.

It's still early, but she dials Josette's number, preferring not to overthink her daughter's reaction to the early-morning call. "I wish you had tried harder to come," Pearline says.

"Mom, it's like you're not hearing what I'm saying. The girls and school. Aftercare. The money . . . It's not a good time for us to spend that kind of money."

"I told you not to worry 'bout the money. It's your grandfather, your last grandparent. You should have been here for this." Pearline knows she should let it go, but she harps on it, angling, it seems, for a chance to say something else. She hears Josette's exaggerated breath, braces for something harsh from her daughter.

"Mom, it's not like I can get on a plane and come now. So what's the use bringing it up? Anyway, how did everything go?"

Pearline pictures Josette sitting on the edge of the bed, head down, tapping her fingers on her knee, waiting to be rid of her

mother. What's the use? Pearline wants to throw the statement back at Josette, wants to ask if a daughter being there for
her grieving mother is too much to ask. "As well as could be
expected," she says instead. Though Pearline is glad no family
members stayed at the house, she craves adult company, wants
to lean back in her father's chair and talk.

"Good."

"How my girls?"

"Still sleeping, but they'll be up any minute now. Yup. Right
on time. I can hear Elana crying about a missing doll. I can see
how my day's going to go." Josette pauses. "All right, Mom. Let
me see if I can stop this before it gets worse. We'll talk later."

Pearline wishes Josette had said something more, had
stayed on the call long enough to ask about Pearline's new
life away from Brooklyn, had given her an opportunity to
tell her about Claudia—the five-year-old girl who is always
somewhere near. Claudia's mother had found a new job in the
Cayman Islands. She left so quickly after Pearline arrived and
took over her father's care that Pearline believes Yvonne must
have been thinking about her departure, planning her escape
to Cayman. Pearline doesn't know if the girl was ever a part of
that plan, but she is Pearline's responsibility now, at least until
her mother returns or another relative steps up to care for the
child. Josette knows nothing about what her mother has been
doing in the two weeks since she gave up her life in Brooklyn.

Pearline has accepted her mistake: the way she told Josette
her plans to move back to Jamaica for good. The memory of
that moment sits like oil on water, always at the top of her
mind. She and Josette are in Pearline's living room, looking

out on the moonlight glinting off fresh snow that has transformed their slice of Brooklyn into a postcard version of its gritty, hard-edged self. Behind Pearline, her granddaughters had built a tent—a king-sized sheet draped over chairs—and spread their cartoon-covered sleeping bags and blankets on the floor. Pearline lies between them and points a flashlight toward the top of the tent, softly dimming the light like that of a partially obscured full moon. She tells the girls Anansi stories, and even though the girls are much too young to understand the fantastical trickster tales, they want more. Pearline talks until the girls' soft snores begin to mingle with her voice.

"If only it were always this easy," Pearline says as she crawls from under the makeshift tent. She stretches, then lowers her body to the sofa, sinking into the soft cushions.

Camping in the living room was Pearline's idea, and with the snow building up now, there was no use in Josette and the girls heading home.

"They would love it if you did that every night." Josette eases into what sounds like a rehearsed speech. "You should move to Long Island, move in with us. You can have the whole apartment in the basement. All yours."

"Not at all." Pearline isn't sure exactly how her words sound. "The only island I'm moving to is Jamaica."

"Mom, we could use the help, somebody to pick up the girls from school, watch them in the afternoon."

"All I think about these days is sitting down on the veranda in the morning with a cup of cocoa tea. Maybe coffee. All I want is to sit down and watch the sun rise. Don't want to *have* to do a thing. When you get to my age, you'll understand how much the little break from obligations means."

"Sounds selfish," Josette says.

"One day your children will tell you something just as hurtful and you'll understand." Pearline's voice is quiet, without emotion. "I didn't raise you that way." Of course she had thought of her grandchildren, how infrequently she would see them once she moved back home. She had thought of Josette too, growing up in Brooklyn away from both sets of grandparents, aunts and uncles, and cousins, dipping into Jamaica for holidays but always standing out as a foreign child. She had weighed it all, and her decision came down to not ever again wanting to fight to take up space. "Anyway, I'm leaving week after next. The house is yours if you want to move back to Brooklyn. No mortgage to pay. You all can save some money. If you don't want it, I'll rent it out, get a company to manage it. Later in the year I'll come back and look 'bout things."

"You really moving, just like that?"

"Don't make it sound impulsive, like I didn't think this through."

"But it sounds rushed. And yes, impulsive."

"Long time I want to go home. See this here?" Pearline holds up a sealed manila envelope with her perfectly slanted handwriting on the front and several stamps fixed in the corner. "This is my green card. I'm sending it back after I finish with all the business I have to do. I'm done with America now. Thirty years I've lived in this country. It's time for me to go back home. When I left Jamaica way back then—1961—I didn't expect to stay away this long. But I got married, had you, worked, buried a husband, and worked and worked and worked some more. All I wanted was to see you settled. And you are—husband, children, good job. My body tired, and now it's my time to rest."

"All this planning and not a word to me."

Josette's comment sits between them like a boulder too heavy for the two of them to roll.

In the kitchen, Pearline turns off the flame under the pot of grated cocoa nut she's boiling with coconut milk and cinnamon and then steps back out with a mug of the steaming chocolate tea. It's the drink of her childhood, cocoa grated and boiled into a rich and creamy hot drink. This time she heads to the chair she had set up beneath the guava tree to contemplate the quiet before the day's work begins. The crows are at it again. She prefers the brown doves' coos, the soft twits of the yellow belly bird, or even the parakeets' caws. She's getting accustomed to the quiet of the countryside, the intrusion of the wildlife's calls. Half a lifetime in Brooklyn, and what she knows are city noises: sirens wailing, horns tooting, rap or reggae or Latin music booming from a passing car, the hum of tires on the asphalt roads. She's slowly getting used to life without twenty-four hours of neon lights, cold air vented into her rooms, the ease of walking to a corner store on Utica Avenue for some necessary thing, the hurried walk to the dank, underground subway station, rushing through hallways to a needy patient. Pearline hasn't rushed for anything since she's been home. Instead, she's relearning her island's concept of time, relishing the slower pace.

In the pasture beyond, gaulins mingle in the tall grass and stand atop the broad backs of the cows, picking at insects. For a moment, she thinks of the artwork on the Jehovah's Witness pamphlets left every Easter in her front door's grillwork, promising the harmony of a pastoral landscape to those who are permitted to cross the heavenly gates. But she is witnessing it on earth, here and now.

Now that she has come home for good, the little things that were ordinary, everyday occurrences in her childhood give her pause: the way a lizard flicks its orange tongue and inches with deliberate slowness from one corner of the ceiling to another, the strength of the thin wisps of a spider's web, the shame o' lady that grows close to the ground and closes up its leaves when touched, the mongoose she saw a few evenings ago creeping across the yard to steal eggs from a dove's nest.

If she could, she would sit and watch all day, but she has to get Claudia to school and get back home before Aileen and Hermina arrive. She moves now with a measure of speed reminiscent of her Brooklyn life, the long-ago days when she got Josette ready and off to school and sprinted toward her own job, intent on juggling it all without a single misstep, intent on showing Josette what hard work and persistence and dogged commitment could yield.

Back home, pacing the living room, she waits for Aileen and Hermina. There are remnants of Irene everywhere—all the things that are such a part of the house that she hadn't seen them for what they are. Each bed has a quilt Irene made from swatches of fabric left over from something else or clothes her children outgrew. The velvet pillows in the living room are among the last things she sewed. There are embroidered doilies and kitchen and tea towels, some stained, some set aside and rarely used but browning now with age. Irene could tell the story behind everything—when she made it and why, which daughter helped and which didn't. She's pleased by this lingering presence, the physical things that seem to be Irene saying *I belong here.*

Pearline climbs in the backseat of the car, next to Hermina's and Aileen's purses. Aileen drives, grasping the steering wheel with both hands and leaning so far forward her breasts brush the steering wheel. She drives slowly, tentatively, like someone unaccustomed to the curves of the road, hugging the corners and brushing up much too often against the overgrown roadside vegetation. On the flat coastal road, Aileen's driving doesn't change. "Gwan," she says now and then as if the drivers bearing down on the car can hear. "You think I going to let you come and run me off the road? Gwan. Pass."

Pearline cracks the window to sniff the air for the acrid scent of the marshes as they pass. But she waits too long. The scent is already behind her, and all she feels is the sharp sting of the heat blowing in on the breeze.

Ocho Rios is bright and manicured in a way that Brown's Town, Mount Pleasant, and the towns and villages in between —the non-tourist towns—are not. Manicured as if the best of the island—the pruned bougainvillea and swept roads—should be reserved only for tourists, as if the island's residents themselves don't deserve proper drains to channel rainwater, smooth roads that aren't a patchwork of potholes hastily filled with marl, markets that don't stink of rotted fruit and vegetables. She counts the places that make her think *for tourists*: the strip in Montego Bay; the stretch of road leading away from the airport through the strip up to the intersection with Queens Drive; Dunn's River Falls, where someone has taken the time to scrub the rocks of slippery moss; horseback tours on the coast; all-inclusive hotels and their cordoned-off beaches. No one has said directly that Jamaicans shouldn't be there. But the idea is culturally ingrained, a relic of the colonial past reinforced by advertisements that show tourists with pale or lightly tanned skin enjoying what the country offers and dark-skinned laborers serving them. Always.

She marks the place where Ocho Rios shifts from tourist town to the residents' town—the clock tower. To the west, where they have come, is Main Street, lined with duty-free gift shops and restaurants catering to tourists. To the east are the open-air market and the non-tourist shops; one side light and airy, the other heavy, the stores denser, both inside and out.

"We're here," Aileen says.

They're in front of a building, a single-story bank of offices the color of pineapple. The lawyer, Jerry Hill, is meticulous, even more organized than the doctors with whom Pearline has worked. He has multiple folders spread out before him, each with a small typewritten label, with their father's surname and the contents of the folder scribbled on the front. He's younger than they are, but not by much, and already gray is sprinkled in his beard.

"I'm going to run through the process," he says. "Then I will go over the specifics of your case. Some of these probate and land issues are never easy. And I find it helps if the family understands what the law says before we get into the particulars of any case."

Pearline, Aileen, and Hermina nod in unison, the first in a long time they have agreed on something. The lawyer talks about stamp and estate duty, transfer taxes, and registering the property in the name of the legal owners.

"This is a hard case." He splays his fingers across the folders as if he's ready to push himself to his feet. "Nothing easy about it at all. Let me just say: Your father willed you a property he doesn't fully own."

"What?" Pearline's one-word question comes out so harsh, so abrupt, she puts a hand to her jaw as if to pull back the word.

"The property in Mount Pleasant is not in your father's name alone. He willed it to the three of you, yes, but he can only will you his share."

"You mean Mama's share isn't included? That would have gone to him when she died, no?" Hermina sits forward, her brow furrowed, her fingers laced before her on the desk.

"It's not in your mother's name."

"If not Mama, then who?"

"Annie Headlam," he says.

Pearline lets out a long breath. Even without all the details, she feels the foundation of her new life shifting, crumbling.

A nervous laugh begins deep in her belly, tickles her throat, and escapes her mouth. "Who the hell is Annie Headlam?"

"I don't know. That's what we have to find out, and make sure she—or her heirs, if it comes to that—know of this property she partly owns. What I have is this." He slides a paper across the table.

The three sisters lean forward. Pearline runs a finger below the photocopied sheet with the name *Annie Headlam* and the plot number for the Mount Pleasant property. The writing is pale, the letters round and squat. She turns to Aileen and Hermina, then swiftly pivots back to the attorney. "Headlam? The same people who owned the plantation? How?"

"I don't know." Jerry shrugs.

Neither Aileen nor Hermina speak. All three sisters are reaching for the collective family story around which their lives are built: their distant blood connection to the Headlam family that dates back to slavery and emancipation; their great-grandfather's refusal to bear the Headlam name; Rupert and Irene's often-told story of repatriation from Cuba and building their house from scratch on land they bought. Pearline feels it all slipping away. She reaches for her father's last words—*Find them for me*—and senses that he delayed his dying to give her his message. She's trying and failing to connect this news to Rupert's last wishes.

She homes in on the second part of Rupert's request: *You are my memory now.* Nothing in Rupert's last words suggested the Headlam family connection is part of the memories Pearline has to carry forward. Headlam wasn't the name Rupert used. It wasn't the name his father used. In the waning days of slavery, Rupert's grandfather, also named Rupert, was born in a small house a short distance from the gleaming estate owned by the man who fathered him but wouldn't claim him. Despite the blood ties, Rupert's grandfather could lay no claim to the estate—not the grand house, not the less conspicuous cut-stone houses that surrounded it, not even the house in which he lived. When he came of age post-emancipation, he moved to Trysee, a free village, where he built his own two-room house and assumed a new surname. Some one hundred fifty years later, that connection to the Headlam name seemed to be coming back to haunt Pearline's family.

"The bottom line is, we can't transfer the property into your names, and the property can't be sold without the other owner." He looks from one to the other. "You need a clean title to sell. Sorry to give you bad news. But we can get to the bottom of this, set everything straight, if you want to spend the money on it."

"What kind of money you talking about?" Hermina glances around as she speaks.

"Research fees alone can run you into the thousands. Paying off back taxes, if any. But it looks like you've been keeping up with the taxes, so from that angle, you're probably set. Hard to say how much exactly, but it won't be cheap. And who knows if any Annie Headlam heirs will want their share. Then there is the business of squatters rights."

"Squatters?" Pearline's voice rises more than she would like. "You calling us squatters?"

"What you telling us?" Hermina says. She gathers her bag as if she's ready to walk away rather than deal with the potential insult.

"No." Jerry speaks slowly. "All of that will have to be

researched—when the property changed hands, who your father bought it from, and so on."

"I see." Pearline's shoulders drop. "So you think this Annie Headlam is from the original Headlam family?"

"Maybe. I don't know." Jerry splays his hands.

"That wouldn't make a drop o' sense," Pearline says.

"Talk it over," Jerry says. "We don't need to rush anything now. The taxes are paid, and I don't see anyone rushing to come claim it. Take your time."

Outside the office, Pearline sucks in the air. "Of all the things I could imagine, never in a million years would I have imagined this."

"Me either," Hermina says. "Annie Headlam!"

"So what we going to do 'bout this news?" Pearline asks.

"Nothing," Aileen says. "We can't do a goddamned thing." There's disappointment in her voice, resignation to what they face.

"He had a plan," Pearline says.

"Everything you see up there was all Mama. Mama planned. Papa was impulsive." Aileen turns in the direction of the car, and the breeze blows back her words.

Hermina looks over the hood of the car, catching both Pearline's and Aileen's eyes. "There's always a way to do something. And if we want to sell, there must be a way to do it, and do it fast before anybody come try to claim it."

"He had a plan," Pearline says again, sliding into the car and slamming the door shut for emphasis. There's something that hasn't yet been revealed that Rupert wanted her to uncover and understand. She repeats her words, slower this time, tapping a hand against her palm.

"I telling you, that was all Mama." Aileen shakes her head, looks up at the rearview mirror at Pearline. "You left long time. Plenty things you don't understand."

"Not this again," Pearline says.

"It matters." Aileen rolls the window down, her body moving forward in an exaggerated effort to turn the crank. "Anyway, this place is like an albatross around our necks. This is what will kill all o' we."

"Could it be our Annie?" Pearline asks.

"How?" Hermina doesn't hide her sarcasm.

"Don't know. Maybe we thinking of the wrong Annie. That's all I'm saying."

"They say cold weather make people go mad in England, but must be same with American cold weather." Hermina laughs at her own joke, and Aileen joins in, their cackling grating on Pearline.

The drive home is as slow as the first leg. A warm breeze blows through the open car window, and when the foliage clears out a bit, Pearline leans right to look at the azure water curved against the land. Pearline is calmer than she thinks she ought to be. One thing is settled: Her sisters can't force her to sell, though she feels that Hermina with her financial background will try to find a way around the law. She can't imagine moving her parents' graves or selling off sections of the land. She can't imagine living anywhere else on the island, not in a mansion in one of the newer developments on the coast, not in the heart of a city that thrums with too many bodies and artificial energy, not cooped up in an air-conditioned house and afraid to let in the natural breeze. No. Her father's— their—hillside house with glimpses of the sea and this winding country road are two of the things she always envisioned in this reclaimed life of hers.

"That must be why that man was stubborn about selling." Hermina speaks softly, almost as if she doesn't want Pearline to hear. "Never even had to sell all of it. Even just a little piece would have been enough. But he wouldn't budge, and now this."

Pearline closes her eyes and feigns sleep. They know what their father wanted. She now knows. They know. She's thinking about his last moments, the way he grabbed her hand and whispered, *Find them for me.* She is sure now that this development is what he was trying to tell her about. Is Annie Headlam their Annie? There's no logical explanation in the family story her parents passed on that explains this change. She suspects her father asked her sisters to fulfill his last wish, and they refused. She's sure of it—sure they heard his request, sure they stepped away laughing, shaking their heads and saying *Not a chance.*

Now, looking at her sisters, hearing of their plan, Pearline knows that her father's request is something she has to hold close. He *chose* her. How long he must have waited for her to come home. She'd seen it often with patients who lingered after life support was turned off, hanging on until a parent, a sibling, a spouse, a child arrived, seeming to give up only then. She knows her father waited and wonders if he'd always known she would come home.

Her decision to come home was based on something else, not her ailing father, not a selfless desire to help her sisters care for him. Thirty years living in Brooklyn and still she was seen only as an immigrant, an other—her accent, the lilt in her tongue and the little green card with *Resident Alien* stamped across the top, forever marking her as one who doesn't belong. She hated the word *alien*. No matter how anyone used it, whether *permanent resident alien* or *illegal alien*, the image she thought of was non-human, elongated head and bulging eyes, an othered being who couldn't be integrated at all. Otherness was a burden, complicated by the various descriptors news reporters and the people she encountered used for people like her.

That year, the popular descriptor was *boat people*. And she hated it for the way it reduced refugees to that single moment when they were found adrift at sea, and the rest of their story, their lives before the decision to board an ill-equipped boat and cross the rough seas, their identities—fishermen, seamstresses, farmers, mechanics, shopkeepers, struggling students, class clowns—reduced to that single moment. Their lives after, whether they were worthy of refuge and rescue, also evaporated in the fight over who would take them in or to whom they would be returned. It was no longer about them, the refugees, but about how their would-be rescuer nations wanted to be seen—as a blinking lighthouse that guides and saves, or a mirage of one.

Repatriation was the third term she hated. It, too, reduced the lives of the repatriated to the single political moment when they were rounded up and returned, unwelcome castaways, no longer wanted by a nation that had once welcomed them. The work they had done for their adopted country and the lives they had built no longer mattered. All that mattered was that they were *other*.

Pearline had been two of those. First, a repatriated child, born in Cuba to Jamaican migrants, expelled from the country of her birth and raised in Jamaica from age four; and later a migrant to America, a permanent resident alien who made a life in Brooklyn. Repatriation is the one that stings most; for her family's ultimate dismissal from Cuba was a stain on her father's life.

But now Pearline thinks something else brought her back. Her father wanted her back. He had prolonged his dying and waited for her to come. She is sure of that. She tells herself again that he chose her and not her sisters to hear his last words: *Find them for me. You are my memory now.* One is her charge, the other her legacy—both intertwined and impossible to deny.

4.

Pearline's grief comes in waves. Sometimes it infuses her nights and she dreams she comes home to Jamaica too late—with her suitcases spilling over and essentials lost—and misses her father's last breaths. Sometimes it's a sound at night, like a distant voice calling "hello," the word blown about by the wind and reverberating like an echo in a valley surrounded by rocky cliffs. It's a haunting sound. The voice keeps her awake. She lies in bed late into the night watching the shadows of nearby trees making patterns on the wall and waiting for the sound to come again. She tells herself it's the voice of an ancient ghost, haunting the land upon which they bore their crosses. Perhaps they are seeking the ones responsible for the crosses. In her mind, it's always a woman, bawling, looking around, stretching toward something that's permanently out of reach—a child, a parent, a lover, or simply peace. Sometimes she thinks it's her mother, also searching and reaching for her lost children, or haunting Rupert, whose stubbornness kept her from them.

Other times Pearline feels the urge to kneel by Rupert's fresh grave, with the dirt soft against her knees. She's there now. Dew has dampened her knees and feet. Her toes, coated with lotion and damp from the dew, slide in her rubber slippers.

She can't yet see the sun behind the trees, but she knows from the sliver of light in the eastern sky that it is beginning to rise. Her mother plotted out the family cemetery, laying out the location of each grave in a circle so she would always be surrounded by her children. There's room for Pearline, Hermina, and Aileen, as well as the others. Her mother died with the hope her lost children would come home to Jamaica someday. In a way, it's easy for Pearline to think of her father's last wish as her mother's, as her father passing on to her what Irene had asked of him before she died. She wavers between the two ideas, still wanting to believe her father did indeed forgive his children at the very end.

Pearline runs her fingers over Irene's tombstone, the cool of the concrete, the epitaph etched into the stone: *Sleep on now, and take your rest. Matthew 26:45.* Soon, Rupert's will say *The Lord hath given him rest from all his enemies. II Samuel 7:1.* He chose the passage himself, asked that the words be printed on a slab of stone made to look like a scroll. He wanted a low iron fence, built as if to keep him within. The stone and fence together will lend an air of opulence to the tomb, making it resemble the aged tombstones of once wealthy planters crumbling to dust in the Anglican and Methodist churchyards.

This is where Pearline wants to be buried when her time comes. She'd made that clear to Josette, filing her wishes alongside her will, telling everyone who would listen, even vowed, with a laugh, that she would haunt those who ignored her final directive. Her body's last resting place shouldn't really matter, but she has made it into a big thing—the thing that will define her afterlife.

Kneeling in the soft dirt, she's back again at her mother's burial with her arms around her father and the convulsions in his body reverberating like the strings of a guitar. She wishes again for Josette, or her grandchildren's tender fingers splayed across her back, or her long-dead husband's steady hold on her body. What comes instead is her father's voice, his last words like a hoarse whisper near her ear. And then comes the lawyer's voice, a hammer of bad news that gives meaning to her father's final request. *Gather the children.* That's what he asked of her. She leans forward, her tears falling on the soft dirt, and tries to catch her breath through the sobs that bubble up uncontrollably. It feels like a decade's worth of emotion catches in her chest and lungs and sputters out in big gasps. She stays on her knees, her toes and palms pressed into the dirt, letting her body convulse.

When she's finished, she looks around, grateful for the cover of the trees and the quiet grove. She takes a leisurely stroll to the gate. The morning damp is slowly dissipating. The traffic is still slow, and it will be another hour or two before the volume picks up and the steady hum of vehicles racing downhill toward the coast or uphill to Brown's Town surges. *Traffic* is not the word she means to use; for that word suggests both highway speed and the sloth-like movement of New York City's gridlocked streets. She won't find either on this rural road with its curves and potholes and gullies inches from the edge of the road.

The remnants of the name her mother gave the property catches her eye. Once, the name read *La Casa de la Pura Verdad. La Casa*—the house—is all that's visible now. She rubs her finger against the rusty metal, pulls back when she remembers it's some time since her last tetanus shot. For reasons Pearline never understood, her father wanted to call the property *La Casa del Jagüe* after a tree that grows in Cuba. But in the end, the name her parents etched in metal was the one Irene chose: The House of Plain Truth.

She relishes the ease of the morning, asks herself again why she waited so long to come back to this little town where rushing is not a concept anyone seems to know. Coming home was always Pearline's plan. She hadn't imagined a grand return, nor had she imagined building an audacious mansion on the side of a cliff with an unobstructed view of the sea. She wanted the simple life—this old house and what it offers, a small garden, and her father's dream of a working farm. The exact timing of her return was always unclear, but she pictured herself with gray in her hair, a softening rather than a muscular body, and with grandchildren looking to her for an explanation much the same way Josette sat with her own mother listening to stories about rolling calves and duppies and making moonshine babies on full-moon nights. And here she is now as she imagined herself—soft in the body, and with Claudia, a distant relative's child, in her care. Since she's come home, she's stopped straightening her hair, and it billows up and out, a pouf of tight coils pulling moisture from the air and shrinking as it pleases.

Like her father, Pearline left for America without Irene's full blessing. Irene was aware—too aware—of how circumstances, even the smallest of blips, can chip away at a person's soul. When Pearline packed, Irene stood nearby, watching her fold clothes in her traveling bag. "Promise me," Irene whispered, "that you won't work as nobody's helper or maid. Promise me you will come back home before you ever do that." Pearline whispered back, "Yes, ma'am." Irene had her share of domestic work when she lived in Cuba, cleaning houses and washing for the Americans who owned or ran the sugar estates in Banes. She made and sold coconut oil, toto, puddings, and cakes at concerts or cricket games at the Jamaican Club. Later, she took up dressmaking. Irene had never wanted her children to struggle as she had. But Pearline didn't become a maid. She worked hard not to fail, and she can proudly say that she didn't.

Like her father, Pearline turned her back on her adopted home. In Brooklyn, it seemed there was always someone waiting to tell her to go on home. It came in waves, sometimes from a patient asking why she left such a beautiful place, as if the beauty of the land was all that mattered, all that should matter to people like her; sometimes from a child misreading Josette's accent and telling her, *Go back to Africa, monkey*, or asking if people lived in trees where she was from; sometimes from the way Pearline's own primary-care doctor asked about her recent travel to the island as if a latent disease was waiting to emerge from her body and take down everyone around her. Pearline carried all of that otherness like a baby she would never birth. Except it wasn't a weight she cradled lovingly. She struggled with it, struggled to overcome it, struggled to move past it. When she could no longer struggle with it, she set it aside, turned her life down like a plate left to dry, wiped her hands clean, and left.

The way she looks at it, looks at every part of her family's story, they were also struggling and clawing through every manner of obstacle to prove their worth, never living but simply trying always to survive. She is tired of the struggle, tired of that narrative in which she is always an *other* proving her worth, always an uninvited being who doesn't fully belong. Really, it has been her nation's lot, bequeathed to this island of survivors the moment their ancestors were taken from West African shores. They hadn't yet stopped fighting to survive, not on their own small island, nor in Cuba, Costa Rica, Panama, the United States, or England.

Pearline, too, had never shed the feeling that she was always behind, running to catch a moving truck, catching up to it, grabbing at the back, grasping but losing her hold as the truck picks up speed. And still she would continue to sprint toward the elusive goal, dropping things here and there, lightening her load to quicken her steps, trying over and over to prove herself worthy of belonging.

Like her father, Pearline comes home without her child's blessing. At least, she thinks her return home mirrors his. It took nearly sixty years for Rupert to call his children's names. She's struggling against making that her legacy as well. Pearline's heart breaks the more she remembers how she turned away from her two granddaughters, how she now puts her time and energy into Claudia, how her father's deathbed regret could also be hers. She doesn't want that for her and Josette, but she could be heading there. She will tackle the outstanding issues with this house first and give Josette a little time to cool down, to reconsider whether Pearline can and should have a life independent of her.

Pearline doesn't just want to survive anymore. She doesn't want to struggle. She wants to live and live fully. This is the narrative she wants, and it's the one she came back home to reclaim.

Pearline brushes the gravel with her foot. *Idle* is what her mother would say, and she relishes this moment, the freedom of doing nothing. But Claudia calls. Her voice is faint, worried, and Pearline heads back toward the house, composing herself, thinking of the ordinary things of running a household and caring for a child. Claudia runs toward her, and she stoops to scoop her up. "I'm right here," she says. "You want porridge or fritters?"

"Fritters."

Near the doorway to the kitchen, Pearline stops at the telephone table, looks down at her own slanted handwriting, and repeats what she had written after the meeting with the attorney: *Find them for me. You are my memory now.*

Pearline stands at the door to her father's room at the back of the house, which she has avoided for three weeks now. The room is musty, the smell so strong she holds her nose as she looks around. The room feels like a museum dedicated to a long-lost person. A hat hangs on a single nail, and beneath it, on an old water-marked table, sits a monkey jar, a hand grinder, a single remaining plate from a china set, an enamel basin, and the rusting iron her mother set on hot coals before pressing the wrinkles out of cloth. In the corner are a pair of shoes, the leather cracked and the rounded toe box curling upward. It doesn't look like a room in which a man had lived but resembles instead the period rooms historians display in old houses and quaint towns that haven't modernized at all. Pearline doesn't remember all these things, doesn't know when her father accumulated them, or why. All these years she has been coming home, she can't remember when last she stepped in here. Her father had kept the room locked, kept it like a shrine to another time. He slept in another room, that one sparse and with nothing that seemed to hold any significance.

It's the steamer trunks that Pearline wants. The trunks are battered, the hinges rusting, and the leather peeling. There are scuff marks and defects in the metal trimming. She has tied together three things—her father naming his children, his last wish, the lawyer's news—all of which point back to Cuba. The trunks do too. They're a bridge to the past and the present, symbols of her childhood and her family's obsession with legends of success and failure. Something about the trunk and her family's return humiliated and demoralized her father.

Pearline falls back to that moment on the wharf in Cuba that is simultaneously the beginning of a new life and the ending of a past one. Her family of seven—soon to be eight again—stands on the wharf, her mother holds a hand beneath her belly, rounded then with what would be her last baby girl; Gerardo stands as if making room for his twin, and Annie and David huddle beside her and Aileen.

Pearline comes back to this moment often, parsing out new details, searching for fresh understanding in what she remembers: Annie pointing toward the sea, and Pearline and Aileen squinting in the sun, looking around the throng gathered on the wharf and across the water for the dot of an island that Annie said was out there. Rupert stands aside, his foot on one trunk that holds their things, his back to the three children who are to remain behind and the two girls who are going on to an island they don't yet know. He seems to want nothing to do with Annie, David, and Gerardo.

"You not saying goodbye?" Irene's belly presses against his side. He says nothing, just stares out at the glistening sea.

"You the oldest." Irene looks at Annie, places her hands on Annie's cheeks. "It's up to you, you know, to take care of your brothers. They nearly men all the same. But you the oldest. You in charge. As soon as I get the money together, I sending for all three of you. But in the meantime, take care of them. And yourself."

"Remember to write," Annie says. "And tell me what name you give the baby."

The family climbs aboard the schooner, each member holding a hand out to steady their unsteady legs.

In the last moment, Gerardo runs up and touches his father's sleeve. "I'm sorry," he says.

"Now you sorry." Rupert sucks his teeth and looks away. "Go on, girls," he says. "Watch where you going." He is again in charge, his heart hardening against the three children standing on the wharf. He looks ahead but never once looks back.

Pearline, four years old, points at the jumble of letters on the side of the schooner.

"*Rapido,*" Aileen says. "That's the name of the boat. *Rapido.*"

"*Rapido. Rapido. Rapido.*" Pearline repeats the word. She knows what it means. Quick. Quick. Quick. The succession of the words on her lips makes the simple word sound like a chant, an urgent appeal to any god or spirit who would listen.

She is too young to worry about all that she's leaving behind, but she has two new things: a word that caresses her tongue and the expansive blue ocean beyond. She says the word again and again and forgets to wave a final goodbye.

Jamaica emerges. Irene points out the blue-gray hills to Pearline and Aileen, keeping one hand beneath her belly to massage the baby's movements. Rupert composes himself, brushes his suit down, smooths his hat with nervous fingers. Irene starts a song, but the first word isn't yet out of her mouth before Rupert hushes her. "*Cállate,*" he says. "Other people on the boat too, you know. You want them to think we don't come from nowhere?"

Irene looks around at the spaces open to the wind. "When we get to land," she quietly says to the girls, "we'll sing."

"This rain look like it don't want to wait," Rupert says. He looks up, rolls his head to look at the clouds behind the boat.

At last, the schooner's engine ceases. Rupert stands ahead of Irene and the girls and commands a porter to haul the trunks. He pushes his shoulders back, brushes his hat again, and sets it on his head. He looks out at the wharf, the youths hustling for small change. A newspaper reporter approaches, pen and paper in hand.

"We're British citizens," Rupert says, mimicking the attitudes of a British gentleman. "And like it or not, it's times like these you learn to welcome the British in Jamaica, because if it wasn't for the British government, we would have been rounded up just like the Haitians. We would have been herded like cattle and put in a holding cell until the ship was ready.

You won't hear me say I want my country to be ruled by a queen, but in these last few years in Cuba, every last one of us was glad to be a British subject."

He looks at his daughters, his wife with her protruding belly, and the trunks at their feet. "I'd rather starve in my own country than in a foreign land," he says. In that single moment, he takes full responsibility for his family's return. Irene looks away as if she knows something else—who was responsible and who wasn't. Rupert says nothing more about it after, sealing away that segment of the family's life in the trunks, packing up the family legacy he had been trying to escape, putting away the names of the children who remained behind—until the very end, when he whispers their names.

And now, all that's been locked away for some sixty years is pushing up, hurtling toward Pearline, threatening to unravel the life she has always known and the new one she came home to create. While she hopes that items in either trunk may solve this mystery her father left, Pearline doesn't have the heart to open either one just yet. *Tomorrow,* she tells herself, wanting to hold off the secrets of the past for a little while longer.

"Sister Pearl," a voice outside calls.

"Coming," Pearline leans toward the open window and shouts. She looks around, grateful for the distraction. She's anxious about what she might find inside the trunks, but she's also simply not sure she's ready for the business of winding down all ninety-three years of her father's life. Having packed up her house so recently, she has no interest in purging another one so soon.

She had done it once before—removed every remnant of her husband's life from their Brooklyn brownstone in batches until every trace of him was gone. And then she regretted it, couldn't recall his scent, the name of his favorite cologne, and not a single shirt or pair of shoes, not his cricket whites, record collection, or stereo were left to remind her. She wanted to play the songs he loved—ska and lovers' rock and older calypsos—wanted to pretend he was there beside her drumming his fingers on his thighs, miming a guitar-playing musician. She wanted to inhale and hold his scent in her nostrils and lungs, to bottle it so she could always return to it. One Saturday afternoon, desperate for his scent, she spent hours sniffing colognes at the Macy's counter until she broke down, so tearful that she ran to the parking garage and cried until she had nothing left in her.

She's thinking, too, of the question of whose memory to let go and whose to keep. She let go of her husband, the man she chose. Yet she is holding on to her father. She has come home to revive his dreams and make them her own, but she fears she will do the opposite and throw nothing of her father's away. Waiting for more messages from him to come through, she fears she will hold on to everything long after the papers have browned and crumpled and Rupert's clothes have rotted.

Outside, Mr. Walker points to a break in the fence where the cows have burst through and trampled the corn. Pearline waves away the damage to the corn. "High time we cut it down and make feed for your cows. That corn too tough for me to eat."

They both chuckle, but Pearline knows what her sisters will say, knows they will insist he pay for the trampled corn.

"You going to plant again?" Mr. Walker asks.

"Soon," Pearline says. "Still figuring out what."

"Your father used to get good yam. Sweet yam and yellow yam. Good crops. The peas never do so well."

"Good to know," she says. She's thinking of how to ask the rate he pays to lease the land. But the telephone rings, and Pearline rushes back inside to catch the call in time.

"Mom," Josette says. "Can't talk long 'cause this long-distance call too expensive."

"I know. That's the price all of us pay when we migrate. We write letters."

"You know me and letters," Josette says.

The house is quiet and lonely without Yvonne, Claudia's mother, the everyday rituals of taking care of an aging man, or Hermina and Aileen dropping by. It's hard for Pearline to get the conversation going. She's waiting for Josette to ask about her new life. In fact, Pearline feels she has been waiting a long time for their relationship to morph into something else. It stalled when Ronnie died. She has remained protector and provider, with none of the softening she usually sees between mothers and daughters who become confidantes and friends in the adult years. She wants what Aileen has with her daughter Terry, what her cousins Marlene and Olive have with their adult daughters—those moments of conspiratorial whispers, exchanging bags and shoes or pants that do not fit. She wants anything but what she senses: Josette holding back and waiting with some barbed comment intent on hurting her. Pearline knows that Josette is still that child who came home to find her father had died, who looked at her mother and saw only a gaping hole that no one else could fill.

The afternoon is a painter's dream, the palette of colors vivid and variegated. A hawk swoops down, its brown plume bright in the afternoon sun. Pearline expects it to light on something—a lizard or insect—but it only swoops and banks, flying away just as quickly as it came into view. She's looking up at the bird rising, its body lost in the glare of sunlight, when she hears car tires crunching on the gravel. All Pearline wants is the afternoon's peace wrapping itself around her, the quiet life she's come to build. The engine is loud, the horn deep. A man steps out, looks the house up and down and around to the side, sizing up the expanse of land. "Long," he says. "Albert Long, the appraiser."

"Appraiser?"

"Yes, we talked last week. Thursday, I think."

"Maybe you spoke to Hermina or Aileen."

He looks down on a notebook, turns a few pages. "Hermina Rattray?"

Pearline steadies her voice, tries not to let her surprise show. "So you're here to assess the land?"

He fumbles again, hands her a business card. *Appraiser and real estate agent*, it says. She wonders how he can do both without conflicts.

"Let me show you around." Pearline leads Mr. Long across the pebbled driveway to the back of the house, through the recently cleared section and past a row of citrus trees. The weeds tickle Pearline's bare ankles. Beyond the trees, she points to the row of croton plants and a patch of newly disturbed earth. "We just buried my father here." She lingers in that spot, letting the newness of death sink in, letting the reasons to hold on to the land emerge like waves. "My mother left room for all her children. My sister must have forgotten that."

He looks up when she says the last. "If I remember what she said, I don't think she wan' sell all of the land. Lot o' land this. You could keep an acre or two for the family and sell the rest." Mr. Long, when he speaks, won't hold Pearline's gaze. He looks away, half turns his body to point at the land he cannot see beyond the grove.

They walk a bit farther back to the edge of the fenced pasture. "All the way back," she says, looking away as Mr. Long jots down his notes. "I forgot I have a pot on the stove. Come back up to the house when you finish."

Pearline walks off as quickly as she can, tamping down the anger that's building second by second. But she waits out his return, waits out his perusal of the house before calling Hermina at work. "How you mean to send appraiser here without telling me? How you mean to make plans to sell the land?"

"You know with everything going on last week, it slip my mind. Totally forgot he was to come today. What he say?"

"Aileen in on this too?"

"What you planning to do with the land, Pearline? What you know 'bout farming? All these years you in America, is farming you were learning?"

Pearline hears the snicker underlying Hermina's words. "Never mind what I know. What bothering me is that the two of you making plans without even saying a word to me. Not one word. As if I don't have a say in this too. And from the look of it, you both planning this long before we even met with the lawyer and heard what was in the will."

"Don't raise your blood pressure over this."

"Really? You trying to sell the land from under me and here telling me not to raise my pressure. See me dying trial and crosses. It not going work so, you know. It not going work so at all." Pearline takes deep breaths, tries to calm herself. She sees her childhood repeating itself—Aileen and Hermina siding together, the oldest protecting the youngest, the youngest looking up to the oldest, and she's in the middle standing alone. She's still convinced it is intentional, this effort of theirs to keep her in the dark about the fate of the family land. What she has is her father's wish, and by extension, her mother's wish: *Find the children and bring them home.* Her parents' wishes are tied up with hers: Find a place where you don't have to fight to belong. This is that place that ends her struggle. This is hers. This is theirs.

Pearline walks again, tattooing a path in the gravel in front of the veranda, building the courage to reenter the back room to find something that will be of some use. It's hard for Pearline to discern her true motive now. What started as her desire to fulfill her father's wish and extend his dream for this property has morphed into a desire to spite her sisters. She's like Irene in that way; she holds grudges and feeds them until they glow like coal. She walks until she remembers she forgot to pick up Claudia from school.

She drives too fast around the corners and on the narrow road, trying to beat time, slamming on the brakes in time to miss the tanker rounding the corner and the wall of rocks and ferns to her left. She hears the truck horn for long moments after, the sound trapped between the rock walls and the canopy of trees, bouncing back over and over, reminding her of how close she just came to an early reunion with her father.

5.

CLAUDIA WAKES PEARLINE WITH A DAMP PALM ON HER
cheek. Pearline stretches her tired limbs, still clinging to sleep.
Already, Claudia has gone into the kitchen and had her morning drink—cold milk from the fridge mixed with Milo. Pearline smells it on Claudia's breath and imagines the mess: Milo
granules on the counter and floor, splashes of brown liquid
on the countertop, and the condensed milk or sugar canister
flecked with bits of brown.

"Somebody come." Claudia's voice is soft, a shy whisper.

A horn toots. From the sound of it, Pearline pictures one
of the late-model Japanese imports common on the island,
a rental perhaps. "Coming." The car has stopped at the far
end of the veranda, and Pearline can't see who is out there.
She grabs a robe and slippers, stumbling over one of the fluffy
shoes as she hurries out of the bedroom.

She glimpses the clock. It's later than she thinks, nearly
midday, in fact, and Pearline is flustered now. She never sleeps
this late and can't remember ever being so exhausted she
missed nearly half the morning. Then she remembers the sleep
aid—the little pill she took just before bed—to try and calm
the dreams fueled by grief that had been filling her nights.

How quiet Claudia had been, feeding herself instead of waking Pearline, but other than Milo, what else would she have had? The bread is on top of the fridge, too high for Claudia to reach. Pearline's mind is foggy, and she tries to clear it, thinking back to the past week—her father, her sisters, the attorney, this house, the mystery she must solve, all building up to the opposite of the rest and relaxation she was seeking when she came home.

The phone in the hallway rings, and she grabs it, speaking into it as she opens the door and steps onto the veranda.

"Good morning. Is this the Greaves residence?"

Pearline doesn't recognize the voice. "Yes." She is cautious as she answers.

"Trying to find Rupert Greaves." There's a hint of a Jamaican accent, but it sounds like what she hears in Brooklyn, that distinct mix of Caribbean, American, and Latino accents.

Pearline stops completely. "May I ask who's calling?" She hears the hesitation on the other end, the man's reluctance to say why he has called. "He died last week. No, not last week, three weeks now," she says. "Can I help you?"

Pearline waves at the men emerging from the car. One begins walking toward her, loping, hesitant, even.

"Hello," she says into the phone.

"Yes, yes, I'm here."

"I'm his daughter. Can I help you?"

"Well . . ."

"I have some visitors," she says. "Can you call back?"

"They reach already? That's what I was calling about."

"I don't understand. Hold a minute." Pearline looks back

at the little girl standing in the doorway like a sentinel and then at the two men—one young, with short dreadlocks, and a slightly older one—stepping away from the car and across the gravel driveway. Pearline wants to pull everything back, restart the morning at a slower pace. "Morning. Can I help you?"

"Looking for my grandfather," the younger one says. He is the only one who continues up the steps.

"Grandfather?" Pearline squints, focusing.

"Yes, Rupert Greaves."

"Your grandfather?" She hears the skepticism in her own voice, remembers the man on the phone, and speaks into it. "Who you said you are again?"

"Victor Greaves," he says. "Rupert is . . . was my father. That must be my son you're talking to."

"Your father? What is this you telling me?" Pearline falls into a chair, holds out her palms to invite the young man to sit. It wasn't simply small-town gossip, she thinks, acknowledging, too, that there's always some truth to every rumor.

"I don't want you to think I'm looking for dead lef or anything. I didn't even hear he died." He pauses, sounding apologetic when he begins again. "We all know how these family situations go sometimes. Everybody have secret. But mi sorry you find out this way."

Pearline doesn't want his apology. It's not his place to apologize for circumstances he didn't create. "So the young man here is what you're calling about?"

"Yes. My son, Derek, needs a place to stay. Since he's family and all, I wanted to ask my father if he could stay there for a little while."

Pearline hadn't pictured this. She's imagined the quiet of the countryside, the mechanical sounds of the civilized world muted, watching leaves fall and leaving them to rot rather than bagging the leaves to have them hauled away and turned to mulch. She's pictured, too, a crew of workers bagging oranges and grapefruits, plantains and bananas, scotch bonnet peppers and pimento, herding cattle or goats, the entire time working together to keep her father's vision alive. Instead, she has the little girl, Claudia, and now this young man with stubs of locked hair, his pants riding on his bony hips and a hint of underwear showing. A nephew and a brother she didn't know existed. And just as quickly, she asks herself if this is who her father meant when he said *Find them.*

"Who's your mother?" she says into the phone, aware of how abrupt and rude her question sounds. She doesn't want Victor's apology, but she wants the other little details of his childhood. She wants to settle the uncertainty that Rupert may have also meant Victor.

"Melba Gordon." The man doesn't hesitate but speaks as if he's used to others questioning his parentage. "She was a secretary up at the secondary school. Light skin, a little on the heavy side."

Pearline reaches back in her memory, picks out a rainy afternoon, a woman and a toddler sheltering alongside her mother under a shop piazza. Her mother looks up, sucks her teeth, and says, "Come on." Without hesitation, Irene steps out into the cold rain, and Pearline follows. Mother and daughter are the only ones out in the drenching rain with water and gravel splashing up their legs. She got no explanation then, and now she suspects the light-skinned woman of her memory is the woman her mother wanted to avoid way back then.

Just as quickly as it comes, Pearline's thoughts about whether Rupert meant Victor disappear. He wouldn't have had to ask about Victor. Victor knew where and how to reach Rupert.

She puts the phone to her shoulder and looks up, trying to slow the thoughts popping up fast. Out loud, she asks the young man, "Exactly how much time you talking about staying?"

The young man shrugs. "Don't know."

"You aren't a deportee, are you?"

"No, ma'am."

"You not in some kind of trouble?"

"No, ma'am."

"The last thing I need in my life right now is trouble." She puts the phone back to her ear and repeats the statement.

"I tried to raise him right," Victor says. "I don't have any other people down there who he can stay with. You see, right now things in Brooklyn kind o' hot. Not a good place for him. And if you have children, you know how it is. You'll do anything to save them."

"Save him from what?"

"The wrong crowd."

"I tell you I don't want any trouble."

"He's a good boy," Victor says.

Derek is fingering a plant, holding his head at an angle, and Pearline can't see his eyes. She has seen his type before: tough or cool on the outside, a scared child on the inside afraid of disappointing. There's something familiar in his features. She can't quite decide whether it's his nose or eyes or simply the shape of his face.

"And his mother's people?" she asks.

"Even more trouble," Victor says. "Not all of them. But two nephews at the yard there . . . just enough to create problems. All these years, I didn't ask for anything. So, trust me, things hard when I call to ask my father for something."

Pearline starts to say no, hesitates, and contemplates the young man—nineteen, perhaps twenty years old, with trouble in his recent past—who has come to complicate her life. She wants to turn him away, wants to get back to the simple, unencumbered life she imagined. Mostly, she doesn't want to invite trouble. But her father's dying wish rises again like a wave: *Find them for me.* While she's sure Rupert meant the children in Cuba, she wonders whether Victor and Derek would fall under her father's concept of *them.* It's curious, she thinks, that when Rupert named his children, he didn't call Victor's name. Once again, Pearline thinks she missed it, missed the true meaning of her father's message to her.

And yet, it's not her father's but her mother's wish to have a place that always welcomes its own, one in which any sense of *otherness* and struggling to belong falls away, that influences Pearline's decision in the moment.

"All right," she says. "I suppose you can stay for a little while. I said before and I going to say it again—I don't want any trouble. First sign of trouble, you're gone from here."

This is her lot, Pearline thinks, taking care of others. She has spent her life doing it in one capacity or another—nursing strangers in hospitals, sending barrel after barrel from Brooklyn to family members here, sending money for school fees and school supplies and medicine and x-rays and myriad emergencies. Just when she thinks she has done it all, when she comes home to rest, she is at it again, mothering Claudia and now this young man on the run from something.

And then, there is the mystery Rupert left for her. Already, the story upon which her family history is built is crumbling. Once, she would have described Rupert's life in the simplest of terms—father, husband, farmer, migrant worker. Now she has to capture the jagged edges of his life and fit them into the puzzle he has left behind—a puzzle that now includes Victor and Derek.

Pearline ends the phone call and ushers Derek inside. Almost immediately, Claudia perks up. The girl giggles, the sound infectious, and grabs Derek's hand as if she's known him her entire life and not a few minutes. From the kitchen window, Pearline watches the two. Claudia leads Derek around the yard, showing him the things she thinks are important, the stick to pick the cherries, the unopened buds on the leaf of life plant that pop when squeezed, the cemetery where the dead relatives sleep. Pearline smiles at the last, the innocence of a child who thinks the dead are only sleeping.

Pearline has her own thoughts about the dead. All these years abroad and she still believes the spirits of the recent dead stay around, some waiting to be summoned to lend help, others unhappy about something or other. She believes that some dead will even haunt the living.

So much time has passed, Pearline forgoes breakfast altogether and makes dinner. She makes chicken exactly as she recalls her mother's, browned in oil and then cooked down with carrots and sweet peppers and thick, slightly sweet gravy. As a child, she and her sisters waited for the strips of the chicken skin that fell off during frying, mouths watering as they watched their mother blow on the strips before handing them off. She chuckles now to think of it, how much now-forbidden foods she ate as a child. Pearline makes carrot juice too, sweetens it with condensed milk.

She sends Claudia to wash up, tells Derek to stay. "Beginning to end," Pearline says. She uses her nurse voice, authoritative yet soft. "I want to know exactly what I'm dealing with."

Derek hesitates, but Pearline is firm, drawing on her years cajoling symptoms out of patients and calming agitated parents. She stops puttering but doesn't look directly at him as he tells her he is neither a deportee nor a criminal on the run but a young man who had done nothing at all, except follow his father's advice to lie low, which translated to an exile from the Brooklyn neighborhood he had known his entire life. With no other plan of his own, he had accepted the airline ticket and left Brooklyn for Mount Pleasant. He was wanted, yes, but not a criminal in the strictest sense of the word. He simply knew too much about neighborhood gang activity. To be exact, he knew too much about the murder of Joey Prieto to remain safely in Brooklyn.

"That can't be all," she says. "To leave the only country you know, the only people you know. You might see gray hairs on my head, but don't take me for a fool." Pearline stops, softens her voice. "I can't help you if I don't know. I told your father yes, but there's nothing, absolutely nothing, to stop me turning you out this house right now. Let me tell you something else. I was a nurse. I worked all over Brooklyn, which means I see everything. The men who sit there bawling after they nearly beat their wives to death. Children shot from stray bullets. The young men your age coming in with gunshot wounds, those hit with so many bullets you don't know where exactly the blood coming from. Too many holes to count. I've seen it and heard it all. I treat the thieves and police officers. It don't matter. They all the same to me. Don't think you sparing me anything. So come now, beginning to end."

She sees Derek shift, sees the knowing in his eyes. Without her, he has nothing.

"Joey was my boy," he says. "We go way back. Elementary school days." Derek hesitates, fiddles with the sticky plastic fruit Pearline has vowed to throw out. "But the thing about Joey is, he talk too much, take things too far. So we had this plan. Nothing big. Just wanted to scare him. Joey had this girl. Heather. Well, she wasn't really his girl. He wanted her to be."

Pearline thinks she knows this story. Young love. That feeling that makes lovers want to rearrange every aspect of their lives to revel in the possibilities a lover's proximity, touch, and smell present. She's seen the consequences of it—broken eye sockets and jaws from a father's fists, gashes, gouges, teenage girls worried about a pregnancy, teenage girls giddy with news of a wanted pregnancy, naïve to the burdens of a newborn.

"The only thing I had to do was tell Joey I was going to meet Heather's friend in Coney Island. Everybody knew Joey would come. Not a thing would stop him. Even if he had to crawl or walk on glass, he would be there. Everybody knew the girls liked the park." Derek looks up at Pearline. "The little park over on the side of Coney Island creek with the ship graveyard. You don't know it?"

Pearline shakes her head.

"All right. Well, it's not much of a park. But it was quiet, kind of dark. Just a ballfield, handball courts."

Pearline tries to picture it—the creek that reeked of putrid seawater, and sometimes sewage, rather than popcorn and hotdogs and funnel cakes. But now that she is back home, she can think only of the brackish seawater in the mangroves, sea grape trees with their sweet, tiny fruit.

"All I had to do was get Joey to the creek. But Joey was my friend. Almost everything I remember about my childhood, Joey was there. And I couldn't do it. Couldn't betray him. So I borrowed my father's car and went to Philly. Stood outside a hospital with the sirens in the background and called Shawn. Told him my mother was in a bad accident. Didn't tell him too much, just that we didn't know if she would be able to walk again.

"And Shawn felt real bad. He believed it. Only Joey knew the real story about my mother."

"What's that story?"

"Prison," he says. "Long story."

"All right. Go on."

"So you see, I wasn't there. But the real sad part is, I hoped that if I couldn't get Joey there, everything would fall apart. There wouldn't be a meeting at the ship graveyard. But I had this feeling that things wouldn't just turn out so. I stayed in

Philly with this girl I used to date. But the whole night, I felt on edge. You know, heart racing, stomach won't keep anything down. The whole night, I just felt scared. Morning come, and I hear what they did. They didn't just scare him. They killed him. And even though I wasn't there, I feel real bad, like if I had done my part, he would still be here. I should have carried him to Philly, told him to go somewhere else. Anything." Derek turns away, but Pearline can see the swift movement of his hands toward his eyes.

The air in the kitchen shifts. It feels heavy, presses down on Pearline. "Sorry to hear that," she says. "That's a lot to carry around inside you."

"Yeah. It's a lot to keep losing all the people who mean something to you."

"You weren't there and you didn't send him to the graveyard," she says. "So why your father sent you away?"

"It took them three days to find Joey. And they only found him 'cause a man who had gone fishing saw his body. Of course, the police start to look for his friends. And I think that if the gang would do that to Joey, they could do anything to me. I knew who was there. I could tell the entire plan and face no consequences 'cause I wasn't there. I just had this feeling my time was going to be cut short. Just had this feeling. Jumpy. A car backfire and I jump. A squirrel run over some leaves and I jump. Couldn't live so. It's like I could hear a clock ticking away. After what happened to my mother, my father don't trust the police. You know how that go. Look at me. Twenty-one. No job. Dreadlocks. Police going to lock me up for something."

Pearline nods, searching for something to say. But she comes up empty. As Derek talks, she pictures his last night in Brooklyn, the thin young man before her cowering in the basement of an abandoned house in Long Island that a friend of his father's had bought for renovation and a quick sale. She magnifies the details, the sound of a pipe dripping, mice scampering across the floor, and sirens that thankfully never came to a stop outside the abandoned house. She magnifies his fear of spending another night alone in that eerie house with the uncertainty of when his time would come to an end. She closes her eyes, pictures him walking up to the counter at the airport, ticket in hand, as if that was the most ordinary thing in his life.

"Even on the plane," Derek says, "my heart wouldn't stop pounding. The pilot could turn the plane around. Police could come and escort me off. The hardest part of all this? Every time I look in the mirror I see Joey's face."

"You did nothing wrong," Pearline says. She holds out her arms, waits for Derek to walk toward her. "If you were my son, I would have done the same thing." And she is in fact thinking of her newborn baby boy, with his head full of curls and with a face that looked like a stamped replica of hers, whose heart gave out before the cardiologist could fix its imperfections. This is him, she wants to think, her boy in another body. But she knows it isn't so, and she cautions herself not to get too far ahead imagining a life for this young man who is still a stranger.

Claudia bounces back into the kitchen. "Let me show you where to sit." She doesn't go to the dining table but instead leads Derek to the veranda, where Pearline has been taking her meals and where Rupert took his own meals when he could still move about with ease.

Much later, after the washing and cleaning up, Pearline picks up the phone to call Aileen and Hermina and tell them of this newfound relative. Then she thinks of the appraiser, their withholding that detail from her, and drops the phone back on the cradle. Outside on the veranda, she sits to take her rest, to summon some semblance of the quiet life she came home to find. Derek and Claudia are lying on the floor with newspapers spread around them. He is teaching her how to dab a brush in watercolor paint and make even strokes on paper. His patience surprises Pearline.

"You sound like somebody who know how to teach children," Pearline says.

"Who me? Not at all." He laughs, but he is gentle when he speaks to Claudia, jovial, and Claudia laughs with him.

Pearline leans in close. His isn't a painting but a pencil sketch of the old house. In Derek's version, the patchwork of new wood mixed with old are no longer flaws, and the old house that sometimes feels like it could crumble with one strong puff of wind regains a semblance of its beauty. He has drawn an old man leaning on the veranda railing, looking out at the lush fruit trees on the stretch of land below the house. He drew what his grandfather must have seen: a land of plenty intended to sustain the generations that followed. The sketch of the old man looks exactly as Pearline remembers her father. How eerie it is to see her father posed as he always stood, drawn by someone who had never seen him standing that way. The old man looks tired, as if his knees will buckle at any minute and he needs to sit and take his rest—an old man fatigued by his mistakes and what the sea sloshed at his feet and the wind churned up around him. She turns away, weeping, tears sliding too quickly down her cheeks and her throat hurting from the effort of holding back her emotions.

6.

PEARLINE WAKES WITH THE SENSE OF A PRESENCE IN THE room. There's no moonlight, but she can make out the bulk of the dresser, the wardrobe, and the shape of the armchair in the corner. She holds still, listening for a breath, for movement in the hallway, the floorboards creaking, a foot sticking to and lifting from the waxy floor. Then she remembers Derek. For a moment, she is paralyzed, waiting for the inevitable, planning her own response. Her heart and blood pump in overdrive, the sound of them frightening in their own way. She considers the possibilities, a helpless Claudia, and flicks on the lamp in haste.

She is alone, her room door still closed, the windows shut. Nothing is out of place. She doesn't wait for her heart to slow but tiptoes down the hallway to look in on Claudia, who is curled in the corner with her face against the wall. She listens for Derek's snores. He, too, is asleep, flat on his back with one arm flung above his head and the sheets tangled around his legs like that of someone who's been wrestling in his sleep. His mouth is slightly open, and the tufts of locks fall away from his face—an askew crown.

Back in her room, Pearline lies down again, but sleep will

not come. A neighbor's dog barks, and another joins in. The feeling she had doesn't return, but, unable to shed the tension, the edginess, she keeps her eyes open, then sits by the window to watch the slow awakening of the night sky. It's still semi-dark when she gets up and heads to the opposite end of the hallway.

Pearline stands in the doorway of her father's room again, watching dust swirl in the early-morning shards of light filtering through the glass and gauze. The dust has a shape to it—or one that her mind projects—a silhouette of a body that's a lot like Rupert's younger one. She sees him as he was—a proud man, hat cocked on his head, his baggy pant legs billowing in the breeze. He removes his hat and brushes his hair, smooths the low-cut curls, and turns with a smile. "Girlie," he says. That was how he always called his daughters, as if they were not distinguishable from one another. But they were: one feisty leader, one quietly defiant, and one just trying to keep the peace between the other two.

Pearline reaches out to touch his hat, and the dust blows and swirls. She watches the image of her father disappear as the dust settles again. Dust powders everything, settling in layers on the mahogany furniture and the old leather trunks in the corner. In this room, there's only a single remnant of her mother: her sewing machine—vintage now. The metal base and treadle are still intact. But the wood is new, the old portions of it replaced with cedar after termites destroyed it.

She looks back at the trunks, takes in a deep breath, then stoops, catching herself before she topples forward. "Lord, have mercy," she says, as if there's someone in the room. "Old age licking me down. Or maybe is Papa." She laughs softly and tries to pull the first trunk closer. It doesn't budge. Pearline inches forward, her knees making small circles in the dust on the floor. Closer now, she tugs at the latch, but it, too, is rusted and doesn't budge. Every piece of metal is rusted. The second trunk is much the same. "Of course," she says. "Why would I think this was going to be easy?"

Pearline walks just as quietly through the house as she did before, stopping briefly to make her morning drink—coffee from beans a neighbor parched. She grabs a broom and dust cloth and returns to the room to give it a once-over. The musty scent of the room softens with lemon-scented furniture polish. There's a wave of familiarity when she picks up the pieces as she dusts, but the memories are locked away or too fleeting to take hold. Overwhelmed, overcome, she doesn't linger any longer.

Except for the floorboards that squeak and dip as Pearline moves, the house is quiet at this hour. Claudia is still snoring gently. Derek has stopped snoring. Pearline shifts the curtains, opens the windows again. The early-morning air is as cool as a late-spring morning in Brooklyn. Pockets of fog hang between the trees, and even at this early hour, the jabbering crows are already at it, their caws loud and raucous. Pearline takes her time though she knows that time is not hers to preserve. Not now when she has to stay ahead of her sisters, has to learn or unlearn the past to see what her father is showing her.

Outside, the morning is warming and the jabbering crows are even louder. Pearline picks up a stone and throws it up toward them, but the stone falls far short of her intended goal, doesn't even lift toward the second row of tree branches, and she laughs at her own weakness. These days she's laughing at everything—the mystery of her father's intentions, this second phase of her life mothering Claudia and now putting up Derek, the rusted locks on the steamer trunks she thinks hold her family's secrets, her shifting view of her parents and the stories they told, the possibility her entire history is a fraud. She refuses to believe this is possible, yet she knows something is awry in the family history around which she has built her life.

She's pacing, again wearing out a little track in the gravel, moving so not to just barge back inside and wake Derek. He's stronger, more likely than her to be able to bust the lock. Again, Pearline has a fleeting sense that she has looked in the trunk before. But she has no clear memory of the moment, no retained image of either parent bending over the trunks or handling the items locked away inside the room.

The cattle are back on this side of the pasture. Sixteen heads she counts. She pauses for a moment to picture what she wants to build here. An estate, she thinks. Not just a farm, not a small-time thing, but an immense operation. She settles on cattle and coconut trees, pictures the house in the middle and her on the veranda watching the fronds dipping and swaying in the breeze. Two coconut trees still stand on the property, and when she looks to them, she says, "Ah," just like Rupert used to. "See there, that is freedom." She mirrors Rupert's stance. He used to point to the coconut palms and explain how every part of the coconut and the tree serve some purpose. The thin leaves, when dried, can be fashioned into a broom. He would point to the branches from which the nuts hang and say, "Even that is a broom." The dried husks can be trimmed and shaped into planters or used as mulch in pots with anthurium. "Coconut oil and milk you already know 'bout," he said. "And you know the water is the source of life. And the shell, if you cut it right, is a bowl." His coconut trees never lasted very long. Each new variety of tree quailed and died from disease. Pearline plans to salvage this part of Rupert's dream by planting dwarf coconut trees on the property, a variety she's heard haven't succumbed to the same disease on the island.

While she waits for Derek to wake, she makes rundown, which she is sure neither Derek nor Claudia will eat. It's not a meal she makes often, but the creamy coconut milk custard with bits of fish and callaloo surfaced in her memory, floating up above everything else that morning. She honors this memory, lets the process and effort of grating coconut by hand take over her mind. She grates and squeezes out the thick, milky liquid, adding water until it's the consistency of cow's milk. She takes her time, boils the coconut milk, chops onion, garlic, bell peppers, and scotch bonnet peppers, adds the chopped vegetables and salted mackerel, and waits for the coconut milk to reduce to an oily custard sauce. She fries dumplings and sets them aside. When Derek and Claudia wake and before either says anything about the food Pearline spoons on the plates, she says, "I made rundown. And all I ask is that you try it before you both say you don't want it."

"Help me with this." Pearline points to the back room.

Derek and Claudia follow closely, their bare feet silent against the wood. Derek stays in the doorway, hesitating, holding his breath, choking on the words he doesn't want to say out loud. The lemon scent has already faded, and the must again overpowers.

"Yes, it musty," Pearline says. "Room lock up long time. Come, come. Don't have all morning." The bed dips with her weight and the springs, rusted too, creak. "Pull that over here for me."

Derek moves, raises his brows. "What's in it?" he asks.

"Papa's body," she says.

Claudia steps back, her eyes wide and mouth open. She's ready to back out of the room, run far away from the trunk.

"Just joking." Pearline reaches out, pulls Claudia against her chest. "Come, baby. There's no body in it. Sit right here so and look."

Claudia hesitates, puts her fingers against her lips instead.

"Remember we bury him outside?" Pearline asks. She has forgotten how easily children get scared. "Come, baby."

Claudia stays in the doorway, tipping her body forward as she peers at the trunk and at Derek, who's leaning toward it and jiggling the rusted locks. He runs his palm over the metal trim, then pulls and jiggles the lock, trying to get the metal to slide. But it doesn't budge.

"You need oil," he says.

"Get the cooking oil."

Together, Pearline and Derek dab the lock with drops of cooking oil and listen for the metal sighing as it moves. Instead, the handle rattles and falls to the floor, the clatter louder than Pearline expects. Claudia jumps, screams, and Pearline stifles a laugh. Again, she reaches for Claudia, lifts her onto her hip, says, "Hush."

The musty smell of a thousand yesterdays trapped too long inside rises, the odor so strong Pearline thinks of it as a loose feather floating before her face, something solid she can grab and put back inside. A life emerges from the trunk in dribbles, each item holding the same musty scent—the scent of sixty years.

"The records of a lifetime." Pearline separates the loose papers from the bound, personal letters apart from official correspondence, paper from cloth, plastic from metal, travel documents from birth papers, trinkets from broken pieces. The black print on brown paper is hard to read and even harder because it is written in Spanish. Among the papers is a single fraying and yellowed piece of newspaper. *The Gleaner.* She unfolds it and holds it up to the light. It's full of advertisements. She rubs her hand over the print, aware of how delicate it is, as she pictures her father holding it, struggling to read through the words. *Plenty work. Good pay. Kind treatment. No railway fare to pay. Embrace the opportunity of going to Jobabo, where you can earn good salary for your family. Kindly do not forget that my Santiago de Cuba passenger service is still going strong. Do not be misled by unscrupulous persons telling you to the contrary.* On that single sheet are seventeen similar advertisements, all promising good pay.

Pearline finds a second batch of newspaper clippings, so old the paperclip holding them together has rusted. She takes her time easing the paperclip across the yellowed paper, careful not to tear the top and bottom sheets. The articles are mostly written in Spanish, and she scans the headlines, trying to make out what they mean. *La Ley de Cinquenta Porciento.* Pearline's Spanish is useless, and she stacks the clippings and sets them aside. There's another set in English, editorials from *The Gleaner*, which she also sets aside.

There's an old pocket watch with a broken chain and missing pin, a cracked teapot, a stained dress with a newspaper clipping showing a sketch of a woman with bare shoulders and back wearing a similar gown. At the top of the dress is a single beaded band. Perhaps it was Annie's, Pearline thinks, because she can't picture her mother wearing such a dress that draped her body and flared at the hem.

At the bottom of the pile of papers is a single blurry photo. Six children and two adults look solemnly at the camera. No one breaks the pose. Their hands hang by their sides, their shoulders drooping. Rupert wears a Panama hat with a dark band, eerily similar to the one hanging from a nail in the room. His dark suit is either black or brown or a blue-black. His cheekbones are prominent, and his chest puffs as if he had been holding his breath when the picture was taken. Irene's high collar hides and elongates her neck, and her face glistens as if she had smothered it with coconut or castor oil. Irene holds a young girl in the crook of one arm. The children's faces glisten as well, their eyebrows thick and smooth. Each holds his or her lips pursed. No one smiles. The biggest of the girls stands in the middle of the boys and she, too, holds a little girl.

"Gerardo, Arturo, David, Annie, Aileen, and me." Pearline is transfixed, awed by the past creeping up on her.

"I can see my father in him," Derek says. He hurries down the hall, returning with his wallet. He pulls out a passport-size photo and lays it next to the dull black-and-white one. "It's hard to see, but my father looks like him."

"Yes." Pearline sees it too: her father's cheeks, the flare of the nostrils, the large ears. "I wish you had met him."

Pearline looks quickly through the pile for another photo or a set of photos. She wants there to be more pictures of them all, especially her older siblings, who would likely be unrecognizable now. But there are no others. Pearline sets the photo aside and turns to a stack of letters written by hand in a halting English. One dated August 1933 reads: *Kiss the baby. Manolo says we going to Havana to find work and start over. He has family there. I will let you know where we are . . . Beg Papa to forgive us. How could he choose not to forgive?* It's signed "Annie," and Pearline gathers this isn't the first letter she sent.

Her hand trembles, and she holds the letter with both hands, imagining Annie thinking in Spanish but translating her words to English. She doesn't try to settle her heart. This letter, this connection to her long-lost sister, feels unreal. For sixty years, she's had nothing, save for snippets of stories, and now she has two sets of concrete and intimate things: a photo of her family together and her sister's handwriting in a handful of letters. Something else paralyzes her momentarily. Which parent stashed the letters away? The letters are Irene's, but she always thought of the trunk as her father's. Nothing about his stubbornness, his easy dismissal of the Cuba years, makes her think he would ever have saved these letters, these artifacts. *Saving the artifacts* was not his intention, she thinks. He simply stashed them, wanting to bury that period of his life in the trunk, lock it up, and forget it.

"You all right, Sister Pearl?" Derek touches her shoulder. His touch is a small comfort.

"Mi all right, man." Pearline looks down on the letter again, rereads the last two lines: *Beg Papa to forgive us. How could he choose not to forgive?* Pearline homes in on the last line, and she knows she will rethink every interaction, every word, every memory for a hint of how this secret is tied to her father's dying wish. The letters don't say. There's no other mention of Rupert, no mention of the deed Rupert refused to forgive. What could teenagers do to warrant lifelong punishment? Now she knows for certain that there's something he held on to, a solid reason Rupert refused to call his children's names.

What a hard man, Pearline thinks. Her mother used to say this about Rupert. And Pearline realizes now that it was Rupert's stubbornness that kept the family apart, that kept her mother from seeing her children, and Pearline and her sisters from knowing their siblings and creating memories wholly their own. Pearline's only true memory of her siblings is not hers alone but a collective memory of a family that waited for three adult children to come home to the family land in Jamaica, where her mother said they truly belonged. They would be in their seventies now, these siblings across the sea. If they were ever to return, it would not be the way the family left—by boat—but by air on a journey measured by the minutes. Pearline wants to tell her long-lost siblings that Rupert forgave them in the very end and bring them back to a home they have never known.

Pearline holds on to one small comfort: Rupert forgave his children in the very end, and she thinks this is what he wanted Annie, David, and Gerardo to know.

She's of a mind to call Hermina and Aileen to tell them what she has found. Again she falls back to how they handled the appraiser, and she knows she must hold on to this find a little longer. Pearline stacks the letters and papers in separate piles. She wants to look through them alone, to unearth this secret thing that would make a man hold a lifetime grudge against his own children. She dabs at her eyes, presses the butts of her palms against her cheekbones and her fingers on her eyelids to stanch her tears. She takes one last look at the photo and the three faces she hasn't seen in nearly sixty years.

Find them for me. Pearline now believes this truly was her mother's dying wish, passed on to Rupert, and now to her. Nothing cooled her mother's anguish over leaving her children in Cuba. It's another of her family's legacies. Nothing cooled Pearline's grandmother's anguish over losing her own children to Panama. As a child, Pearline didn't understand why her grandmother—her mother's mother—got so sad when anybody mentioned Panama either. Her face drew down and her eyes filled up with water, mouth pushed out as if she wanted her lips to touch her nose. Of the five children her grandmother had, four went to Panama, and only two returned to give her grandchildren she could see and touch and love. It was a hard thing for a woman in that time to see her children, adult or not, go off, unsure if they'd ever come back home. Now Pearline knows how hard it was for her mother and grandmother to live the rest of their lives with that question mark. Irene lived with her mother's pain and her own. Four of her own children were lost to her—one dead too young and three left on a wharf in Cuba. For the rest of her life, Irene spent half her energy wishing Annie, David, and Gerardo would appear walking down the drive to the house and the other half resenting her husband for them not being there.

What comes to Pearline is the rhythm of her family's stories—footsteps pacing back and forth. It's the rhythm of waiting, stepping forward to peer over a railing at the road rounding a corner, and falling back to an empty chair. It's her father listening for a song on the waves, hoping to catch a long-lost relative's message. It's her mother waiting for the December breeze to bring its news, voices from the sea— David's, Annie's, Gerardo's—the word from Banes, Ciego de Ávila, Havana, Santiago de Cuba.

Irene pruned the plants they called Christmas flowers so the small white blossoms would be ready in December. They transformed the front of the house, whitewashing every-thing—the stone wall, the tree trunks, the old tire around the almond tree. The poinsettia bloomed red, adding its dash of color. Irene washed the curtains, and for at least one day, the scent of soap powder fluttered from the window. She blended raisins, prunes, and mixed peel with rum and wine for the black Christmas cake and pounded ginger root to steep with the sorrel. When everything was ready and the scent of cinnamon, nutmeg, and warm vanilla hung in the air, Irene would sit with her children on the veranda in the dark, night after night, as she waited to receive the voices from the sea, their stories dripping sea salt, sweat, and tears, or for her long-lost children to come round a corner and up the driveway.

In the stillness of the empty room, Pearline hears her mother singing a folk song. It's been years since she has heard her mother's voice, but the memory of it is clear when she closes her eyes. She sees her mother as well, bent over a tub of clothes with her hands deep in suds. She always sang as she washed. Pearline can't remember all the words, but she sings the words she remembers, letting the rhythm sink in and each word settle in her bones and hold her body like a wave rolling gently toward shore. She knows this song always made Irene's eyes water. Pearline waits for her own tears to slow and stop. Now, though Pearline knows why her mother cried, she still doesn't understand precisely how her family's time in Cuba altered their lives forever.

It's best to let buried stories remain unprovoked, she thinks. But then again, the center of the story, she knows, is right there in the trunk, crumbling like aged paper, giving off the scent of decay. It will itself decay if she doesn't claim it as her own.

7.

FOR A MOMENT, THE AIR IS STILL, THE BIRDS SETTLED AND quiet, the road noise nonexistent, the house empty of Claudia's laughter now that she is in school and filled instead with the outrage of persons calling in to the daytime radio programs. Pearline flicks it off. There's nothing new—bad roads, water locked off, electricity or telephone service or running water slow to come to a hillside district, the devaluation of the Jamaican dollar, public service employees threatening to strike. Tomorrow the complaints will be the same.

Derek has gone to explore Mt. Pleasant. Pearline hadn't bothered to tell him there's nothing to explore, just a single roadside bar and corner shop within walking distance. Runaway Bay, the closest town center, is farther along the road, a walkable distance but a trek she's sure he wouldn't want to make. She's at the concrete laundry sink with suds up to her elbows. Already her knuckles are raw, and for a brief second, she regrets turning down Hermina's and Aileen's offer to lend their helper a couple days a week. She declined, bothered by the idea of "borrowing" a person, as if the woman had no say in where she worked or for whom.

With the radio off, Pearline's mind is now free to drift

wherever it wants to. A memory begins to form with absolute clarity as if it were truly her own: The year was 1916. Montego Freeport didn't exist. The Bogue Islands were still separate parcels of land, and nearly eighty years passed before the islands were artificially joined to create the commercial and residential strip now known as Montego Freeport. Rupert stood on a strip of beach, his eyes trained at the small islands. On the water before him, thin palm fronds and a single red leaf—almond, perhaps—drifted out to sea.

He always started his story like that, Pearline remembers, describing a version of himself that Pearline couldn't then and even now still can't really imagine. In his version of events, he is contemplative, a man sitting still, watching leaves bob on the waves. The man she knew was defined by his movement, his attitude toward physical labor, the stories he told, and his rumbling laughter that consumed his entire being, jiggled his belly, and bounced his shoulders like limbs set on springs. In the version of the story Rupert told, he is sitting by the seaside thinking about salt, not the salt of the seawater but the salt of labor. He worked as a gardener and general handyman for a local doctor. He knew about trimming bougainvillea and ixora, cutting back roses, stacking rocks to make mini garden beds. The work wasn't easy, especially in the midday sun, especially under the critical eye of the doctor's wife, who considered ginger a cure for every ailment. Rupert spent many a morning digging up ginger root or snipping peppermint for her morning and afternoon tea. Sometimes he slipped a bit of the ginger into his pocket so he could chew on it and calm his unsettled stomach. For his own family's plot, he did much of the same, except he concentrated on food rather than on ornamental plants, learning when to unearth yam from the little mounds, when the sweet potato vines indicated the root vegetables were ready, how to shimmy up a coconut tree to pick the fit nuts, when to plant gungo peas for a December crop, and how to keep worms away from cabbage leaves.

But on that morning by the sea, he was also contemplating a different kind of labor in a different country altogether, ninety miles north. Rupert, that year, was not interested in Europe's war, nor was he interested in joining the British West Indies Regiment, which was lending help to the distant war. He was of that age, between sixteen and forty-one years, where he was liable to be called for military service. "No, sah," he says, when he tells his story. "Not me. Not fighting nobody war. Not then. Not now. Not ever."

What he knew was that sugar estates in Cuba paid laborers much more than he could earn in Jamaica—as much as two dollars a day. When he said two dollars, he paused to explain that he didn't know the value in present-day dollars. "But it must be plenty," he always said, "'cause it had me thinking 'bout taking a boat to Cuba, making enough money to come back and buy a piece a land and build a house. Those times, I wanted to grow banana. Those times, we called banana green gold. Anybody growing banana was making money. What I wanted, you see, was my own likkle army of men cutting and carrying bananas to the pier. No middleman between me and the ship." He had seen the silk shirts and gold migrant workers brought back from Panama. What he wanted was simple: He wanted wealth, the very thing that had eluded his parents, neither of whom was privileged nor white nor educated. He couldn't change his skin—which was the color of coffee beans and just as smooth and unblemished—but he could change the texture of the shirt that whispered against his back and arms. He could dream of an expanse of land with banana or coconut, a hill rising to a small cut-stone house, his wife within and children without. He could dream about a piece of property to pass on.

Those thoughts had brought him to the seaside. Pearline simultaneously pictures him telling her this story when she was a child and as he must have been on the day he described, walking with his head down, kicking at dry coconuts, sinking his bare toes into the sand, listening to the swishing and slapping of waves against the rocks. She imagines those sounds wrapping around his body like a soft sheet. He was a man of symbols, and he had come to the seaside to wait for a sign, the universe spitting back or accepting his dream.

"What difference," Irene had asked him, "between what you do here and what you goin' do over there? Same work with cutlass. Same white man is the boss. If you caan do better, stay wid wha' you know."

But Rupert couldn't let go of the dream, couldn't let go of what the advertisements tacked on the poles and printed in the daily newspapers promised. The rocks along the beach jutted out like a natural pier, and that was where he knelt, not exactly praying but asking that Irene understand and forgive his deception.

"You see, I was waiting for a sign, but I done already tell Carlton I going wid him. We had plans to meet at the train station." He had planned in advance, saved five pounds to secure his passage, cover the head tax, doctor's certificate, police permit, and British passport. Everything was set, except for the permission he felt he needed from his wife.

Rupert talked about Carlton with reverence. He respected traveling men; history had taught him that men could make their fortunes by traveling to other countries. The British, Spanish, French, Dutch made their fortunes by traveling to and colonizing distant lands. Post-slavery, Panama and its canal offered both his father's generation and his a chance at riches they didn't have here on their own island. Why wait for riches to come to him? Carlton had already gone to Cuba and returned several times over, and he knew the details: the dates on which the boats sailed, where and how to get a passport and doctor's certificate, and which plantations in Cuba treated its workers poorly. Rupert briefly wanted to be Carlton, calling the names of Cuban places with ease: Ciego de Ávila, Holguín, Manatí, Santiago de Cuba. He wanted to sound like a man with book knowledge. He wanted to sound and look like a man of importance.

Again, Pearline pictures her father with his eyes closed, listening to the shifting sounds of the waves, the urgency of water lapping against the shore and gurgling softly in rocky pools. It was always at this point in his story that the sounds he described shifted, and he talked of a voice saying *yes, yes*. Sometimes when he told the story, the voice said, *Gwan, me bwoy*. Sometimes the voice was that of a granduncle who went to sea and never returned, and sometimes he said it was just the wind bringing him an anonymous voice from the sea.

Whatever it was, it was all the permission he needed. Rupert sprinted away from the solitary beach for the rail station and the journey across the island to the port in Kingston.

Pearline envisions a version of her father who is light on his feet, running toward a future, picking meaning from everything: the robust "walk good" that a childhood friend called out to him near the station, the higgler who pressed a baked sweet potato into his hand, and even the sun's rays bursting from behind a cloud as if nothing could hold its light back. His last task was sending word to Irene. Just before he got on the train, he pressed a small paper and some coins into the hand of a boy who haunted the waterfront shops looking for odd jobs. On that paper, Rupert had written eight words: *Gone to Cuba. Be back in six months.*

Pearline thinks about her father's cowardly and secretive departure, how Irene made do without him. All her life when Pearline heard her father's story, she had chuckled, praising his bravery, the gumption it took to run toward an unknown country without his wife's support. Only now does she think about it from her mother's perspective, and it bothers her that she has for so long thought only of her father's drive to succeed and not the selfishness of his departure. Irene, too, usually downplayed it, waving at the air whenever Rupert told the story, as if his departure was just an ordinary, everyday thing, as if sending a boy to deliver a hastily scribbled note with such news was normal.

Irene told her version to her girls away from Rupert's audience, usually in a quiet domestic moment, standing in the very spot where Pearline now stands, hands plunged in the soapy water, or when she was squatting in front of a basin, rubbing a brush against Rupert's clothes. She hummed mostly. When she spoke, her voice was soft, as if she, too, was keeping a secret from Rupert.

"Somebody come. Only way I know was 'cause the chickens start scatter and squawk. Dem chicken use' to act like guard dog. And de one lazy dog never bodda bark." That's where Irene always began her version of the story. She and Rupert were living in Montego Bay then in a little house behind her aunt's. Irene was trying to cook dinner in a pot over a fire that seemed unwilling to catch when two boys appeared by the side of the road, watching the dog and the house and the panicked chickens strutting back and forth.

"Mi have a message," the taller boy said.

"From who?"

"A man down by the station. Him say to gi you dis."

Irene took the paper, and the boys scattered, kicking up a bit of dust as they ran through the yard pecked over and over by the chickens. Irene read the hastily written words: *Gone to Cuba. Be back in six months.* Irene expected nothing less and nothing more. She crumpled the paper, turned back toward the anemic fire, and dropped the paper in. She fanned the fire and shifted the pieces of wood, watching for the orange glow, then she tipped some water from the pot and returned a piece of yam to the storage box, for there was one less person to feed that night.

When Irene told the story, she slowed down here, stopped scrubbing, and let the drip-drip of the water falling back into the basin be the only sound. Her face often took on a faraway look. Pearline came to see that her mother was hiding some-thing: the hurt that had settled deep inside. It was years before Irene told Pearline why she was so weary of wandering men. Her father and uncles dug ditches for the construction of the Panama Canal. Her father, when he returned in 1905, wasn't draped in gold as many a Colón man, but he spoke with an American twang and laced his English with Spanish words that no members of his family understood. Irene's uncle Stan, however, returned the same year with gold ringing his fingers and neck. He was the image of success and progress—a flashy Colón man—but spirits haunted him day and night. So strong was the haunting that he leveled the cotton tree growing in the yard, believing, like many, that the spirits lived in the cotton tree. Still, even after he cut the tree down, the spirits gave him no rest. Her uncle Stan moved from room to room in the small house, seeking solace from the spirits he alone could see. He dribbled rum in every corner of the house and later left food cooked without salt in conspicuous places to feed the spirits. Still the haunting persisted, and he moved to a cave, believing until he died that the spirits would never find him there.

It was Irene who took him food—boiled yellow or sweet yams, boiled bananas, steamed cabbage, hot cocoa in a glass jar—taking away bit by bit the gold pieces that would no longer serve his needs, returning them to her aunt, who had chil-dren to feed. Later, she took only his words, *mi querida, mi hija, enamorada.* Once, he held and kissed her open palm. She turned away, her clean hand grabbing her stomach and then her mouth. She heaved until her stomach calmed. Three days later, when she returned, he was still at the mouth of the cave, no longer on his knees but toppled on his side, his body stiff and covered with flies. Nothing good, she thought, comes of travel abroad.

Irene would hold that belief always, along with the image of a Colón man in tattered clothing, crawling from the mouth of a cave, blood oozing from cuts on his knees, the soles of his feet hardened and crusted with dirt, and his mouth opened always to form the words *"Mi querida, queda conmigo!"* My love, stay with me.

To Irene, men came and went like peenie wallies in the night, flashing a bright light and then disappearing to Panama, Cuba, Costa Rica, America, England, to war or for work. Rupert left and made her into a girl again. The night the boy delivered the note, she dreamt of Rupert, standing at the edge of a wharf, holding his hat, shouting from a distance, *"Mi querida, queda conmigo!"* Rupert didn't know Spanish, but that's the language he spoke in her dream. His words carried over the water, and his mouth stayed round for that final "o." When Irene woke, there was a speck of blood on her lips.

Irene spent no time worrying about the type of man Rupert would be when he returned or whether he would indeed return. She bid her few friends and distant relatives in the immediate area goodbye and headed back to St. Ann, two parishes away, where her people, lured by the whims of her father, had gone to make a living from pimento farming. Irene took her time traveling by donkey cart, on foot, and by train. She couldn't and wouldn't sit down and cry. She simply left and went home to build a different life without Rupert.

The sheets flap in the breeze, the cattle moo, and for a minute it feels like Pearline is a child again, and her father is in the fields a little way from the house tending to his crops. She watches a gaulin high-stepping among the cattle. There's something familiar about the day, the way the sunlight hits and the clouds move, that feels like the lazy early afternoons of her childhood. Derek has still not returned, and she tells herself she should drive toward Runaway Bay in search of him before she has to pick up Claudia.

Instead of heading out to look for Derek, she returns to the room in the back, looking around, waiting like her father always did for a sign. Once, when she was little, she asked Rupert how he knew he was meant to be in Cuba. "What was the sign?"

"A tree," Rupert said. "After the voice, it was a tree. You gwan laugh. Everything I tell you is the truth."

Rupert didn't know immediately though. When he told this part of the story, he leaned back in the chair and stretched his legs out, or he stood up and paced as if the very act of retelling it put him back into the quarantine station in Cayo Duán. He deepened his voice too, as if to reflect the man he wanted to be, measuring himself with every word against the man he was. He hadn't expected to be quarantined. All his thoughts had focused exclusively on the work and the pay and not on the details of a migrant worker's life—the quarantine station, doctors and government officials inspecting his body and papers and standing between him and his desire to set foot on Cuban soil. He hadn't given thought to the type of men who made the journey—teachers whose speech mimicked the Queen's English, carpenters, cobblers, machinists who'd come back from Panama and found life on their islands too hard, farmers like himself—all of them lured by the same propaganda of money flowing.

"The heat and the stench," Rupert said. "That alone make me wan' come back home. But there was a teacher man there. Him make me stay. That was the first sign." There were no baths, no washbasins, no conveniences. "Before you know it, everybody sick. All night you just hear man a cough."

The teacher carried with him a folded newspaper sheet, where he had circled a portion of the editorial. Rupert knew the passage by heart, and he recited it when he told his story. *One, in fact, can earn enough in Cuba in six months to keep one for a whole year, with ordinary forethought and prudence; and what several of our people have formerly done is this. They have labored in Cuba all through the sugar season, saved a tiny bit of money, returned to Jamaica, and either set up in trade for themselves or purchased a piece of agricultural land, which they have cultivated.* These words were a road map of sorts, a plan for how he'd build his life.

Lying in the quarantine station among other laborers like himself—some on beds, others on the floor—the newspaper was all they had, and the men passed it among themselves. "I never so happy to see the sun as when the fifteen days up."

Miles and miles of cane slipped by, the vegetation no more green than what he had left behind in Jamaica. And yet, he said, the countryside looked more fertile, the cane more vibrant, the flowering poinciana a more distinct red-orange. When he left for Jobabo, he carried six things: a hammock, which he bought in Santiago de Cuba for two dollars; a cutlass, not yet sharpened; a clean shirt; a clean pair of pants; some paper; and a pen to write his first letter to Irene. He tucked deep inside himself the memory of those first two weeks, and even then, he knew his letters home would say nothing of his quarantine.

The way he told it, that time of year, November, 1916, the plains off Río Jobabo were forest green, the cane leaves as sharp as blades and stalks packed so tight only a whisper of wind blew between them. Snakes, rats, and mongoose moved on the ground, each species slithering toward or scampering away from the other. And in the clearing beyond the expansive cane fields, wagons lay around the mill yard like discarded skeletons, the front of their wooden bodies pressed into the earth and the back held aloft by oversized metal wheels. Absent the mechanical whirs of cane grinding, the constant hum of the machines, the strikes that signal sugar is nearly ready to drop into the bags below, the mill was mostly quiet. But the dead season, as it was called, was coming to an end, the cane cutters were arriving in batches, the nearby trains clacking along the tracks. A few palm trees waved near some of the larger houses. And he realized then that even with the swath of fields, the place looked barren. There were hardly any trees on the flat plains, all cut down, it seemed, for banana, sugar, and tobacco crops. Trees filled the hillsides though.

What did he know of Jobabo, this place where he would live and work for six months at least? Nothing. He knew the pay would be good. The contract listed the owner of the mill as The

Cuba Company, but it was no more Cuban than he was. The company operated out of New York.

When he arrived, someone pointed out the *batey*, the center of the plantation, the shops where he could stock up on food, the pristine grounds of the managers' homes, the barracks where the American workers lived, the other barracks where he would stay. No one described the housing structure by race but by job functions. Yet Rupert knew exactly how the housing arrangements fell across racial lines. One *barracones* housed white managers, and the other housed black field laborers. Another person pointed to a jagüe tree, which grew away from the batey and stood alone, triumphant. "Parasite. A vine. You wouldn't believe a tree big so is a vine. You know what the name mean? The tree of a thousand feet or the tree that walks."

The vine wrapped itself around a tree and anchored itself with thousands of roots to survive. "When mi see how the tree survive, mi know. That tree is me. I am that tree." He wanted to see no mistakes in his actions, to harbor no regrets.

That's where their circumstances diverged. Rupert had time to wait and see; Pearline doesn't.

8.

PEARLINE DRAGS THE CHAIR OUT OF THE BEDROOM, NOT caring that the feet may scratch the floor. For the second morning in a row, she has awakened with the sense that her father is sitting in the chair looking at her. The trees, lit by moonlight, cast moving shadows against the chair and wall, and the being that is her father moves as well, lifting a hand to smooth his jawline and resting the other on the chair's arm. He stretches out his legs, leans back in the chair the way he always did after a long day in the fields. He'd sit with a tin cup at his feet and a bowl or plate balanced on his palm, just looking out at everything and nothing, digging into whatever Irene had cooked. Then he'd say, "Well, well. Thank the Lord."

Now, in these nighttime visitations, Rupert, or the shape of him in the chair, calls for Arturo just as he did on his last day. He never calls the other children by name. There's something in his voice, guilt or fear or love or disappointment, that Pearline feels he can't let go. The voice and the call haunt her, burying into her, until the voice she hears is like a patter on her eardrums, close and loud. Even now when she's halfway down the hall, she hears his voice drawing out Arturo's name.

The chair bucks on a raised floorboard, and Pearline stops,

stretches her back. She looks around the already cluttered living room, at the overstuffed sofa that has been reupholstered many times, the spare chairs from an older dining room set, the whatnot unit in the corner, the large vintage stereo. Plastic floral arrangements, which she's promised to throw out, are still on the center table. A pair of brown ceramic dogs sit in the corner closest to her. There's no room for the overstuffed armchair.

"You need help?" Derek is standing by his bedroom door, shifting his glances between the chair and Pearline.

"No." Pearline is paralyzed. She's caught between her desire to move the chair out of her bedroom to stop her father's visitations and wanting her father to come so she can find out why he calls for Arturo. What is it that haunts him? What is that specific moment that Rupert's spirit has not been able to let go? It aches not to know what Rupert would say if the boy answered him. "Help me move this back in the room. Too crowded inside there."

Pearline is still on edge, jittery, and she stands at the threshold of the living room, waiting until she's heard the last push and pull of the chair and Derek's footsteps coming back toward her.

"Anything else?" Derek looks at her warily, as if he's wondering what he's run away from and into.

"No, that's it." Pearline heads back toward her bedroom, her slippers making swooshing sounds on the wood.

"Next time, just call me," Derek says. "Don't want you to hurt yourself."

Pearline lifts her hand, gives Derek a backward wave. "I so

used to doing things by myself I forget I have a big strong-back man like you around."

Derek chuckles and she hears him gently close his door. Pearline heads to the window. It's barely light outside, and she feels bad now about waking Derek and disturbing the early-morning solitude with her misplaced desire to stop her nighttime awakenings. Pearline sits in the chair and props her feet up on the bed. This time she sleeps, and sleeps deeply without interruption.

From her bedroom, Pearline hears the soft purr of Hermina's late-model Toyota pulling up outside and her sisters' laughter. Both her sisters step out. It's been a full week since she's heard from either of them. They are laughing hard, one bending forward and leaning against the car hood for support, the other holding on to the doorframe.

"Mind you burn yourself on that hot metal," Pearline calls. She's on the veranda now, waiting to hear what has tickled them so. "My nursing days done."

Still they laugh, each holding the bottom of their bellies, acting like schoolgirls. The sound of their cackling is as loud as the jabbering crows' caws. By the time they stop and climb the steps, Derek has come outside. He stands in the doorway behind Pearline, shirtless, leaning against the doorframe.

"Eh, she take up with young man." Hermina starts laughing anew and, weakened again, plops herself on the steps. "Mi belly."

Aileen, laughing too, turns away from the steps and leans against the car, and Pearline watches them, once again feeling far removed from the connection her sisters have. She's excluded from their silent and coded way of communicating that's built upon their shared adult experiences and the family stories they now tell that don't include Pearline at all. They have stories about her father she suspects she'll never hear.

This feeling of estrangement is not new. All her time in America she has felt it, always felt she was a step behind understanding cultural references, making small talk at parties to people with a background that wasn't quite like hers. But here, with her sisters, she didn't expect it. She thought she would ease back in to the way it was when they were children, when the order of their birth mattered and Hermina followed her lead. Instead, she is the returned resident, the foreigner, the one who doesn't understand how things work here.

Surprisingly, Pearline is calm. She doesn't try to fit in, doesn't think of a way to join in their laughter as she would once have done. She has never sought or needed their validation. Why should she seek it now? The space between them widens, and she pictures them like two groups on opposite riverbanks, each needing the other to get across but thinking of separate, distinct ways to do so. Pearline steps back to the low-slung chair, lowers herself, drops her elbows to her knees, and waits. In that moment, she feels like her mother waiting on the girls to explain some misdeed or another, except back then they wouldn't have been laughing. Their faces would have been tight and serious, their eyes darting back and forth between Irene's switch and her face.

When her sisters both sober up, Aileen is the first to speak. "So you not introducing us to your young man?"

"Derek," Pearline says, "come meet your two aunts."

"Aunts?" Hermina says. She glances quickly at Aileen, raises her brows. "Who fa pickney that? Where you find nephew?"

"Don't tell me you have a secret son all these years." Aileen is at the top of the steps now, inspecting Derek, her eyes taking in every detail, looking for some feature or other that marks him as a blood relative.

Derek's complexion is a shade lighter than theirs, and there's a splash of spots on his forehead and temple with less pigment—some type of vitiligo, Pearline thinks. The way her sisters look at Derek tells Pearline exactly what they're thinking. She knows that look—the single dismissive, scornful glance that betrays their preconceived notion of his entire history and foretells his future. Pearline knows how it plays out in different scenarios: a security guard looking him up and down and repositioning himself by the exit; strangers taking in the diamond studs dotting his ears and his dreadlocks in the early stages of matting and turning away as if he mattered little; a doctor looking at him and assuming gangster or drug dealer. His locks, fuzzy and puffy uncontrollable stubs that weren't yet ready to lie neatly against his scalp, and his pants, which drooped a little too low, low enough for the band of his briefs to show above his belt, convey to them his entire story. Even here in Jamaica, the response is similar because he doesn't conform to the conservative looks Pearline's generation and the generations before prefer—a look that binds them to European ideals. It's taken Pearline nearly half a lifetime to dismiss those cares and shed the standards taught alongside the alphabet and basic subtraction and addition.

"Tell them," Pearline says.

"But wait?" Aileen holds up a hand. "From when you come?"

"Sunday," Derek says.

"So you here six days and is now we meeting you? Not even a phone call? Not a 'come meet your nephew'?"

Hermina leans toward Aileen. "Could be she have something to hide. That might just be what women call dem young boys nowadays. Me an' you too backward to know these things."

"All right, enough," Pearline says, her response so brusque her sisters share another glance.

"So who you now?" Aileen turns to Derek, stares at him as hard as she would have stared at a student.

There's uncertainty in Derek's voice. He leaves out a lot, skirts around the primary reason he is on the island and at his grandfather's house. But he tells them of his father, Victor, his relatives in the communities around Brown's Town.

"Bring me some of whatever drink you have round there." Hermina lifts her chin in Derek's direction.

"Carrot juice in the fridge," Pearline says. "And bring some slices of the bun."

No one speaks until Derek is out of sight and his footsteps fall away.

"So he come just so and you let him stay here?" Aileen tries not to raise her voice. Yet her words are harsh, sharp. "You wouldn't do this in Brooklyn, and yet you come back here and let a complete stranger sleep in the house with you and Claudia. What you thinking?"

"And keep so quiet about it too." Hermina glances at Aileen with a slight lift of her brows. "Like is you who have something to hide. Not a word about it. Not a drop."

"Fussing with us 'bout the appraiser we forget to tell you 'bout and then turn 'round and keep big secret like this. For all we know, he could kill you in the night. Then poor us have to go tell police say we never know you have man in the house."

"Lawd, Aileen, no say it like that." Hermina laughs. "Serious business. You can't trust any- and everybody."

Pearline doesn't like the insinuation, but she waves her hand, downplays it. "Never mind that. He's family." For a moment, she feels like a child being chastised by her mother in this very same spot on the veranda, shame blooming through her body like a spreading fever. Except now she feels no shame, just a certainty that welcoming Derek was right and exactly what her parents would have done—both doing it for wholly different reasons: one spiteful, the other stubborn, but neither letting the young man feel unwelcome.

"How you so sure he's family?" Hermina again looks at Aileen and shifts her eyes quickly away. Her eyes skitter across the veranda and remain fixed on the yard. "And even if he's family, he can still turn on you. Even family will turn on you."

"You don't seem surprised to hear about Victor." Pearline cocks her head, shifts her eyes from Aileen to Hermina and back again. "You knew about him? His mother?"

"You hear things, and when you begin to hear the same thing over and over, you believe it," Aileen says. "Besides, when you live in a small, small place, everybody take your business and make it theirs. You should remember that. And there's always somebody who feel you must know the *truth*, who carry news come give you even when you don't want to hear it. Even if they can't verify it, so long as they think is the truth or very nearly the truth, they coming to tell you."

"So you knew about him? That's all I want to know."

"Pearline, mi caan tell you if is true or not. Mi can only tell you what mi hear." Aileen emphasizes every word, leaning back after she speaks and stretching her legs out before her.

"You're the only one who thinks Papa was a saint." Hermina keeps her eyes fixed, staring at something in the distance. "That man was no saint. Mama knew it. We knew it. Only you think he was a saint."

"He tried," Pearline says. "How that man tried."

They hear Derek's footsteps, the drinking glasses clinking, and Aileen rushes out what she wants to say. "Anyway, you can't let people take advantage of you. Look at Claudia. Even now, her mother don't come back yet. And if you don't watch it, you raising that child till she turn eighteen."

"Don't bring Claudia into this. You know I couldn't tell Yvonne no. After all she did for Papa, you wanted me to tell her I couldn't keep her child while she go off to find work?"

"You say it like she just have a day job in Ochie or Falmouth and come home to her child every day. Look how far Cayman is. Who to tell when she coming back? That I know I couldn't do. No matter how life hard, I swore I would never leave my children."

"Easy for you to say."

"What you mean by that?"

"Some of us have to do things we never imagined we would.

Anyway, forget 'bout that. Claudia is my responsibility, and I'm not complaining."

"One thing I telling you—you can't save everybody, and if you not careful, people will bleed you dry." Aileen brushes her hands together as if to say *Argument done.*

Derek is closer now. He's brought three glasses of the milky carrot drink. Aileen wastes no time, takes charge as she's wont to do. "So tell me what it is you running from."

"Running?" Derek looks at Pearline, and she opens a palm as if to say *I don't know what she means.*

"Yes," Aileen says, dropping back into schoolteacher mode. "Young man like you leave America all of a sudden to come here to Mount Pleasant. You must be running from something."

Pearline watches his chest rise and fall, imagines his quickening heart. She could save him from the questions, but she doesn't. She's working through where the question fails, not the inappropriateness of it, but how it suggests such limited possibilities, as if migration from Mount Pleasant, or Jamaica itself, should be only a one-way road. Migrating in search of work is all her family has known. Every generation it's the same, except that her generation, and perhaps the one after, no longer expects those who leave to return to Jamaica.

As if Derek senses the inappropriateness of Aileen's question, he answers as directly as she asks. "I wasn't there," he says. "I didn't kill Joey." The way he pauses, he knows the effect of his words.

Hermina and Aileen suck in and hold their breath. "Lord God Almighty," Aileen says.

Pearline almost laughs, but she holds it back, watches the

horror and disgust spreading across her sisters' faces. She almost expects the dramatic hand upon the chest and the exaggerated intake of breath when they hear the rest of it. But Hermina squirms instead, and Aileen sits upright with a hand on her chin, waiting. Pearline admires his honesty, how forthright he is with the details.

"All I know," Derek says, "is the gang had a plan to scare Joey."

"Gang?" Aileen looks at Pearline when she speaks, her lips curling up in a sneer. "Murder?"

"It wasn't really a gang," Derek says. "We just called ourselves that. Anyway, initially, they just wanted to scare him. But then they started plotting it out and it turned real. Really fast."

Derek adds more details, exaggerating the events he told Pearline. The story sounds manufactured, like the plot of a television series. She no longer knows what's true. The plan Derek sketches out was a grid made to look like a game of tic-tac-toe, with Joey at its center, surrounded by the elements necessary to lure Joey to the ship graveyard. Every element had fallen into place, except that a detective examining Joey's body on the rocks reported that the awkward angle at which his body was found suggested murder and not an accident. One thing Derek didn't know: the exact cause of Joey's death.

"I know you going to judge me. But I didn't kill Joey. And I don't know how he died."

"So if you don't know anything, why you run down here to hide?"

"I know who was there," he says. "And they are some people I don't want to mess with."

"Your own friends?" Hermina asks.

"Joey was their friend too."

Pearline has misread him. She sees now that he's not responding to the inappropriateness of the question but is desperate to be accepted. He wants her to save him. He is a frightened young man, unsure of himself, of his place, afraid, too, of losing his only refuge. "All right," she says. "You never come here to interrogate Derek. So it must be something else."

When Derek goes back inside, Pearline says, "You of all people, a principal, should know better than to judge the boy just so. Give him a chance. And you know me all my life. You know my judgment. That alone should be enough."

"Is long time you gone," Aileen says. "Who knows what kind of woman you've become."

"What an indictment," Pearline says, exactly how her mother would have said it. But she doesn't know exactly what Aileen means. "I know you didn't come all this way to chastise me," Pearline says.

"Matter of fact, no." Hermina sets her glass on the floor. "I meant to ask you this all week. Some friends holding a clinic up in Alexandria, and I wanted to see if you could help out."

"Doing what?"

"You're the nurse."

"You the one asking for a favor. So tell me what they need help with."

"Anything they need a nurse to do."

"I hang up that hat, mi dear. Thirty years of that, no way."

"Suit yourself. But if I knew a thing about medicine, I would be up there helping out. So many people showed up yesterday they couldn't keep up. And they have two more days of it."

"You act like I don't have anything else to do."

"Like I said, suit yourself."

"Leave her to her things," Aileen says. "She have nuff things to do."

"Another thing," Hermina says. "We looking for some papers."

"What papers?" Pearline feels a deep need to close the house to them.

"Birth certificate, burial papers."

"Not you have them? One of you, anyway."

"I put the burial paper on top the fridge after the funeral. Didn't want to lose it. As for his birth certificate, it here somewhere."

"What you want birth papers for?" Pearline is wary again. She has a distinct feeling her sisters are plotting something else she'll learn about after the fact.

"You so suspicious," Aileen says. She glances at Hermina, her eyes moving so quickly that Pearline could easily have missed it. "I don't know how things go in America, but we need all them papers to close Papa bank account."

"The two of us on the accounts," Hermina adds. She says it sheepishly, as if she knows exactly what Pearline is thinking.

"All right."

Pearline steers her sisters away from the room in the back with the trunks and toward the chest of drawers in her bedroom that she hasn't yet gone through. She's not ready to reveal what she has found back there. The top drawer is stacked with envelopes—aged bank statements, yellowing Christmas and birthday cards, handwritten receipts for appliances and tuition —artifacts of a family's life. All three of them bend forward, heads almost touching, and for a moment, it feels like they are one unit committed to the same cause. Rupert and Irene's girls, pretending they are triplets, working together on a common goal.

9.

PEARLINE'S A CHILD AGAIN, SITTING ON THE FLOOR BY Rupert's feet. He's not in the armchair across from her but on the veranda, legs stretched out before him. Night has crept up around them. The breeze tickles her bare arms. June bugs fly into the lamps, their bodies making soft pings against the glass before they fall to the floor, stunned. Pearline picks up the bugs one by one, and Aileen glares, warning her against throwing the bugs in her direction. Rupert's voice is like a low and constant hum. He's talking about Jobabo, describing a night much like the present: the pitch is at its deepest and the nighttime sounds—a slight rustling, like leaves brushing against the roof, frogs croaking, crickets chirping—creep closer. Except the sound her father describes is inside the field barracks where he's living, close to him. Mice, perhaps, he thinks, or maybe a rat bat returning before daylight. He lies still, lets his eyes adjust to the dark, waiting to see what, if anything, moves.

Pearline wakes with a start. She's afraid to move, worried that if she shifts to her right she will see Rupert sitting in the chair in the corner, talking. Every night now for the past month she wakes to this feeling. Pearline lies still as if danger or something else lurks outside her window, as if any movement will disturb that unseen or invisible thing, or she will indeed see movement from the chair in the corner. She closes her eyes tight, trying to shut out the vision or the dream. Instead, her father's voice comes back clearer, his presence more vivid.

Her mother, sisters, an uncle and his wife, and two neighbors are all gathered on the veranda. Only, the chair on the veranda is peach, not the aqua color it is now. Her uncle has just finished telling a story about a man who died in Cuba and another one who wrote home to say life there is good.

"No, no," Rupert says. "Cuba was hell. A living hell. It's a wonder all o' we live to come back home."

"It wasn't all bad." Irene waves her hand from side to side, drops her chin to her chest.

"No. Let me talk, nuh." Rupert tells the group about the night he heard the scratching in the barracks. He isn't sure what woke him that night, whether it was the scratching sound or a dream.

Rupert pauses, lifts up an arm, rolls his sleeve back, and shows a scar he wore like a tattoo. "See this? Every day I look at this and remember."

Silence slips over the night like a veil. Pearline and the others sit waiting for Rupert to continue the story he began.

He hears paper against wood, the whisper of a shoe against the floor. When he shifts, he sees his friend Carlton slowly untying his hammock, rolling it, bundling his belongings into a small bag. Carlton moves with deliberate slowness, his silhouette like a marionette controlled by an external source. Carlton, his closest friend here, the man who had lured him to

Cuba, is leaving, taking off in the dead of night without telling him. Carlton disappears.

Rupert turns away from the door so as not to watch his friend leave, or ask, "Where you going?" But Carlton doesn't get very far. A group of three men burst inside. Lamplight floods the room. Rupert jumps, swings his legs toward the floor, his momentum pushing the hammock into a full swing. Rupert can't make out the color of the men's skin, can't see their faces. But he smells their sweat and the pungent odor of a bush he doesn't recognize. The room becomes alive.

Rupert's knees and legs are weak, fear bubbling up inside him, his heart beating out a fast rhythm in his chest. He moves without thinking, bounding across the tamped dirt floor toward the lamplight, his fists raised, ready to tackle whoever it is. Rupert is no fighter, yet he pounces, swinging once, twice. His fist lands on flesh and bone, and the pain of it reverberates up his arm. A lamp falls, the flame quickly going out, and two fists come toward his face.

"*Cállate y muévete!*" The man's voice is harsh, his movements quick.

Rupert reaches out again, swinging at the man's body, kicking at the air, rolling to avoid a boot coming toward his stomach. The machete lands, breaks Rupert's skin.

"Rupert. Rupert." Carlton shouts at Rupert, a desperation in his voice that Rupert hadn't heard before. He feels Carlton's hands on his arms. "No, man. Don't do it."

Rupert pushes back against Carlton, slowing only when he notices that the men have guns. Neither Rupert nor the rest of the workers in the barracks have weapons. And only then does he realize these are rebels. There's a war. Cuban insurgents are rising up against their government, raiding, burning, and looting American-owned sugarcane estates, blowing up bridges and railway tracks.

Rupert stumbles backward toward the thatch wall, watching and measuring the rebels who move across the room as if they have memorized every inch of it, know which man sleeps where and what he possesses. The rebels loosen and roll the hammocks, pack the men's single pairs of boots, moving through the room as if fire is behind them. The sounds traveling across the barracks are more distinct now—raised voices, Spanish and English, rustling, metal clanging against wood, a sharp slap, more scuffling.

Within minutes, the rebels are gone, the room barren without the hammocks strung across it. At least, Rupert thinks, the rebels hadn't searched for money. He has a little stashed away, the one thing he is counting on to prove to Irene that this trip was worth it. And yet, each day now, there is another reason for him to question why he stays.

"Man, what you thinking? They could a shoot all o' we."

Rupert brushes Carlton aside. The entire barracks is awake now, the excitement like any daytime rhythm, one then another recounting what happened, Carlton making out Rupert not as the reluctant hero he wants to see in himself but as a fool. Rupert wants none of it. And he steps away from the men he once called brothers to put a cold rag on his swollen face and wash away the blood.

"My wife did warn me," Rupert says. "If she could see me now."

Slowly, the night quiets, settles. Smoke lingers in the air; the charred smell of sugarcane is buried in every fiber of Rupert's clothes, lingering, too, below his nostrils, so close it feels like he could taste it. Regret steeps in him, taking over his body, but he refuses to acknowledge that he should not have come to Cuba, should not have left his little island to come to this one. He wants to go back to another time, a simpler one, and he wants to know if anything should happen to him, who would tell Irene.

Just then, Claudia cries out, her scream piercing. Pearline jumps up. The dream and the sense of her father's presence slip away instantly. Claudia is pointing at the window, saying, "Papa gone." But she's not awake. She's still in the midst of a dream herself, moving, thrashing, talking. Pearline gathers Claudia and tucks her in with her in the larger bed. She lies awake, holding back the dreams of her father.

It dawns on her that he will come again and again to make sure she doesn't rest until she does what he has asked. She lies like she's comatose until restlessness eats at her, brushes against her legs like tall grass. If he won't rest, neither will she.

Nights when Rupert told stories about Cuba were plentiful in her early childhood. The three siblings and their parents would sit by the candlelight, Rupert or Irene—mostly Rupert—telling Anansi or duppy stories or some tale of a time before the girls were born. Sometimes, when Rupert had harvested and dried produce, the sound of pea or corn grains or pimento hitting the tin bowls would ring out. Other times they ate roasted corn and played a guessing game, each of them taking turns asking, "Ship sail. How many men?" The others had to guess how many corn grains the speaker held in a closed fist.

Pearline remembers a night like this, similar to the one she was dreaming about before Claudia woke up. It was the night that Rupert first spoke about what happened in 1917. The crops on their farm that year were plentiful, and her grandparents were present, helping to shell corn and sieve the stems from dried pimento. Someone, an uncle or neighbor, said Rupert could go off on farm work in America now that the crops have come in. "Bring in something extra to add on to the house."

"Gwan now before you plant the yam. By the time you come back, groun' ready again."

The memory seeps into Pearline like water, and she's back there with her family. Rupert shakes his head. At first, he doesn't speak, but the jokes continue. Someone calls him a coward, says he's afraid of foreign. Quick money, another says. But again and again, the gentle ribbing comes back to Rupert's fear.

Rupert leans back. "Let me tell you something." He pauses, and Pearline knows that what he'll say is serious and will be nothing like the Anansi stories she's come to expect. "Unu don't know nutten 'bout foreign. Don't know what we live through in Cuba. Irene can tell you. But I going to tell you about my first time. And after this, argument done. I don't need to ever set foot in another country, you hear me?"

He stretches his legs. Pearline is too young to know this is the contemplative man her father sometimes is. "Nineteen seventeen," he begins. "Don't know nutten and too young to know what I don't know." The young man he describes doesn't understand American economic imperialism, the vast ways in which the United States expands its territories, or how American companies come to dominate the sugarcane estates on the northern coast of Oriente Province. But he knows the companies are advertising for labor, black men from Jamaica and Haiti and Barbados and the small Antillean islands who can cut cane. What Rupert knows is simple: There is work and money. Anyone who wants to work can. And what he stands to earn in six months is enough to keep him and his family for a year.

He can recite from memory the language of the fliers posted around Montego Bay and on full pages in *The Gleaner*— advertisement after advertisement offering passage and clearance. *Cuba! Cuba! The cheapest, reliable, and bona fide service in Kingston . . . No need to go to so-called Agents who have no boats to take you . . . The Motor Schooner "Emerson Faye" will also sail to Santiago de Cuba 18th, 28th Jan., 10th Feb. Please book early to avoid disappointment . . . The schooner "Lovenia" sails every Friday . . . Females wanted in abundance . . . Millions of pounds already noted for laborers to earn . . .*

"It don't take long for everything to go wrong," he says. "When you work in a cane field, you used to the smell of smoke. You used to cane burning 'cause you have to burn the fields before man go in and start to chop. But what I telling you about is not just that. This was a revolt. Cane and buildings and bridge. Everything burning."

Rupert sits up straighter. He leans forward. Irene tenses, and the girls mirror Irene's response. Even now, Pearline does the same, shifting as if she experiences the overwhelming scent of smoke Rupert describes. Soot—sprinkled around on broad, flat leaves and on the pots in the kitchen—disintegrates under his fingers. Pearline moves her fingers as if she too feels the soot, as if she is also moving her hands to brush soot from everything.

Rupert is keen to the sound of hoofbeats, sometimes as loud as a hundred fingers on drums. When he hears the thunderous sound, he never knows what to expect—another influx of government troops or rebels, another round of fire in the canes. Men are leaving for other estates. But Rupert, still new to Cuba, can't determine where to go—Camagüey, Jatibonico, Ciego de Ávila—or which routes are safest.

Nights, Rupert doesn't sleep. He lies awake tracking the sounds, those distant and near, that come unfiltered to him in the cabin, and imagining his death, his lungs strangled with smoke as fire spreads from the fields to the barracks, his body charred black, the brittle remains of him buried somewhere in the fields, or rebels again coming in the night in search of clothes or food or money. He's aware that Irene and his parents may never know what happens to him.

He is acutely aware of every sound, the distant crackle of cane leaves burning and animals, low to the ground, scampering away from the heat. He is acutely aware of the hunger in his belly, gas bubbling deep in his stomach, the hunger pangs that move from his shoulder, to his chest, to the bottom of his belly. He pictures Irene, her face hardening and her lips puckering to say "I told you so." Except she would say it differently: "Wha' sweet nanny goat going run him belly," cutting her eyes away the moment the last word leaves her lips.

"February, March, April. Nutten change." There are rumors that government troops have fanned out across the provinces and restored order. There are rumors that two Jamaican men are killed at the Elia Sugar Mill, just up the road from Jobabo. There are rumors that the shooters were government troops who had first taken some new shirts belonging to the two Jamaican men, rumors that the men asked to have their shirts returned but were instead flogged with machetes. There are rumors that when the men talked about their ordeal, a snitch told the troops, who retaliated by leading the men outside and shooting them dead.

"April 1917," he says. "I will never forget."

Around the field barracks, everything is calm, the morning punctuated by the subtle sounds of waking—water trickling, spoons clanging against metal, here and there a yawn and a man groaning as he stretches, birds twittering. There's little to eat, sweet potatoes mostly, for the shops are empty. And there's little work to do. Instead of cutting cane or seeing to the business of making sugar, the men have been fencing fields, herding cattle to the fenced area, and cutting and hauling firewood and cane tops for the horses and oxen. He misses the rattle of train wheels on the track, the hiss of steam, the rhythm of cane moving from field to mill, the mill's machines banging and hissing and pressing cane juice into sugar crystals. Where vapor should have been suspended in the air, there is nothing, not haze, not steam. Absent, too, is the familiar crunch of stone caught between ox-drawn cart wheels and hard-packed earth, the clop of horses' hooves, the heavy, slow advance of carts pulling cut cane toward the *batey*, the rhythmic rise and fall of men bending forward to chop at cane stalks just above the roots.

That morning, Rupert looks at his body and measures the changes by what he sees in the men around him. Their cheeks are hollow, faces long and drawn, and their complexions shades darker from the sun. Wendell's shirt moves freely around his body, puffing up when tucked in, his body within it looking more skeletal as the khaki puffs and blooms like a balloon filling with air. He imagines his own cheeks and the defined muscles in his shoulders and back. Sometimes he pictures Irene rubbing his sore muscles with bay rum or packing herbs in brown paper to tie as a pack on his aching joints. But he tries not to think about her, for she had warned him, not specifically about a revolt and near famine, simply that nothing good comes of travel abroad.

Irene tenses again, and so does Pearline. The sounds around her fall away, and there's a depth to the quiet she can't explain.

"Easter come," Rupert says, "and is like everything break loose. I don't tell you what kin' a name them call we. Savage. Thief. Blame us for everything, looting, assault. So April come. We waiting 'cause we hear government troop coming to protect the workers."

Easter comes and goes, and the sweet potato and flour supplies dwindle. Government troops come and try to restore order. The American families have mostly left. Still, he waits, not sleeping, keeping watch, learning to detect from the weight of sound whether it is a lizard or mouse skittering in the undergrowth or a man's stealthy footsteps.

"April 17," he says. "I will never forget. That mawning I get up to cook. We never have much lef'. Likkle cornmeal, little bit o' dis and dat. Rustle up something and call the man dem to eat."

From outside comes the sound of something breaking, a boom, and another and another. The sound occupies every fiber of Rupert's body. It rings in his ears like a church bell, and he feels every ricochet like the bell's tongue clanging the bronze sides. He holds his body tight, feels his hand moving to cover his lips as if to hold back any sound that might escape. "Gunshots." Rupert doesn't know who speaks, but he hushes the men, each of whom makes themselves small and quiet. Rupert peers out through a sliver of a hole in the wall. Each heartbeat feels like drumbeats in his ears, and his legs are as unsteady as rotting cane bending at the root. He can't hold his body up, but as he slips to the floor, he hears a gun fire again, hears the sharp barks of a machine gun reverberating. The bones in his body feel loose, like sticks bobbing in a water tank.

The kitchen is deathly quiet, each man lying on the ground afraid to move. But Rupert looks around, counting the men beside him, trying to figure out who might have gone outside, who may have been shot and why. Rupert strains to hear the words, make out the commands in a mixture of Spanish and halting English. "Think it done now," he says at last.

But again and again a gun blasts. How long Rupert lies on the ground, shivering, he can't say. But he stays there long after the morning has quieted, thinking over and over, if he should die, who would tell Irene of his demise? He isn't the first to move. And when he does move, when he looks through the tiny hole, he counts two bodies, sees blood oozing into the black earth.

Across the barracks, the survivors are slow to emerge, stepping slowly as if they, too, have been shot, carefully, then frenzied, shock and anger pulsing through them all.

McLeod points toward a guava tree, but Rupert turns away rather than look. Slowly, the story comes out. Seventeen men have died, all lined up like schoolchildren and told they would take photographs. There was no camera, just bullets.

Sounds emerge again, and Pearline wraps her arm around herself, warding off the chill from both the air and the sounds she hears: the rasp of the shovels against gravel, the ping of the metal against stone as the men dig graves to bury their friends. Rupert names the men, and another chill runs through Pearline. The man they called Coco. The man they called Irish because of the sprinkling of red in his hair. Everton. Jerry. Claude. Some names Rupert can't remember. He prays though for each one, holding each face in his mind as if he were picturing a blurry photograph. He pictures the men as he wants to remember them—each leaning against the base of a mango or coconut tree, their long fingers wrapped around a bowl of stew with dumplings and the waning evening sun filtering through the leaves and splashing their bodies with yellow. He hears their laughter, sees Everton standing up and belching after each meal, his eyes as he gets ready to tell a story Rupert knows couldn't be true.

Rupert doesn't look back at Jobabo, the fields of burnt cane that would yield no crop that season, the charred remains of buildings. He keeps his eyes forward. He is alive and riding in an oxcart covered with thatch. The smell of smoke lingers, and he longs for something else—the scent of ripe mangoes, the scent of rotting fruit fermenting, the stench even of cane in production.

"That was my first time," Rupert says.

"And after all that you go back and carry us go there." There's a bitterness to Irene's voice that cuts and burns. "If it wasn't for you, I woulda have all my pickney dem wid me here."

"What to do?" Rupert says. "Them days I couldn't do no better. Hurricane wash way everything. Everything gone."

"If I did follow my mind, I woulda never set foot there," Irene says. She stands up, forgetting the bowl of grains on her lap. The clatter of the metal pan and the grains scattering across the floor shatters the quiet, marking for Pearline how deep her mother's anger runs. And if she's correct, Rupert never told that story again, never opened himself to be publicly blamed for what her family endured.

10.

Tiptoeing to the back room in the early-morning hours to escape the sleeplessness and Rupert's haunting is becoming Pearline's second new ritual. She's learned which floorboards squeak, how to sidestep them, how to move with whisper quiet so as not to wake Derek or Claudia. She's later this morning, slower, even. The sun is already up, the birds chirping and cawing, the hum of traffic getting louder.

She's already in the room in front of the trunk when the telephone rings. It's much too early in the morning, and she answers with a tone she hopes says that. It's Hermina asking, "You decide yet?"

"About what?"

"The clinic."

"No."

"They need you. They were overwhelmed yesterday. And you know this the only care some of these people up in the hills going to get for a long while."

Pearline breathes in deeply. It can't hurt, she thinks, and perhaps this one deed will get her back on the right side of her sisters' thoughts. "All right, yes. What time?"

"Good. They start early. But whatever time you can make it. Ask for Cynthia McGhee. She expecting you."

Pearline takes her time winding through the hills on the way to Alexandria, careful at every turn to remember to stay on the left-hand side of the road. She's dropped Claudia at Hermina's. And Derek is planning to take a bus to Ocho Rios. Ahead of Pearline, a laden truck belches smoke. She hangs back and lets the bus drivers, anxious for an opportunity to pass, go ahead. She doesn't know the road well and worries she will overtake the truck too close to a corner. She's more nervous on this road than she has ever been driving in Jamaica.

Here, the asphalt road is tinged with the red dirt that the bauxite company is mining and carting away to be processed into aluminum. What had once been farmland or hillside communities are now enormous pits of bright red dirt. Bit by bit, the bauxite companies chip away at communities, buying up land, relocating people to brand-new neighborhoods that don't resemble their own. Now, she thinks, the bauxite companies fill in the gouged land and return it to some form of use. But at what price, she thinks. It's one of the issues her father talked about—how much of the island's resources were taken away, how little of it was left for Jamaicans.

There's a line outside the church hall, mostly children whose parents want the children's eyes examined. The hall's windows are blurred by dust and the morning dew, and she bends her head, momentarily shutting out the cracks in the concrete wall, the freshly patched hole that hasn't yet been painted to match the fading yellow wall. She's not a praying woman, but she prays because she already knows that the team won't have nearly enough to meet the community's needs, and it will take more than a day to get through all the complaints here.

The church hall looks like a field hospital. The dental team is in one corner, examining and cleaning teeth. In another corner, a nurse swabs the upper arms of children and gives them injections, mouthing *hush, hush* to calm the wails. A mother calms a baby with bits of ice from a frozen drink and wipes his face with a rag, already dirty from sweat and dust and tears.

Pearline checks in with the staff, finds the young woman Aileen said would be expecting her. "Mi glad say you come," the woman says. "Everybody need some kind o' help."

"Ah, cataracts," a doctor nearby says. "This is something that can be fixed. But you can't wait too long. We don't have the equipment for that this time." He writes out a script and refers the patient to an ophthalmologist in Montego Bay.

"The Lord will provide," the patient says.

"You can't afford to wait," the doctor says again.

Pearline takes the stethoscope and moves to the other end of the hall to help triage the patients. She takes blood pressure and temperature and a quick pinch of blood to check for diabetes.

There was a time when this was her family's life—getting medical care at clinics like this and extra food from a charity that imported bulgur and powdered milk and other rations they would not normally have eaten. Those were the days when the crops failed, when her father miscalculated, or when a drought dried up the breadfruit and ackee on their trees. And she's grateful now that she came, that the clinic in the church hall reminds her that what she has in Mount Pleasant is plenty. She doesn't need Hermina's grand house on the hill or a house on the coast among the other returning residents as her sisters have suggested.

When Pearline leaves, she's exhausted, as tired as if she has been walking miles from ward to ward. It's the stories that have tired her: the pregnant woman drinking cerasee to cleanse her blood so she doesn't give birth to a baby with skin as dark as the baby's father; the woman with sarcoma who's still waiting for her family abroad to get her the money to buy the chemotherapy drug that isn't available on the island; the man drinking soursop leaf tea to bring his blood pressure down because he can't afford the pills; the woman who's there because her health insurance covers only a small part of her annual medical costs.

Pearline thought her nursing days were behind her. But she revives an old idea to drive through the small communities in the countryside taking blood pressure and testing blood sugar, doing what little she can to ward off strokes and amputations and heart attacks. Something like the Red Cross's blood mobile or a book van. Or more low-key, like the fudge man with a cooler on the back of a motorbike from which he sells ice cream and creamsicles. She chuckles at the latter image, pictures herself on a motorbike hurtling through hillside communities on dirt roads.

She's still thinking of it when she gets to Hermina's house, and Claudia runs toward her as if she's been gone forever.

"Sister Pearl." Claudia presses her head into the soft folds of Pearline's stomach, and for a moment, Pearline thinks of her granddaughters, the joy they brought her back in that other life in New York.

"Did you behave?" It's becoming her signature greeting.

From Hermina's veranda, the view of the sea before them is a solid blue—perfect. Pearline thinks no painter could do the horizon justice. Yellow and peach hibiscus flowers on the periphery of her vision lilt inward, forming a floral frame around the blue sea. Out in the garden are aged wooden stumps around which orchids sprout white and purple. The pink bougainvillea is perfectly trimmed, and the birds-of-paradise delicate and wispy. There are two frangipani trees— one with pink blooms and the other with white blooms—and a range of plants whose names she doesn't know. In the midst of one garden bed are leaf of life plants—their leaves plump and a handful of bulbs hanging like bells. On the veranda itself are potted anthuriums, each stalk of flower richly colored, the palette of colors so vivid, so variegated, that at first glance they don't seem real. Hermina's green thumb is her gift from their father. Where their father planted crops to feed his family, Hermina grows ornamental plants and pulls from her garden to arrange elaborate bouquets for church altars and various ceremonies.

Pearline grabs her things. "Night coming," she says. "Till tomorrow."

Derek is pacing the veranda when Pearline drives up. He looks as if he wants to ask how she stayed away so long. "Two men came by," he says and leans forward to take Claudia from Pearline's arms. "The appraiser. Said he was here last week.

Came with his client and wanted to look at the property, but I told them to come back when you're home. Something didn't seem right."

"What time they came?" Already Pearline is calculating the exact time she spoke with Hermina about the clinic. If Hermina, or perhaps her sisters together, wanted her out of the house and away from the property that day, then they succeeded.

"Around twelve."

"You did the right thing." She pats Derek's shoulder. He's still holding Claudia, who hasn't stirred at all. "Just put her on the bed."

Pearline leans on the railing, her stance mirroring her father's. Her throat is tight. She is straining to hold back the tears, muttering "coincidence, coincidence, coincidence," trying to convince herself the timing was purely coincidental. And even as she says it, she knows she has to move faster, not just to counter her sisters' moves but to anticipate and block them. Her sisters know something, she thinks. There's a reason they're so anxious to sell the land so quickly.

Pearline doesn't head inside immediately. Her exhaustion disappears, replaced by an anger that burns deep, sears her insides. It's not a feeling she wants to contain or retain. So she walks, stomping on the shame o' lady, kicking at pebbles, childlike in her manner, stopping only when she looks up to see Derek standing in the doorway and holding Claudia against his chest, both of them bearing witness to the new woman she is becoming. When she tires of walking, Pearline sits with the gift Rupert has left her.

She's holding steadfast to the belief that he trusted her with his gift—his memory and his story—when he didn't trust Aileen or Hermina. Unlike Irene and Hermina and Aileen, Pearline always believed in Rupert's dreams and his mission, a belief that goes back to 1967 when the bauxite plant in Discovery Bay first opened. That year, Rupert's crops failed, and Irene, tired of the failures and the struggle, encouraged Rupert to find a job at the nearby bauxite plant. She didn't care if the job was at the drying facility or the port, whether he worked in maintenance or swept the roads. She wanted something concrete. And Rupert, distraught at the possibility of giving up his livelihood, wrote his first letter to Pearline, who was already a married woman in Brooklyn with a newborn. Pearline sent seeds and money to finance Rupert's shift away from his reliance on crops alone. He built pens for goats, fenced off the land for cattle.

Pearline looks out as Rupert used to. The successes and failures of his farming are as much hers as his. She believed in his dreams then, and she believes in them now. Sometimes she thinks that fighting to save this place Irene called *La Casa de la Pura Verdad*—The House of Plain Truth—directly opposes her desire to end her family's long struggle. But she has come to understand that the heart of that struggle was always to find a place to fully belong.

She's in that place—The House of Plain Truth—where Claudia is loved in the absence of her mother, where Derek has discovered his family and found safety, where she is coming back into her rightful identity. The old house is still here for them—so many generations of tears and sweat poured into its surrounding fields by her ancestors, keeping the land fertile. She has it now. It's a gift, the only legacy a man like Rupert, without the privilege of education or wealth or any other currency valid in the colonial era, could have left to his children. How can Aileen and Hermina not see that?

11.

Too tired to read the Sunday *Gleaner*, Pearline nods off. The paper slumps in her lap, catching drool and crinkling when she startles and tries to force herself to wake fully. A dream holds her, paralyzes her, and she fights herself to rise out of it. She hears hooves beating, tamping the ground in rhythm. There's the sound of a truck engine too, and she can't tell which is closer—the horses or the truck—or whether the truck's rumble is coming from the main road outside her gate. Around her, people run, grabbing children too young to make great strides, leaving clothes out to dry, a tin of kerosene, a young goat tethered to a tree and bleating loudly, a jar of money buried in a soft mound of earth rounded to look like a yam hill. The action spinning around Pearline is like a movie, as bright and loud as any action film. She doesn't feel like she's a part of it, but she knows she is.

"Any money you have," a man begs. "If they take me, I want to go back home with something."

Pearline backs away, waves her hand, spins around. She knows she should be running too. But she doesn't. Pearline turns in the direction of the sun and calls for Arturo, Gerardo, and David. None of the boys come. She turns again. The truck is nearer now, and she feels the sound in her chest wall. Men lean against wood rails, their mouths open to shout messages for the families they can't see or reach. Pearline scans the faces, all shiny with sweat and oil, contorted with anger and despair and uncertainty. Spanish, French, and English words flutter from the men's lips like leaves blown about by a strong wind, a babble of voices that sound like a hundred parrots screeching. She wants to reach out and tell the men everything will be all right, but just then, a voice shouts, "You. *Jamaiquino.* You are next." A finger levels at her face, and a whoosh of air breezes her forehead. A woman's scream rips through the air. And then another, and another.

Pearline spins and shouts again for Arturo, her call more urgent now. She stretches out a hand and grabs a child's collar, turning the child to see whether it's Arturo or Gerardo or David. She turns again, and it is her father who is holding the boy and shouting. Except her father is not a young man. He's elderly, grayed, and weak, the very way he looked when he lay outside on the veranda insisting on calling Claudia "Arturo." They're both stuck there in that moment, calling a child who never comes. Except Pearline feels the cloth rough against her fingers, the child's clammy skin, and the child pulling away from her. She holds on tighter, hears another scream, feels a soft hand against her own and then a stronger, firmer pull.

"Sister Pearl."

Another voice, deeper, more urgent, is close to her ears. Fingers pull at hers, shake her shoulders, and the grip gets stronger, rough almost. "Aunt Pearline. Aunt Pearline, wake up."

Pearline jumps, raises her hand to her face, and tries to reorient herself. And when she opens her eyes, Claudia is pressed up against the railing, brushing her collarbone, and Derek stands over Pearline asking, "You all right, Aunt Pearline?"

"What you mean if I all right? I just doze off."

"That was some nightmare, or daymare. You hold on to Claudia's dress and wouldn't let go."

"Eh?"

"Yes, and calling out Arturo's name."

"No, sah." Pearline hesitates. Slowly the dream takes shape, and what she sees is her father on his last day alive, calling Arturo's name, mistaking Claudia for Arturo. She has dreamt of the moment that was among Rupert's last memories. Pearline holds on to the dream, presses the details into the crevices of her mind. She knows she'll need to reach for these details again.

She looks up at Claudia's face, crumpling with the effort to hold back her tears.

Derek nods. "Thought I had to get the jaws of life to get your hand off her collar."

"Boy, why you must exaggerate so?"

Derek laughs, the sound freeing something within Pearline. "Must be a real serious dream."

Pieces of the dream, details of a time in Cuba Pearline has no right or reason to know, come back to her. The action, the movement, the voices are all so vivid, more present than in any dream she has ever had. She closes her eyes, momentarily shuts out Claudia and Derek, and thinks of the clarity of the other dreams that have come to her recently. Even though she wants to think these are repressed memories, they are not necessarily events she experienced. "Mus' be spirit tek me." Pearline laughs, but she is almost certain her father is inhabiting her body in a way she can't explain.

Pearline moves to shake off the thought. She bends to rub Claudia's head. "Sorry, baby. Never mean to frighten you."

Claudia flinches, pulls herself away from Pearline's touch. Her eyes are watery. The details from Pearline's dream slide into place, each so vivid and so real that Pearline looks around to confirm she is in Mount Pleasant and there are no horses and no truck full of angry men here. She wants to know where the men were headed, what would have come next in the dream, whether that truck has something to do with Arturo's death and the thing her father refused to forgive his living children. She's dreaming her father's life, down to reaching for Claudia in her dream and calling for Arturo, and it spooks her. She doesn't understand the significance of this specific moment that replays in her subconscious or Rupert calling for Arturo in the last moments of his life.

Irene cried if somebody said Arturo's name. Just closed up, folded in on herself like a crab hiding in its shell. Pearline remembers now that she, Aileen, and Hermina learned very early in their childhood that their siblings' names were taboo. All she has is a single clear memory about Gerardo, David, and Annie standing on the wharf on the last day the family stood together as one. Sons and brothers and a daughter and a sister deliberately erased and forgotten.

There's a clearing in the field that Pearline likes. From there, she can see the sea clearly, make out ships in the distance and the white froth of waves churning. The clearing is far enough from the house and the road that she doesn't hear the hum of vehicles and can pretend for a little while that she is all alone. On Sundays it's even quieter, with most every store closed and few trucks or minibuses on the road blaring horns or music or braking hard downhill. She heads there now to wrangle the dream into the ordered life she prefers, to parse out what her father is still telling her. Things have changed. He's ramped up his efforts. He's no longer just a presence in the chair in her bedroom. Now he's occupying her dreams, refusing to rest. He will not rest until what he wants is done. And neither will she.

When things get overwhelming, Pearline thinks through her issues as she does the components of a patient care plan. Assess. Diagnose. Plan for desired outcomes. Implement. Evaluate. She has assessed and diagnosed, and she knows her goals. *One more week,* she tells herself. Just get through this Easter holiday week and Easter dinner at Aileen's with the extended family in a week's time, then work on giving her father his rest. Pearline has held on to the belief that the dead, if not appeased, do not rest. She carried those beliefs with her across the seas, to every hospital where she worked, to the homes of every elderly patient in her care, cajoling family members of the dying to take care to follow through on the dying person's wishes.

Pearline wants Rupert to rest. She wants him to know peace, which will come only with her following through and finding the children he asked her to find.

It's nearly eight in the morning, but Pearline is already in the car driving, her body still trembling from last night's dream. A separate dream coming so soon after the daydream in which she grabbed ahold of Claudia has made Pearline realize that she needs to stay ahead, stay on top of her father's restless spirit. She also wants to sleep and wake up rested. So she heads out now, days earlier than she had originally planned.

Fog is still suspended between the trees as she drives, with Claudia sitting tucked up against the rear passenger-side door. The scent of the periwinkles is strong. Bruised by the night's rain, they're perking up again, the purple flowers bright against the green leaves. Her clothes hold on to the scent of the bread-fruit she roasted and the scent of smoke from the coal stove she'd set up to roast it. Though she wants to roll the window all the way down and let the air blow the scent of smoke from her clothes, the air outside is too cool for Claudia, who is stealing glances at Pearline. It seems Claudia wants to be as far away from Pearline as possible; she hasn't forgotten Pearline's hand tight against the collar of her dress. Pearline hasn't forgotten the dream either, how vivid it was and how forcefully she acted it out. In that dream, she was Rupert, wrangling with a stubborn boy. And she wants to know why.

The minibuses and vans come upon Pearline's car in groups. She hears the music before she knows the vehicles are bearing down upon her. Dance hall music spills out, the beat persistent and loud, much too loud for her taste. Pearline hasn't driven this distance since she returned, and though she should have asked Aileen or Hermina to come along, she doesn't want them to know where she's headed. At least, not yet. Even Derek would have been a good companion, but she's left him to keep watch over the house lest her sisters try something new. Even so, his idleness bothers her. She wants to tell him that it's past time he begin thinking about what he's doing here, time to look about a job at the bauxite company where Hermina's husband works, or think about returning to Brooklyn. For now though, what she needs him to do—keep watch over the house—is more pressing. Selfish, she knows. But she suspects he won't complain. Without her, he's homeless, trapped for the time being into doing what she wants or what he anticipates she'll ask. Without her, without this house, he has nothing.

Just three days earlier, when she got back from the market, she found Derek pulling weeds from her little garden. A mound of Spanish needle and water grass sat at his feet. He was careful not to pull out the tomatoes and callaloo seedlings, the pepper plants, the gungo pea plants marked with a stake and a tiny card bearing the name. His shirt, soaked with sweat, clung to his rounded back, and every now and then he wiped an arm across his forehead. Pearline pictured her father at Derek's age, a man in Cuba, a husband and father. What would her father think of Derek, this wayward grandson whose young life had already fallen off track? How would he right it? For sure, Rupert, who demanded so much of himself, would set him on another path.

Rupert learned early the sting of failure, how it coats everything, how the loss of a crop—whether to flood or drought or worms—infected every decision, determined whether he or his siblings went to school, what his mother put on the table for supper, the heft of the basket she took to the market to sell the produce they'd planted and reaped. He learned early how easily a family's dream crumbled with a single failing. And he fought for something more for his girls. He bought three heads of

cattle, one for each of his girls. "This is so unu can go to school."
He didn't know then what his daughters would choose or what
it would cost. But when the time came, he sold each daughter's
cow and fattened another calf, setting aside every penny of it
for Pearline's nursing school fees and Aileen's and Hermina's
teacher's college fees. Later, Hermina chose a bank training
program and finance. And when Pearline talked of America,
he smiled, proud, it seemed, and said, "Gwan, mi girl."

All three of Rupert and Irene's daughters have done well.
She immediately corrects herself: Rupert and Irene's last
three daughters have done well. They have succeeded, cata-
pulted themselves from the struggling farmer's daughters to
middle-class professionals. They succeeded where their father
didn't. She wonders how different their lives would have been
had Rupert given in to Irene's suggestion and gone to look for
a job at the new bauxite company headquarters. She doesn't
know what her father would have done given his limited
education, or, so many years post-Cuba, if any of the skills
he acquired then would have been transferrable to a bauxite
mining operation. Stubborn, Pearline thinks. That was also her
mother's assessment, the descriptor she used over and over to
describe Rupert.

Pearline wants to mirror the part of her father that wanted
to see the next generation succeed. But Pearline knows she can
be stubbornly insistent on seeing through only one big goal at
a time and blocking out the small inconveniences that get in
the way or threaten to make her fail. She built a life in New
York and doubled down on work to put a daughter through
college, pay off a mortgage, and fund her retirement after her

husband died. She succeeded, but she never paused to think about what she had lost to get back here to this very place or what she could lose in the fight to hold on to it.

She won't admit that she misses the hustle, the adrenaline of Brooklyn and her multiple jobs. Back in Brooklyn, constant movement kept her from thinking about her failures with Ronnie and Josette and the baby boy she couldn't save, and she thanks Rupert for giving her this charge, this search that fills the gap.

Pearline drives slowly, carefully, along the coast to Ocho Rios and up into the hills through Fern Gully. She's surprised at the health and variety of the ferns along the three-mile stretch of road, surprised the exhaust and fumes haven't combined to kill the plants over the years. Claudia is quiet. They're both in separate worlds, Claudia looking out as if the country is new to her, and Pearline snatching glimpses of the countryside she has missed—Moneague, home to the teacher's college Aileen attended and an underground lake that rises once in a while to submerge a valley and whole buildings; the steep and winding Mount Rosser; the Bog Walk Gorge. The river is clear in some places and green and slow-moving in others.

Highways are what Pearline misses most about her former life, and the long drives from state to state, watching farms pressed up against the highway, cattle and horses and sometimes goats carrying on with chewing and sleeping, completely unfazed by the semi–tractor trailers and cars blowing by at tremendous speeds. She always wished the rural towns were more visible, more present on the highway, so she could peek at the lives within, not too close to the road but just close enough to see who lived there, the clothes hanging out to dry, and children at play. Much too often what was visible from the highways were more modern buildings, larger and larger homes sprouting up on tracts of land that was once sprawling farmland. It's the latter that bothers her most, how suburbs have eroded a way of life, how her sisters, without fully understanding what they're offering up, have suggested they do the same with their family land—sell it to developers to build a community of modern homes. Even though they cannot sell the land—at least not yet—the suggestion is imprinted on the forefront of Pearline's mind, and she wants to do all she can to squash this plan of theirs.

Near Spanish Town she slows, looking left and right for the records office.

"There," she says.

"Where?" Claudia asks, perking up to see the treat—a zoo or park or a national landmark like the one her class visited on its most recent outing. She looks up and out the window, her eyes shifting quickly.

"I have some business first," Pearline says, knowing now that she has to do something else for Claudia, something to make this long drive worthwhile.

She wastes no time in getting out, tramping across the dusty parking lot, her feet moving like a version of her younger self. A lightheadedness comes on. Pearline has felt it before—a shortness of breath, a tightening in her chest, weakness in her legs—and she stops, leans on a railing, and lets it pass. She tallies what she ate this morning—two slices of breadfruit, a single sardine, black coffee—and reminds herself that she must eat fuller, more complete meals. She finds candy in her bag—how old it is, she doesn't know—but she sucks on it as she waits for the feeling to pass. *Stress*, she tells herself. This whole business with the house and these dreams that invade her sleep are stresses she doesn't need. She should think more of it, she knows, but she brushes it aside as she's always done. It's how she got through life in America—head down against the wind, pushing through, pulling Josette along through every trial and every setback, refusing to cry and bend.

The air inside is cold, uncomfortably so. In fact, there's nothing comfortable about the building or the counter at which several people stand as they page through ledgers filled with details on wills and deeds.

"Sit on the bench over there," Pearline tells Claudia.

But Claudia looks around and refuses to move. She presses against Pearline's leg, turns her face into Pearline's thigh, and holds on tight. Pearline doesn't shake Claudia off but continues toward the receptionist at the counter and on to the ledgers that hold the secret history of the land in Mount Pleasant. She's not exactly sure what she's looking for. She knows the Headlam family owned the land at one time. Knows, too, that post-emancipation, the Headlams split the once vast estate and sold blocks of it. Yet their piece of the vast estate, the house her parents built when they returned from Cuba, has the Headlam name.

Pearline makes her way through the ledgers, moving her fingers slowly line by line over the handwritten script until she finds the records from 1900. It was deeded to Annie Headlam, from one George Headlam upon his death in 1900. Irene and

Rupert's names do not appear until 1956. Much later, 1972, the names shift again; Annie Headlam's name replaces Irene's. Though she has known of it for several weeks now, it's still surprising to see her mother's name replaced by Annie Headlam. As far as she knows, the Headlams and their immediate descendants were long gone from the island.

Pearline moves her finger back to 1956, twenty-three years after her family boarded the schooner in Santiago de Cuba and came back home. Another feeling seeps through Pearline, settling into her bones, pulling her toward the ground. She grabs on to the counter and holds herself up, waiting again for the feeling to pass. The truth settles into her, leaches her insides: Her parents hadn't built that house in 1933 as they claimed. The house is older. All her life, Pearline has lived on the land in Mount Pleasant believing that her parents bought the property with the money they'd earned in Cuba and built the house themselves. She's sure this tidbit is not something she imagined. Irene repeated it, saying time and time again, "You know how hard me and Rupert work to buy this place and build this house? We save every likkle penny we have. When you grown and gone 'bout you' business, this the only place we still have. So you take time with it."

What would she have known? She was three years old, watching her father whitewashing the stone, hammering nails into the wooden floor, building a legacy and fulfilling a dream. Pearline tries, but she can't think of what transpired in 1956 or 1972. Can't think of what would have prompted her mother in that particular year to change the ownership.

Claudia starts to fidget. Comfortable now, she twirls away

from Pearline, anxious to move. Pearline gathers what she has, swallows hard, tucks away what she doesn't want to believe: They are squatters. Or at some time it seemed they were.

The foundation upon which Pearline has built her life and raised Josette is crumbling. Grief creeps back into her, lodges itself squarely in her chest like a hand compressing her heart. She can't separate the physical discomfort from the heartbreak of betrayal. They're one and the same, a sharp pain in her chest and upper shoulder, her breath coming heavy, the urgent need to sit. She holds fast to the counter, steadies herself, repeats "Just breathe." She worked so hard abroad to be able to come back home with something, to fulfill her dream—an immigrant's dream. Except now she thinks she may have come home only to watch her dreams die.

Pearline walks out certain of two things: She won't let her dream go without a fight. She won't let Hermina and Aileen finish shattering this dream of hers to build upon and finish what Rupert couldn't.

Pearline drives past the road up to Mount Pleasant and continues along the coast past Pear Tree Bottom, the little river she's long suspected runs under their property before appearing again aboveground and pouring out into the sea. She heads to the Green Grotto Caves. As a child, Josette hated it, the musty scent, the bats, the closeness. Yet she takes Claudia there to fulfill her promise of an outing, to show off the rock formations, the stalactites and stalagmites and the subterranean lake.

But the outing is as much for her. She's not ready to return yet to the house of her childhood, to return to picking apart every memory and every story her parents ever told about purchasing the house and the land upon their return from Cuba, of building a family home with their earnings. She wants to exhaust herself so fully that she sleeps deeply and doesn't dream of events she has no right to know.

Pearline takes a deep breath, tries to stem her growing anxiety and the pounding in her heart. These kinds of outings are the things she missed doing with Josette—showing off Brooklyn or Jamaica or the whole eastern coast of the United States. She was too tired for much of anything, and that became her husband's job. He handled the vacation outings, boat rides, bus rides, hikes. She's absent from most of the vacation pictures, from the photos of the two of them halfway up Dunn's River Falls, screaming on roller coasters, at the top of the Statue of Liberty. She's making amends now, though she knows she's making amends to the wrong girl.

She breathes in the stale air, holds it. It reminds her of the mustiness of her father's room, the things she must parse through once again with a new eye. What she's missing isn't yet clear, but she thinks the answer is in that trunk, tucked away in the papers her father saved. She watches Claudia's eyes widen as she quickens her step, filled with the surprise and fear of being underground. Claudia inches toward the cave wall, rubs her hand along it, pulls back quickly, and looks at Pearline. Pearline nods, smiles, and Claudia touches it again, inching even farther away from Pearline. Pearline can't help but picture Josette, standing close to Pearline, refusing to lean in to the experience, and Ronnie coddling Josette, ushering her out in haste.

Pearline takes her time driving back, pushing off the inevitable return of the dreams. She is searching for a better name for them. They are not so much dreams as they are moments of the past that have eased into her life, inhabiting her waking moments and haunting her dreams. When Pearline gets back, Derek is on the veranda looking out. Three men came to clean the yard, trim the overgrown bougainvillea, and brush the grass with cutlasses, he tells her. Again, Aileen and Hermina made plans without consulting her.

He points to the kitchen garden, bigger now than it was when she left this morning.

"Told them you wanted to plant more," he says.

"Good boy," Pearline says. "The two o' them think they running this show. But me an' them."

Pearline waits until midnight when the house has settled into a quietness like death. She moves gingerly across the creaking floorboards and lets the musty scent fill her nostrils. When she opens the trunk, the scent again overwhelms. "Papa," she says softly as if he is in that room waiting for her to call his name.

The papers rustle, the sound thin and fragile in the semi-darkness. Pearline doesn't know what exactly she's looking for, but she looks at the papers with a new lens, with this new knowledge that the family history her parents passed down was a lie. She lays out her three tasks to discover: how her parents came to own this house, who Annie Headlam is, and the secret her father wouldn't forgive.

First, Pearline rereads Annie's letter, parses every word for clues about what her father wouldn't forgive, and reorders the rest of the letters by date. The letters are bare, formal in their structure, informal in their tone, and the handwriting slanted and cramped. They're five letters in all, each from Annie, all written to Irene, who had kept the letters tucked away as if they were letters from lost lovers. *I was certain you were going to have the baby on the ship. What name did you give the baby? Did you name the baby after the ship?*

She reads letter after letter, but there's still no clue as to what her father forgave only at the very end of his life. Pearline puts the letters back. Pearline is frustrated by how little she knows about her family's return in 1933. All she knows is that Irene said things were hard: "No work, no money, no food. So we come on home." When she said it, her voice was flat, without emotion, and her eyes took on a faraway look. "Nothing we could do but leave." Any deeper probing made Irene's eyes water, made her sing a soulful, plaintive song. Now, when Pearline thinks about it, there's another discrepancy in the story; for both parents said, "We work hard and come back and build this house." Still, they could have sent money back home, had it waiting for their return.

Babsy, Pearline thinks. Irene's good friend Babsy would likely know. As quickly as Pearline thinks of the name, she dismisses it, preferring not to reopen old wounds.

She sets the newspapers aside. Her Spanish is minimal, just sufficient enough to get her a name and pertinent demographic information from patients. There are copies of birth papers as well—hers, Aileen's, Hermina's. Pearline again holds the photo, angling it toward the light. She has a blurry memory of a photographer's studio, an old-time camera contraption, but again she's not sure the memory is hers or one collated from family stories told throughout the years. How could she remember such seemingly inconsequential details? How could she remember Arturo saying, "We should take a family portrait. All of us. Before you and Annie go to Santiago."

"Of course." Irene leans in, kisses Arturo on his head. "All of us together before we leave."

"So today, then. Come about lunchtime."

The conversation sounds familiar, but she doesn't know which member of the family was leaving or why. She remembers Irene always said she wanted all her children together, none sent to be raised by relatives, none left with better-off family friends for a chance at greater opportunities, none leaving her house until they were grown and ready to face life on their own. But she remembers this moment preceding somebody's departure, remembers Irene smoothing her eyebrows with oil, smoothing the curls around her hairline that refused to be tamed, and rubbing oil all over her face. They'd dressed in their church clothes, Pearline wearing a little dress that Aileen had outgrown, which was still a bit too long and roomy for Pearline's slight body. She's sure of the origin of the dress because that's the way it had always been—new dresses for Aileen and hand-me-downs for Pearline and Hermina, worn until the threads frayed. The family wasted nothing. Pearline skipped. She's not sure of it, but she thinks she must have skipped, must have smelled the coconut oil in her hair and on her face as the breeze moved over her body.

Pearline sees Rupert brushing real and imaginary flecks of dust from his suit. He always did that. In the photo, the coat hangs limply from his shoulders. And she pictures him later in life, wearing suits that fit better, posing like royalty, his body more imposing. She remembers they stopped outside the photographer's studio and watched Arturo seat the customers who came in for photographs—the women wearing dresses too flamboyant for daytime wear, the boys who fidgeted and tugged at their pants riding up at the crotch, the girls who held their smiles like china dolls, the mothers and fathers who stared at the camera with solemn faces. She remembers—or imagines—her father beaming, watching his son perfecting the customers' poses, encouraging them to look directly at the camera, then running back to the black box to snap the photos before the perfect pose unraveled and the girls' china-doll smiles cracked.

Once inside, Arturo moves his siblings and parents around like mannequins, taking a moment to right Rupert's Panama hat and adjust the shoulders of his jacket. He tickles Pearline, the youngest of his siblings, tells her to look at the funny box in front of the old man, and adjusts the collar of Gerardo's shirt. Then Arturo stands behind the old man, takes his turn looking through the camera's lens. "Nobody move," he says and sprints forward, positions himself between his father and Annie, away from his twin, away from the face that looked exactly like his.

The old man snaps the photograph, and Rupert releases a pent-up breath.

"Uno más. Uno más."

Pearline holds her breath again, just like her father holds his, puffing up her chest but this time smiling too late.

Pearline shakes her head, trying to unravel whether she is confusing this photo session with another one from later in her life or borrowing from a story her mother told. She looks again at the photo, certain she's never seen it, and even more certain her sisters haven't seen it either. Besides the photo and this little memory of the photographer's studio, there's nothing to help her current quest. She closes the lid, locks it again, forcing her burgeoning sense of disappointment down and holding on to a tiny shard of anger that her father or mother or both secreted away this little piece of family history.

The cocks haven't started crowing when Pearline begins making breakfast—boiled green bananas, callaloo, fried plantains, and chocolate tea. She takes the mug onto the veranda and watches until the morning finally begins to sharpen. The sky shifts from a blue-black, the stars twinkle off one by one, and slivers of color appear as the sun cracks above the horizon and the fog slowly dissipates. Closer to her, the hibiscus flowers unfurl, and cobwebs strung between branches glisten with dew. The roosters to the right of their house begin crowing, setting their coops aflutter. She's thinking hard about what must come next, trying not to succumb to helplessness, trying to be her father's daughter—stubborn and strong in her convictions and refusing to fail or accept defeat.

12.

Aileen's house no longer smells of fresh concrete and, up close, the Spanish brown paint on the wooden louvers is beginning to fade. Red dirt stains the base of the light peach outer and inner walls, streaked where a broom or mop brushed against them, or rainwater beating against the ground splashed up. The fronds of two of the seven dwarf coconut trees lining the driveway are yellowing, no doubt succumbing to the plant disease that's wiping out coconut trees across the island. Rupert's trees suffered the same fate. She has to rethink her own plans to plant dwarf coconut trees. Pearline looks for more imperfections, anything to remind her that what her sisters have is no better than the old house they scorn. Inside, patches of the terrazzo tile have lost their sheen, and the cabinets and ceiling show signs of termite damage. The house is sturdy, nothing like the much older family home, but Pearline wants to point to each of these imperfections and say, "Look at the shape your nearly new house is in." And at twenty years old, it is new compared to the house Pearline now thinks of as hers.

If Pearline is counting correctly, it's been twenty-five years, perhaps more, since she's spent Easter in Jamaica. That last time, Josette was still a child, six years old, easily impressed by the novelty of the island and the old traditions Irene practiced. That time, Irene set an egg white in a glass of water to predict her granddaughter's future. She got up early before the sun rose and woke Josette. Then the two of them sat and watched the pattern the egg white formed. Josette wished for a ship, a sign of more travel in her future, and indeed the egg white expanded and blossomed into whispery sails.

"Somebody traveling," Irene had said.

Now, walking through the house with the pan of buns and escoveitched fish, she wishes she had held on to a concrete tradition like that, something beyond making Easter buns.

"Arturo," Aileen says. She's looking at Derek. "All this time I trying to think who you remind me of. And is just now I see it. You remind me of Arturo."

"You remember him?" Pearline tries to picture the faces in the photo.

"Sort of. You know when you have a vague mental image of something? Well, that's it. When I picture Arturo, Derek's face is exactly what I see. He had a way about him. And you have a way about you too. I can't exactly put it into words, but I know it."

Pearline hesitates, but then she says, "I have something to show you. Next time you come to the house."

"What?"

"When you and Hermina come."

"Why so secretive?"

"No big secret. Just one of those things that you have to see for yourself. That's all." Pearline isn't sure why she doesn't describe the old photo from the trunk, but Aileen is so suspicious Pearline thinks again that there's something else her sisters are withholding from her. The photo isn't too much to share, she thinks.

Relatives cluster around the yard and settle in chairs on the veranda—a fragile aunt, another aunt who peddles herbs and bush teas, an uncle who lords over the domino table, cousins on both her mother's and father's sides, and more children than she can count. Two cousins, Wendell and Gerry, each with a plate of oxtail and rice, lean against coconut trees in the yard, quietly reasoning.

"How you get everybody to come?" Pearline asks.

"I have my ways." Aileen winks and reaches for the pan of fish.

Once, Irene was the grand marshal who gathered the family and hosted the Easter and Christmas dinners. Now Aileen does it, bigger than any Irene hosted. She gathers everyone, and for the first time, Pearline thinks Aileen is more like their mother than she or Hermina. Claudia loosens up and runs with the cousins she remembers. Derek leans against a chair by the domino table, watching the players' exaggerated moves. Pearline drifts inside to the kitchen and then to the back, where a coal stove is set up to boil a massive pot of goat head soup. Her cousin Denton is scraping the goat head and prepping the pieces of meat to drop into the boiling water.

Coming so soon after Rupert's death, the gathering feels like a delayed wake. Family stories float in from every corner of the house and yard. On the veranda, two cousins talk about their wheelchair-bound aunt, her dressmaking skills, and the "perfect dress" she made for Cynthia's baby girl; how neatly she trims the inner seams of every garment she makes, so neat the garments could readily be worn inside out; Rosalee's chiffon bridal gown, with a deep neckline and even deeper back; her cakes at Christmas; and buns at Easter. These are the stories that build a eulogy. The stories that make the rounds at wakes.

"You dream see him yet?" Pearline's aunt Del leans in close. She's sucking on an oxtail bone and loudly chewing the last remnants of meat.

Pearline looks up, surprised by the knowing comment. But not wanting to explain the nighttime awakenings, she simply says, "No."

"Is a matter of time," Del says. "Is what, three months now?" She's whispering still, leaning close to Pearline as if they're conspiring on something big. "Me, now, I never put chalk on the door like everybody say. Any duppy coming to talk to me, let him come. If you live good wid people, you shouldn't have nutten to worry 'bout when they spirit come back."

Pearline's eyes drift across the yard. It's too late now to say yes, to tell her aunt that Rupert is inhabiting her dreams and ask what this unusual recollection of memory means. There must be a word for this state, these visions where she is living someone else's experience. *Vision* simultaneously seems like the correct word and the wrong one. And she suspects she may never be able to fully describe this state.

Del is still talking. "I tell you, when my mother died, I dream see her every day. Never fight it. Just lie down every night, and if she come to me in my dream, is just so. Some people frighten o' duppy, but not me. Make she come. She never hurt me when she was alive. What make me think she would hurt me when she dead?"

"Give me a second." Pearline squeezes Del's wrist, eases herself away, and drifts toward the kitchen.

"Here." Hermina hands Pearline a knife and a bag of oranges. "Help me with this. Drink finish, and we need more, quick."

"Of course." Pearline stands at the window looking out, watching Derek near the pot, waiting for the cook to ladle out a cup of soup. None of the relatives question Derek's presence. They accept him as if his father's status—outside child—and his are the most ordinary of things. She wonders now if everyone but her knew about Derek's father.

Pearline tenses when Aileen approaches Derek. He's moved from near the pot to the veranda. Steam twirls from the paper cup toward his face. Pearline bends her head, blocks out the noise to try and catch Aileen's words.

"So what you doing now, young man? You find work yet?"

"No, ma'am."

"Big blanket mek man sleep late," Aileen says. She's staring directly at him with the knowing look of a teacher who has dropped on her students a complicated concept she knows they won't understand. She waits for a minute, feeling him out with her eyes. "Too many luxuries make you complacent and take everything you have for granted. All that to say, it's time for you to do something. You can't sit around all day and waste your life. Everybody must have a purpose."

Derek is quieter than Pearline expects.

"So tell me something," Aileen says. "What kind of skills you have? What kind of training?"

He drops the spoon back into the cup before he speaks. "I draw," he says. "I always wanted to study art."

"Art. Hmm. There's no money in art. Young women these days want a man with money. How you going to keep a woman?"

Derek shrugs. It doesn't seem to be a concept he's given any thought. Pearline tamps down the urge to swoop in like a bird protecting her hatchlings and rescue him. *Another minute,* Pearline thinks. In that light, the sun against his skin, Pearline looks to see what Aileen sees—Derek's resemblance to Arturo. Though she recently looked at the photo, she can't bring up the faces of her brothers. She wants to remember something more, wants to remember a scent, the way one of her missing siblings pronounced a word, a favorite food. All she has are memories of Aileen and Hermina, and again she resents how her other siblings were erased.

Pearline shakes it off, presses her shoulders back, leans her neck left and right. There's tension in her shoulders, tension in her body, rising by the second. But she waits a minute, feels out the direction of the conversation before she calls Derek.

"Don't mind her," she whispers. She waves the knife and half a squeezed lemon. "Bossy from the day she was born. Carry this to the veranda and pour it in the Igloo."

By the time Pearline sits down to eat, the sun is getting low. She makes her way back to the veranda that looks down on a valley and across to the main road. There's a story that a river once ran through there, and Pearline can picture it meandering through the flat valley where houses now sit. Even now, the valley is lush, much brighter and greener than the grass on Aileen's hilly lawn. Once, long ago in high school, Pearline learned about Jamaica's limestone rocks succumbing to rivers flowing aboveground. The water eats the rocks through, and eventually the river disappears belowground. She can picture what happened here, how the underground water still feeds the plants in the valley below.

She looks down the hill, at the dwarf coconut trees, across the valley at the community college high up on the hill. She pictures her father standing there, looking out the way he did at his own house in Mount Pleasant. Her people once worked this land and got nothing in return for their labor. And now Aileen owns a piece of it, paying again for the very piece of land their ancestors had already paid for with their labor and their lives. Acres of pastures separate Aileen's house from Mount Pleasant, where their house sits on land that had been part of another plantation. It's whirling in her head, the idea that the circumstances surrounding their house in Mount Pleasant are similar. Her ancestors worked that land. Her family had earned that piece of land over and over. Her father knew it, had always known it. How could she not have thought of this before? All these years, how could she not have seen it?

The sun is going down when Pearline leaves, and the road, sheltered by trees on both sides, is nearly dark. Claudia falls asleep almost as soon as she leans back against the seat. Her snores are soft. Derek, too, is quiet, and Pearline welcomes it. Pearline takes her time around the deep corners and the potholes that pop up without warning. But when she nears the gate, she turns right instead of left, following the winding hill directly across from their property toward the Headlam house. For as long as Pearline has lived in Mount Pleasant, she has never climbed this hill, never seen the house up close, but she feels as if she knows it. Palm trees line the drive, spaced like colonnades holding up an invisible roof. She equates palm trees lining a driveway with the wealth and grandeur that once escaped people with skin as brown as hers. Equates it, too, with the skeletons of her father's lifelong attempt to achieve for himself something resembling that wealthy life.

The residence is grand, with a sweeping view of the Caribbean Sea, wide verandas that run the length of the house, and balconies that look straight out to sea. Sheer curtains hang outside open bedroom windows, and she imagines the front door opening to reveal a curved, solid wood staircase. The house is ringed by a cut-stone wall that's crumbling in places but is nevertheless a beautiful piece of masonry. She sees her house, which had been part of the estate, in the flats below. She's thinking of it differently now, thinking of the way her father saw the piece of property he claimed.

From the left of the house, Pearline sees movement, and she puts the car in gear. "Wrong turn," she shouts out the window, waves, and eases back down the hill before she has to answer more fully for her presence.

This house, behind her now and no longer visible from the rearview mirror, mocked her father's dreams, and she is determined not to let it consume hers. She eases across the main road and onto their own rough driveway. The remnants of the name her mother gave the property catch her eye. *La Casa de la Pura Verdad*. The House of Plain Truth—the very thing she's struggling to uncover.

13.

ANOTHER MEMORY SLIPS INTO PLACE. PEARLINE ISN'T dreaming this time. She's fully awake, putting white clothes soaked in bleach water out on a zinc sheet to sun. The memory is well formed, concrete, so clear that Pearline can make out the patches of facial hair on Arturo's face, the slight gap between his front teeth, the light brown mark on his face where the skin had made less pigment. He is close enough that she can smell the coconut oil on his body, see the sheen of it on his brow and nose.

Still at that age when she shortens or mispronounces her words, she calls out, "Turo. Turo." But he doesn't respond to her. She waves. Arturo doesn't wave in return.

David runs in breathless, his bare, brown feet making slapping sounds against the floor. "They're picking them up," he says, and stops to catch his breath.

David's face is clear too. He's another shade of brown, with a thin and angular face and body to match.

"Who?" Rupert's voice is gruff, weighted with irritation and fear and anger.

"All the Haitians. La Guardia."

"Stay here. Don't leave the house. Hear me, bwoy."

Rupert rushes outside and through the gate, and Pearline and David move to a window, kneel, and lift the curtains to watch their father sprint and dodge yapping dogs, frightened mothers, excited children, fearful men. Already they know that Rupert, too, may not return. "Arturo." Rupert's voice has a jagged edge to it. "Arturo. *Ven acá.*" His voice is sharp. It cuts and then it disappears, a chorus of voices swelling up and around Rupert's voice, swallowing his words.

Martine! Martine!

Izarac.

"Arturo. *Ven acá.*"

Tell Mattie.

Tell Drina.

They are all ants in a disturbed nest, scurrying, running, burying, hiding. The trucks come, their engines loud. One, then another man in uniform jump down. There is one scream, and another, and another, and again the calls for Martine and Izarac and Arturo. In the crowd, Pearline spots Rupert's shirt. She knows him by the shape of his head. He runs, his mouth open, Arturo's name falling from his lips. Dust billows. Time and space shift. Seconds and minutes and hours lose meaning. Two men come close. By the color of their uniforms, Pearline knows they are *La Guardia.* One has a machete. The other reaches out and grabs the fleeing man. The machete glints in the sun, then comes down flat against the man's back and arms.

The curtain hides Pearline and David, who lifts a finger against his lips, whispers, "Shh. Don't make a sound."

Again and again the machete glints. Again and again the cries come. But there is no blood, just the agonizing sound of a grown man bawling. Behind David and Pearline, the door opens, the soft creak frightening them. Pearline screams, and David again says, "Shh." Rupert and Gerardo walk in, drop to the floor, crawling to Pearline and David.

"Where's Arturo?" David looks from Gerardo to Rupert, searching.

"Didn't find him," Rupert says.

Gerardo, shaking his head, looks away, saying, "Last I saw him, he was running to the photographer's studio to get the old man."

Rupert shakes his head, lowers his chin to his chest. "Haitians they picking up. But who to tell how they will know whether a boy like him is Cuban or Jamaican or Haitian. Unu stay here, and don't you leave."

Together, the three watch their father run and dodge, just one more desperate parent in the midst of the commotion of rural guards grabbing at panicked men and women. The evening turns cloudy, the shades of blue and gray and white deceptive in the waning sun. When the sun sets, the clouds gush, the rain so heavy it stings, and the water moves like a swollen river down the road. Together, they sit, Pearline on her father's lap rubbing her fingers against his chin, waiting for Arturo to come home, watching and waiting for a movement in the dark, a flicker of light, a twig snapping underfoot. Every now and then, lightning flickers in the sky and thunder booms. Near midnight, the rain eases, and Rupert and Pearline take one last look for the rain-soaked boy.

The memory is too heavy for Pearline to carry. It's a continuation of the daydream she was having when she held Claudia's collar. It's the same moment when Rupert calls Arturo. Her mind keeps looping back to it, sharpening the details. She wraps her arms around herself, rubbing away the goose bumps emerging. She steps back directly into the sun to let the heat ease the chill settling into her bones.

"Beach," Pearline says out loud. She turns to Claudia, puts a singsong lilt in her voice. "You wan' go beach? Come quick. Go change your clothes and come." Pearline looks to Derek. "You too."

He raises his eyebrows, silently asking if she's sure she wants to leave the house unattended.

"It's all right. All the other times, they knew I was going somewhere. Now they don't know. Two hours," she adds.

Derek looks back as if he thinks the house is already lost. She watches his eyes looking at the front door and the windows, a habit honed and sharpened in Brooklyn. She hasn't missed being on constant alert, securing her car with a steering-wheel lock, draping her purse around her neck. But out of habit, she looks back through the rearview mirror at the shrubs and trees, looking for movement, a body stepping out of the shadows.

Pearline walks into the water, shuddering at the first wave that splashes her back. It's cold, so she keeps moving, splashing the water around. She doesn't stop walking until the water is at her neck and the moss tangles in her toes. She hates the way the moss feels, but she waits for another wave to roll over her. Pearline wants to wash the memory away, lighten the load her father has left for her to carry. If only temporarily. She flips on her back, floats, lets the waves bounce her body about. She is nothing here, not a mother or grandmother or daughter balancing generations of grief and loss, just a weightless blob soaking in the sun, imagining her complicated memories floating away, and pushing away any thought that comes.

When the three of them return from the beach, there's an X marked with chalk on the upper-left corner of the door. Certainly, the mark wasn't there when they left. Pearline's sure of it. The mark is childish but positioned too high for Claudia to have made it even if she pushed a chair up against the wall. And which chair would she have been strong enough to push so far without Pearline or Derek hearing the feet scrape across the floor? Pearline points to the mark, raising her eyebrows and silently questioning Derek. He raises his brows in return, and Pearline looks around at the veranda for anything else that's out of place. At the foot of the chair that had been Rupert's favorite is a bowl with ten pebbles, presumably gravel from the driveway. Everything else is normal.

"Back door," Derek whispers.

Pearline nods. She reaches for Claudia's hand, and together the three walk along the worn path to the back door. Every sound is sharp. The grass crackles. The parrots in the cherry tree caw and chatter like a bickering family, then scatter when they sense danger. Pearline's pants swoosh. Claudia is quiet. She has picked up that something isn't right, and she tightens her grip on Pearline's hand. There's a chalk mark above the kitchen door, too, and another set of ten pebbles on a plastic, disposable plate.

"You want me go in first?" Derek whispers again.

"House quiet," Pearline says. "Don't think whoever make

the mark still here. All the same, go in through the front. I'll stand here in case anybody try run out this way. Kuff." She punches at the air and lifts a leg, miming a kick. She's not as young as she thinks, and she struggles to right her body.

Claudia takes a step as if to go with Derek, but Pearline tightens her grip, and Claudia edges a little behind Pearline.

"Hello." Derek's voice sounds far away, like a sound coming from the bottom of a steel pan or deep in a cavernous pit. More seconds pass, and then the back door creaks. "Nobody. But look here."

Inside, the living room furniture has been rearranged. The sofa is up against the wall opposite where it had been, angled now to fit the shorter wall, and the two armchairs are on the side of the longer wall. Where the coffee table and straw mat had been there's an oval shape marking the faded floor polish.

"Must be Aileen or Hermina come to run duppy." Pearline peers into the dining room at the curio cabinet too heavy and full to be moved. "Old-time something. People used to move furniture so when duppy come back, the house won't be familiar to them."

Pearline chuckles and sits. The jitters that weakened her knees leave her body, easing out into the sofa cushions, spreading out and forming a new shape around her body. Moving the furniture around is something they should have done from the very day Rupert passed. But she had overlooked it, as had her sisters—all of them too modern for these old-time beliefs.

"You know what this mean?" Pearline asks. There's a smile on her face again. "Papa must be haunting them. Conscience bothering them, and they think is duppy."

Pearline laughs. But hers is a nervous laughter because Rupert has taken over her dreams, and she knows what her sisters must be feeling. She won't say out loud, though, exactly what she believes or how Rupert's haunting is spreading into every space in her life. Pearline's blood runs cold, and she shudders, exaggerating the movement. "Warm up the soup and give Claudia some in the little green bowl," she says. "Then I'll wash your hair." Afraid of what her eyes will show, she looks at neither of her two charges.

There's no question Rupert is telling his children something. Pearline welcomes his presence. Unlike her sisters, she wants to hear what he has to say. How desperately she wants to be the daughter who gives Rupert's wandering spirit the message it needs to take its rest. There's only one way: do what he asked and ramp up her efforts to find them.

Pearline waits until the sunlight dims, the moon is a sliver in the sky, and the nighttime chirps are loud. She doesn't fear the night here as she did in Brooklyn, doesn't bolt herself in as soon as the night comes. Instead, she welcomes it, embraces the cooler air, the chirps, the bugs that emerge to swarm the light. She heads back to the veranda with a damp cloth and bowl of soapy water. Outside, the air is cooler and the leaves are damp with dew. Beads of sweat form on her forehead as she moves her arm to wipe away the chalk mark. She wipes around the doorframe as well, steps back, and chucks the pebbles one at a time at the driveway.

"Let him come," she says.

Pearline is leaning against the railing, looking out at the

pitch, when Derek comes outside and leans on the other side of the railing, mimicking Pearline's stance. He reaches for a leaf, and a lizard jumps and scuttles in the brush. Pearline and Derek both jump, momentarily frightened by the sudden movement. Then Pearline waves her hand, swatting at the air. They are silent for a while, with just the chirps and croaks and twits surrounding them.

"I want to ask you something," Pearline says. "Just listen before you answer. And take your time to think about it."

"Sound heavy."

Pearline doesn't know how to begin. She hasn't planned for this—not just yet. "Don't answer me now. Take tomorrow and think about it."

"Making me curious. And nervous." Derek utters a sound between a grunt and a laugh.

Pearline takes the old photo from her bosom, where she placed it when she picked up the bowl with soapy water. "Aileen said you remind her of him—Arturo. Me too. Though I don't remember him. Not like how you remember people you grow up with. But all this time I trying to think of why you remind me of him. And is not the way you look—though there's a little resemblance there. The nose and mouth. All of us Greaveses have that nose. But is something else that you can't see in a picture."

Derek looks down at the photo, angles it so the light hits it differently. He nods and Pearline isn't sure whether he agrees about the resemblance.

"You know how people say somebody born again. Not the church way, I mean. It's when somebody dead and they say another person in the family is that person reincarnated. Something like that." Derek starts to chuckle at the thought. "No, no. Don't laugh. You see, Arturo was a photographer's assistant. He was going to be somebody big. One time I hear my mother say Papa treated Arturo like gold, like he was destined to live an extraordinary life. That's how she put it. You see, my parents didn't have much education. Mama could barely read. Papa not so much. Papa had big plans for Arturo. You have that same creative side. Just like Arturo. And that's what I mean when I say you are Arturo reincarnated."

"I see." Derek shifts, turns, and leans back against the railing.

Pearline is also thinking of her baby boy who lived for only a few hours before his heart gave out. In the back of her mind, a thought forms. He would have been nearly Derek's age, perhaps in a similar position, floundering to find himself in a city too busy to stop and see his needs, with a parent too caught up in succeeding that she fails him too.

Pearline steps back to the chair, picks up Derek's drawing of the little girl aloft in the air. Derek looks down at it too, surprise blooming on his face as if this is the first time anyone has embraced this dream of his. Pearline knows too well how easily a dream can be shattered, remembers how with just one word she nipped Josette's dream of a life in film and watched her daughter stifle one creative project after another and replace it all with a corporate life in Midtown. In this second life of hers, she sees what she is becoming: a midwife to half-formed dreams—her father's dreams and now Derek's.

"I want you to think of what you can be."

"My father says there's no money in art. 'You'll be dead before anybody recognize your work and you start to make money. How that going help you?' I can still hear him. Can still hear the scorn in his voice, his laugh when he said, 'You don't have any trust fund to get.'"

Pearline shifts too. The air is cooler now, and she rubs her hands across her chilled arms. She's working out what else to say, and thinking, too, about how she once told Josette not to allow her professors to fool her into thinking that all the roles in the film business were open to her. "Watch any awards show," she had said, "and see who makes it up on the stage."

Now Pearline takes her time answering. "Your father and I come from a different school. A whole different time. My parents' generation knew one kind of labor. They worked with their hands. My generation now—your father, me, my sisters —we had it a little different. We had education. We finish school. We could teach or nurse or do secretarial work. We could work in a bank. When it come on to getting a job, that's what we know. I know what you going to say. I hear the argument from Josette already. But the difference, you see, is that we know what doctors do. We know what lawyers do. We know what police do. All those jobs that my parents couldn't imagine for themselves, they could imagine for their children because they know what the doctors and lawyers and nurses and teachers do.

"But this other creative world is not something any of us know about. We hear that so-and-so died penniless. We hear 'bout the starving artist. So you have to understand that when our children say they want to do something like draw or make movies, we don't really understand, we don't know how to protect you from disappointment, we don't know how to guide you. We don't personally know anybody who has done that. We don't know how you going to put food on the table. We don't know how you going to pay your rent or buy land and build a house. We just don't know.

"But I can see you have talent. And I don't want to see you waste it." This speech is what she wishes she had said to Josette. She wishes that she could say it to her now and reset Josette's career. But the time has passed, she thinks, and Josette is on another path—commercial videography. It's not something she fully understands, but Josette is independent and successful, settled. Pearline has another chance to right her wrong with the young man before her. She wants him to do what Arturo never had the chance to do and make the kind of name for himself that Rupert never managed to do. He can be the one who breaks the family curse of dreaming too big and failing.

What Pearline doesn't say is that she is a different woman now, more aware, and willing to take chances.

"The Edna Manley School of Art is one of the best. You don't have to worry about the tuition. I'll pay it."

"I can't let you do that," Derek says.

She sees his pride, his fear of appearing weak, senses, too, his hesitation comes from something else. "Going to school here doesn't mean you can never go back home. You have to do something in the meantime. Can't just sit around and watch your life fritter away. Think about it, but don't take too long. As my mother used to say, 'If you caan get turkey, you haffi satisfy wid jancro.' I know you don't know what that mean. Basically, what you have now may not be what you want. But sometimes, that second-best thing is just the right thing."

"You've done enough," he says. "Can't let you do that."

"You caan stay here just so withering away to nothing."

This gift that Pearline offers will come with something else. She wants something in return, something she isn't quite ready to name.

For the second time this week, Pearline drives through Fern Gully and on into Moneague, down Mount Rosser and through the Bog Walk Gorge. She takes Derek but leaves a radio blaring and windows partially open. The man who leases the land is working in the nearby pasture as well, chopping out bush and weeds that are threatening to overrun the grass. This trip is different. Pearline plays tour guide, pointing out places that Derek cares little about, though he's too polite to say so. He nods as she talks, her voice authoritative, her stories unoriginal, borrowed from history and geography books. She brakes when she points out the places she thinks he should know—Fern Gully; Moneague, with its disappearing lake, barely visible then in the valley below; the red mud lake that holds the caustic residue from the bauxite manufacturing plant; the flat, single-lane bridge, known simply as Flat Bridge, that crosses the Rio Cobre; the hidden train tracks that run on the other side of the gorge through a hillside tunnel. The river is swollen, the water gray-brown, and the rocks that typically jut out of the water are submerged.

"Water don't reach the road yet," she says. "And I hope it stays that way 'cause I don't even know the detour. It's somewhere up on that side of the hill." She waves her left hand, but there's nothing but a dense forest on the cliffside, no hint of what lies on the other side of the rocks.

Claudia twines her fingers in a doll's hair and every now and then looks up to catch Pearline's eyes in the rearview mirror. Clouds hang low, seemingly swallowing the tips of hills and treetops. Outside the gorge, on the front end of Spanish Town, the clouds lift, and a hint of sun burns behind the overcast sky. Before long, the sun shines in full glory, illuminating the hills in the distance and the shacks built on captured land, highlighting the stark contrast between the sleepy countryside and the city, between the rusting zinc fences that give some semblance of privacy to the tenements along the highway and the massive mansions on the hillside looking down on the capital. It always surprises her how vast the differences are—extreme wealth, or the semblance of it, and extreme poverty jutting into the roadside.

They arrive at the records office. Pearline goes in on her own, leaving Derek and Claudia in the parking lot in the shade of a massive tree. She doesn't plan to be long. This time, she knows exactly what she wants: birth and death records for any Headlam in Mount Pleasant and for Annie. She looks for Annie's first, halfheartedly so, because she knows that most people at that time were not registered at all. But when she finds it, she stops, runs her finger over the names again and again. Mother's name: Irene Greaves. Child's name: Annie Marie Headlam. The father's name is missing. But the birthdate matches Annie's; the district matches her grandparents'.

Pearline's response is almost comical. She presses her hand against her chest like any old British madam shocked into silence. All along they had been thinking of the wrong Annie. She leaves the other records, takes only a copy of Annie's birth papers to show Aileen and Hermina. Annie's birth papers change nothing. They still can't sell the land. To do so, they have to prove Annie had passed and had no direct heirs to receive her share. This is what Rupert meant when he said, "Find them." Her father's final wish begins to make more sense.

Had her mother planned the little coup they learned about at the lawyer's office by deeding her portion of the property to her first-born child? Was it her last attempt to gather her brood, to lock them forever to this place and give her children a home to which they could always return? The more Pearline contemplates it, the more she thinks that's what her mother did. But why the *Headlam* name? In the early days, before Irene went to Cuba, she worked at the Headlam house. Could it be, Pearline asks herself, Annie isn't Rupert's child but a daughter he accepted as his?

Still, it's clear to her now what her father and mother meant all these years about coming back to Jamaica to claim what was theirs. As Pearline sees it, her father claimed the Headlam property, simply took it over as his own because he was done paying for land his family had already paid for with their lives.

Pearline tries to picture the house as Rupert and Irene saw

it when they arrived in Mount Pleasant. She pictures a partial roof, the walls strong, and the floor intact. She pictures Rupert leveling the cane growing near it, replacing the shingles on the roof, patching the floor, and making the house theirs. It wasn't and still isn't the house on the hill, but from a certain point behind the house, he could see exactly what the residents of the mansion on the hill once saw: the Caribbean Sea spread out like an aqua blanket and the never-ending possibilities of distant lands.

When Pearline leaves the records office, she doesn't head back home but turns toward Kingston, winding through the city cautiously. She is anxious for many reasons—the family secret she thinks she has uncovered, the unfamiliar streets, and busy roads. She is recalling the difficulty of city driving, double-parked cars along the streets of Flatbush, taxis, dollar vans, and city buses pulling in and out of traffic, pedestrians stepping off the curb as if daring drivers to hit their bodies. She hasn't missed it. Here, there are vendors hawking sweets and fruit and fuzzy steering-wheel covers and newspapers or stepping up to wash her windshield. She wants no trouble. She closes the windows and turns on the air conditioner, blasting cold air onto her bare arms. Derek perks up, looking as if he, too, is thinking of that other life in Brooklyn.

"This is Kingston." Pearline looks up at the rearview mirror, catching Claudia's eye. "This is the capital." She wonders what Claudia even knows about cities and towns and capitals. Then she adds, "This is where the prime minister lives."

Claudia looks out, whispers, "Where?"

"We can't see it yet. But I'll show you on the way back."

She winds through New Kingston's congested streets and downtown to the waterfront. "The National Gallery of Art," she says to Derek. "This is what I wanted you to see."

"Okay," he says. He draws out the word. There's skepticism in his voice, but it's dawning on him why she brought him here.

Inside, Pearline hesitates, looks around at the stark whiteness of the walls, the cavernous center hall. It's been a long time since she has been in any building like this. At another time in her life, before her husband died, she frequented museums in Manhattan and downtown Brooklyn, peering into another world far removed from hers and feeling like an imposter. Her world was simpler—bouquets of plastic flowers atop crocheted doilies, a curio of shot glasses and spoons from the cities she had visited, plastic coverings on the sofa and dining room chairs, heavy draperies that both darkened and warmed her rooms. The white lights and walls of the museum are intimidating, but she shakes it off, reaching forward for this moment she thinks is her second chance at mothering. "Imagine that this is yours." Pearline dips into her bag, an oversized tote, and pulls out a scrolled sheet of thick paper. "Imagine," she says, holding up the pencil sketch of Claudia jumping rope, "this hanging on the wall right here." She focuses on a single painting, grasping for a word to describe the style, but only comes up with *mythic*.

"I want you to look around, see what you, too, can do. Go on."

Claudia moves as if to walk with Derek, but Pearline pulls her back. "You stay with me. Right here where I can see you."

She watches Derek go, watches him linger in front of a bold red image, imagines his fingers itching to touch and trace over the whorls of dried paint. She can almost feel on her fingers the ridges of dried oil paint, the smooth canvas beneath. More than anything, she wants to see his work here, see Derek fulfill her father's dream for Arturo, the boy her father believed was destined to live an extraordinary life. She hopes that she and Derek together can achieve what Rupert hadn't and finally put her father's spirit to rest. She has one more request for Derek, but she holds it close.

14.

Thirty years on, Pearline stands outside a gate, looking up at a house she never imagined she would see again. The house still glimmers. The paint is fresh, helping make the house look new. The glass windows sparkle and the roof's shingles burn a steadfast red under the unrelenting sun, glinting in places as if someone splashed shards of glass in the paint. Pearline smiles a little, pulls her shoulders back, and steps up to the gate to call to the man pruning a bougainvillea shrub. He stops, shears in hand, and when Pearline looks more closely, she sees it is him, still trim, his body looking so youthful she thought for a moment he was the man hired to maintain the yard. He shades his eyes, hesitates.

"Eddie," she says. "Pearline *Greaves*." She hasn't called herself Greaves in more than thirty years. She no longer feels like the immigrant with the armor but the young woman she left behind when she boarded the plane in 1961 for America.

"Pearline." He draws out her name, surprise lighting up his eyes. "Long time. Long, long time. How long now?"

Pearline waves away the question, though she knows it's been exactly thirty-two years, and wraps her arm around his waist. His shirt is damp, as is her cheek when she lifts her face.

"I heard about your father. Sorry we couldn't make it to the funeral. How you holding up?"

"Holding up all right. So it is. Not a one of us going to live forever. How your mother?"

"Sharp same way. Strong. She will be glad to see you."

He is waiting, she knows, for the reason for her impromptu visit. Pearline wants to say something profound. But her mind empties, becomes for a moment a barren shore exposed after a wave recedes. She has come to the only person she thinks would know the details about her parents' early days back in Mount Pleasant, the only person who would know if her sister Annie was her father's daughter or a descendant of a Headlam.

"Come, come out o' the sun," Eddie says.

The heat from the concrete driveway wraps itself around her toes. "Nothing like the cool breeze in the country," she says. "Mount Pleasant no feel like this at all. But you would know."

"The price you pay for progress and city life." He laughs as he speaks, holds the door, and steps back to allow her to enter the small entryway.

It's the same as it was then—plastic flowers in a vase, a curio with glass ornaments, and the polished wood stairs curving away to the bedrooms. Then, the house was new, still so new it smelled of freshly poured concrete. The living room, still empty, felt cavernous and crushing. Pearline was new to Kingston. *They*, Eddie and Pearline as a couple, were new. She found him on campus, the boy from her childhood who had moved to Kingston, to a different life, with his mother, once her teacher, who married up and became a city woman and who thought Pearline to be unsuitable for her son. Pearline experienced a crushing moment in this house. She replays it like a movie, the mother and son just off camera arguing in hushed whispers; his mother asking about some other girl, a doctor's daughter, whom his mother deemed more suitable than the daughter of a poor farmer. An emotional Pearline stands inside the doorway, soothing her crushed heart and fighting the urge to run. She pictures it ending differently, with Eddie running away from his mother toward her. In reality, it was Pearline who, not in that moment but weeks later, ran away from Kingston, away from school, and, like her father and her mother's male relatives, away from the island altogether. Her reason for leaving was different—heartbreak and loss—but what she sought was the same—a fulfilled life.

The old lady, Babsy, is exactly as Pearline remembers her. She wears her hair in two braids wrapped around her head like a crown.

"Greaves," she says. She is indeed sharp. "You think I too old to remember? Live on the Headlam property, just below the great house up on the hill. Which one are you?"

"Pearline. The second one." She reverts to her childhood ways, counting herself as one of three instead of one of seven.

Pearline hasn't heard her family's place called the Headlam property before. To her, it was and has always been her family's, a house without a history, walls without stories before her family's. The feeling that she was so wrong spins again inside her like river water gurgling around a massive rock. Pearline leans in, brushes her cheek against the old lady's.

"I can tell you Greaves girls anywhere. All of you the dead stamp of your mother. You the one who went to America?"

It's the closest the old lady comes to that long-ago day.

"Long time now I don't go up that way. Used to go up there all the time and stop and see your father and mother when she was alive. But not anymore. Too old for all that now. These roads will kill you."

Pearline never understood her mother's friendship with Babsy. They'd met at the Headlam house weeks after Rupert left for Cuba. They were just two young women doing day's work for the family whose land stretched far and wide, both pregnant. "She wasn't married," Irene had said. "Wouldn't talk to me 'bout the father of the baby. So mi no tell her nothing 'bout Rupert. Just say father gone. Shut that argument down."

Eddie comes out with a tray, three glasses with ice clinking. "Cherry and guava," he says.

The reason for Pearline's visit still looms, and she eases into it, talking about how well Eddie's house has aged, comparing it to the Mount Pleasant house that creaks and threatens to fall, backing slowly into what she wants from his mother, fishing for tidbits of information without seeming to. "You're the last living person who knew my mother well."

"From school days. Ninety-four years old this year. I think I last longer on this earth than every one of them people I grow up with."

"And not an ache or pain," Eddie says. "These days, that's all I can hope for—reaching old age with my senses. And the ability to take care of myself."

"You don't come all this way to talk 'bout old age. So tell me, why Miss America come back to Mount Pleasant?"

"Miss America?" Pearline isn't sure how to take that. She's

heard it from her sisters, and now from an old family friend. "Hardly that. When you spend your whole life in a place wishing you were somewhere else . . . there comes a time when you just have to go to the place you long to be. That's it. Nothing profound. No deportation. Nothing I running from. No big story. Just time to come back home."

"Not everybody have the luxury of being where they want to be," Eddie says, and Pearline knows he's sending a coded message to his mother.

"Back in the old house and trying to save it from my sisters, who want to sell it or knock it down."

"But they can't sell it," the old lady says, and Pearline knows she was right to have come.

"Why?" Pearline says. Her breath and anxiety almost stifle the word.

"All who could lay claim to that land didn't. Only your father would. And from what I know, he never had the papers to claim it."

"How so?"

"Anybody can squat on a piece of land," she says so matter-of-factly that both Pearline and Eddie look up. "And if you stay on the land long enough, the government give you papers for it. You're nothing but squatters. That's it. Nothing more than that."

"Mama." Eddie's face is distorted by disgust. "You have to excuse her." He looks steadfastly at Pearline. "Sometimes she act like she senile."

But Pearline knows it's not old age but the underlying thing her mother didn't like about Babsy.

"What mi saying that not true? You know nothing about those times." She's slowly twirling the glass of juice. "Besides, that's why you come. No other reason than you find you don't have the papers for the land."

Eddie, increasingly uncomfortable, opens and closes his mouth, holds back what he wants to say.

"We own that house." Pearline isn't convinced, and her voice betrays her. "We have the papers to prove it."

"Papers? What papers? Them Headlam people never sell that house. She would be dead long time anyway, but I can tell you your father and your mother never buy that land from her or her people. Your father and mother come back from Cuba with you and your sister. Mother pregnant with the third one, who born here. And they take over the house. You think I old and don't remember nothing? But is the truth I talking. My brain still work. I remember. I can't tell you what happen after that, but they never buy that house. Hurricane take the roof, and it was there abandoned until your father come back and take it over." She holds the glass out again, swirls the juice so the ice clinks. "Was a time when Manley giving away land, redistributing land and wealth, he called it. Maybe then they got it. But I telling you, they never buy that place, and far as I know, unu don't have no papers to sell that property."

There's something unpleasant in the old lady's voice that Pearline doesn't like. Disdain, Pearline thinks. But Pearline goes back again to that long-ago day here in this house, when the old lady chose another girl for her son, and knows there was something more. She doesn't have what she needs, not the full story anyway, but she gathers her things, gathers what's left of her dignity. "Long way back to Mount Pleasant."

"Sorry." They're outside when Eddie speaks. "What you should know is this. What my mother was hinting at is that my brother's father, the man everyone knows as his father, isn't really his father. That Headlam man was."

Pearline nods. The specific details don't matter. She already knows how the story plays out.

"You have to understand," he says. "My mother was just doing day's work at the house. Washing clothes. Cleaning."

Pearline nods, places a hand on his arm. "Almost every woman her age has some kind of story like that." She waves off the rest of his story.

"No. No. She thinks your mother had the same experience she had, has thought for a long time that your oldest sister is my brother's sister too. Thinks that's what your parents used to claim the land."

He has a pained look on his face, and for a moment, Pearline thinks he sees her as his mother sees her family—as nothing more than squatters occupying land to which they have no rightful claim.

"You know I was an attorney." He waits for Pearline to nod. "Gave up engineering. Took up law. Some of what my mother says is true. I won't get into all of it. But if you live on a piece of land for seven years and can show you were taking care of it, you can file for the deed to the land. That's the gist of it."

Again, Pearline feels her childhood and everything she has believed of herself and her parents falling away. "So what she said is true? We're squatters?"

"Your mother came to me a long time ago. Asked me to help her put her share in her daughter's name. Annie, the firstborn. Said it was her daughter's money that paid for the house, and she wanted to be sure that when her daughter came home to Jamaica she had her place. Wanted to make sure your father didn't sell it. Your father didn't know all that. Then I saw the name Headlam, and I thought my mother was right all those years ago when she said you weren't right for me. But your mother tell me 'bout Rupert's rightful name and how she named her firstborn Headlam out of spite." He waves his hand. "So I did what any good lawyer would do. I looked it up. I believe your mother. What's done is done. And it's all legal."

"Thank you. It makes sense now."

"I'm not practicing anymore—give up the law long time. But if you want help sorting it out, just give me a call." His eyes are soft, and it looks like he wants to say something more.

She, too, wants to say something. But she pictures his mother at a window looking out, her old ways returning.

"We shouldn't let this much time pass again," he says.

Pearline nods, his presence now a little too much. She's wary of promises, but she lets his hand linger on her arm. "You know where I am."

It's miles before Pearline feels the breeze turning cool as it blows through the car. She's in the Bog Walk Gorge, stealing glances at the river running alongside the road. The river is calm today, the water frothing in places and moving steadily over and around rocks jutting from the riverbed. She's trying hard not to think about Eddie or his mother, the grudge her mother's good friend has held all this while. Relief works its way in waves through her body. Her eyes tear up, and she wipes them away quickly before they tickle her cheeks and chin. She rubs the goose bumps on her bare arm and finds a spot where she can pull over and compose herself. She walks around the car to stretch her legs, but they're weak, unwilling to hold her up.

Back on the coast, she forces herself to think about something else. The breeze whips through the car. There's a stretch of road where the coconut trees are dying. The branches, brown now, hang limp, and it's only a matter of time before they fall, before the entire length of the trees rot. She catches glimpses of the sea, the distant waves cresting and the water pushing up in the mangroves. She pictures her and Eddie at another time, before his mother stepped in and severed their relationship. They're on a beach, the waves too rough and water too cold for swimming. Too afraid to get in, they sit on the sand looking out, watching the water rise and fall.

"Tell me," Eddie says, "what you most want in the world."

"I don't know." Pearline holds her voice for a second longer than she should. She hasn't yet allowed herself to own her dreams. "Shh. Just listen."

After a time he asks, "What you want to hear?"

"Let the water speak," Pearline says, and he looks at her as if she has said the strangest thing in the world. "There are thousands of stories buried in this water, which we'll never hear. We could be gone in an instant, and nobody would hear our stories."

Eddie traces pictures on her back, starting low and moving his finger up her spine and across her shoulder blades. "What is this now?" he asks.

"A tree."

"What kind?"

"Coconut."

He moves his fingers again, tracing a mango, the map of Jamaica, an almond, none of which she guesses correctly.

Pearline thinks of it now, Eddie tracing maps on her back, because that is where she'd rather be: on a beach with the water rolling up over her calves, the wet sand around her shifting and her body settling into it, making its own cocoon.

For the first time, Pearline thinks that all of this is too much—the history, her father's wish, the crumbling old house, her sisters' disdain for the house and what it means, Claudia and Derek and Josette. She wonders if she was wrong to give up her New York life. She could return to Brooklyn now and leave this headache behind, pick up exactly where she left off. But she's been dreaming of this return for thirty years, and she can't or won't let it go. There are millions of others like her who promised to return and didn't, who left their families listening for footsteps that would never come. She's come back the way Rupert and Irene hadn't—settled, financially secure, able to build a legacy in Jamaica so that leaving the country isn't the only option for other members of her family.

Pearline has no way of knowing whether Eddie's mother's version of her family's story is true and her father claimed Annie because no one else would, later using her as leverage to squat on the land indefinitely. But, deep in her soul, she believes her mother's version.

Find them for me swirls in Pearline's head. Pearline tacks a map onto the wall below a smaller map she has torn from the *Concise*

Encyclopedia of Geography. This tourist map is larger and more detailed. Both maps are a reminder of her charge. She traces the red lines marking major roadways from Santiago de Cuba, north to Holguín and Banes. She looks for other cities Rupert and Irene talked about—Ciego de Ávila, Camagüey—traces her fingers along the length of the entire island to Havana, the last known address for Annie. On the other side is the more detailed map of Havana, and she traces her fingers grid by grid looking for the street, imagining Annie, or the fuzzy image she has of her, making a life in this city. *"La Habana,"* she says, pronouncing it the way it's written on the map.

Pearline traces the road back across the island to Banes on the northeastern tip. She tries to remember something about Cuba, tries to place her three-year-old self in the house in Banes. But her memories are not hers. They are her father's and her mother's, stories they passed on and told over and over until she took them as her own, until she hears even now the heavy rains pounding the roof the day Arturo and Gerardo were born. Even now she sees herself at an Emancipation Day festival, a little girl with ribbons in her hair dancing the maypole, keeping time with the other dancers to braid the extended ribbons. Though she knows she would have been too small at that age to reach the ribbon or match the adults' movements, she still sees herself on the field, still sees the multicolored ribbons, herself in a white dress, her mother and her father cheering her on, and her mother with a basket of sweets she sells to anyone who stops by.

When she closes her eyes, she sees the house clearly— yellow, with red floors and coconut trees lined up next to it. She sees thin curtains fluttering, her brothers, sisters, and parents on the veranda. Her mother has her head down. She's been crying. Annie stands up and rubs her mother's back. It's the clearest memory she has had outside the dreams. And even so, she wonders if it's truly her memory or her father's, another one of his appearances. She can't think of the occasion, wonders if perhaps it was after Arturo's funeral or a Sunday evening after church. What else would have made her mother cry? She tries to picture her father as well. But he is a fuzzy figure, more dreamlike than real. And so are the others; her mother's image is the only clear one.

She drops her hand back to the tiny circle on the map that represents Banes, the place where she was born and about which she knows very little—the equivalent of a short paragraph at most and essentially a documentarian's or historian's view. She knows this: Banes was a company town that owed its growth to the United Fruit Company, one of the many American companies that owned sugar plantations in the northeastern section of Cuba. The company built mills, transforming the little banana-growing town to a sugar-producing town, bringing in laborers from Haiti and Jamaica and Barbados and a host of islands in between. In the beginning, there was nothing but fields. The workers who came transformed it with the wood and thatch they were given to build their houses. The little township became theirs with names for sections like Jamaica Town and Bajan Town and the Salvation Army, Wesleyan, Anglican, Baptist churches. It was theirs, populated with people who wanted to hold on to the cultures they had left behind.

Pearline pictures the gentle rolling hills of La Güira. She

tries to picture the street where they lived but can't pick up the details. She closes her eyes to focus, but all she can see is the yellow house, the coconut trees towering above it, the branches dipping with the breeze and playing peek-a-boo with the orbs of fruit, and her father in the backyard standing over a mound of earth, burying something—a yam head, money, or something else of value, which he may never have had time to recover. She hears Babsy saying, "All that Cuba business. Every day your mother lived, she regretted that she ever follow your father and go and come back without all her children."

15.

"I HAVE SOMETHING TO SHOW YOU," PEARLINE SAYS. THIS
is her second call. She has already told Aileen, and as she tells
Hermina, her heart quickens again, and the heady, short-of-
breath feeling she attributes to nerves and uncertainty over
what her sisters will think of her discoveries spreads through
her upper body. She pulls a chair closer to the telephone table
and bows her head to her knees. "Aileen passing through in
the morning."

"All right. I have an appointment at ten tomorrow in Ochi.
Will stop on my way in."

Pearline tips her head back, waits for the feeling to pass.
This has always been her strength: powering through, always
beating a path forward despite pain or discomfort of any kind.
It's partly stubbornness she thinks she inherited from Rupert,
partly built out of the desire not to fail, to carry forward her
family's legacy, and partly due to the fact she's seen so many
patients come through much worse. She promises her body
rest when she comes out on the other end of this.

When the feeling passes as Pearline expects, she lines up
the papers and artifacts she has gathered—the age-old family
photo, Annie's letters, birth records, property deed and transfer

papers. She jots down the details she learned from Babsy, stopping every now and then to shake out the numbness in her arm. *Retirement making me soft,* she thinks. Pearline doesn't yet know what her father wouldn't forgive, but she thinks it's within reach.

Pearline pushes a pillow beneath her neck and lets her head loll back. It's not comfort that she wants, for comfort brings sleep, and she's trying not to sleep—she's trying to head off the dreams she's sure will come. Not now. She flips, sure she won't sleep this way, on the couch, sprawled like a lizard in the sun. But her eyes are heavy, her body tired from days of heading off the urge to rest and dream. At the moment, Pearline both wants and doesn't want to own her father's memory. It is a heavy weight to carry, and she envies her sisters' ability to focus on a future that isn't strung to the past through half dreams.

Outside, Claudia and the girl from the neighboring house are making mud pies, setting dirt and water to dry in an old cheese tin. She's promised to take them to the beach, but even that is too much trouble, and Pearline thinks they'll have to make do with splashing in the enormous galvanized washtub. They won't mind. The sound of their voices is a calming lull. Her body, a dead weight, sinks deeper into the cushions, and she falls into sleep with the sound of water sloshing and the cooling feel of water sprinkling at her feet.

She dreams of water, just droplets of it on the underbrush and dry leaves that make a cushion on the ground. Irene is a silhouette in the dark who disappears in the thicket of banana and plantain plants. The dry leaves rustle beneath her feet.

Soon, the sound Pearline hears falls away, but she senses that Irene is present. She is not; Pearline is the one walking through the banana grove. Rupert is there too. It is he who Pearline sees among the banana plants, waiting for her to emerge on the other side.

A breeze tickles Pearline's bare toes, and she relaxes even more. Her toes list outward, and one arm falls from the couch to dangle on the floor. Outside, the trees whistle, and Claudia and her friend giggle and pull chairs across the veranda. The sound of scraping wood infuses Pearline's dream. They move a crate of toys, pulling it across the floor. Pearline hears the scraping and pushing, but it sounds distant. Pearline, too, dreams of giggles, except the giggling makes no sense in the context of the banana grove. Pearline tries to wake. But she can't pull herself out of sleep, can't move her body from the couch. She feels trapped, feels like something is sitting on her chest and back, holding her in place and preventing her from moving her arms to push it off. Pearline wants to call out, but even that seems impossible. She bides her time, waiting for the moment when the thing on her torso eases its hold.

Derek wakes Pearline—not intentionally—when he returns. It's the sounds from the kitchen that finally pull her from the throes of the dream that grabbed her. She feels she is clawing her way out of a deep sleep, overturning a barrel, tumbling out and upright. Sitting up, she reaches for the remnants of the dream.

Claudia comes tumbling in. Her friend has left. Pearline finally moves, lowering her legs in stages, as if each limb requires a separate, distinct set of instructions.

"You had a good old time, nuh true?" Pearline asks.

"Yes, Sister Pearl."

"Tomorrow, we go beach. Old lady like me get tired easy."

Claudia nods and runs off to the kitchen, toward Derek.

"Derek, what you in there making?"

"Fried rice," he calls back. "I miss the corner Chinese shops."

"I know what you mean," she says. She wants to move from the couch but can't. There was nothing restful about her sleep, and what she wants most is to close her eyes again, turn a valve that shuts off her dreams, and sleep fully.

Night comes quickly. The electricity goes out, plunging the house into complete darkness. With no television, no music on the radio, and Pearline unwilling to play a game of Ludo, Derek and Claudia retire early. Except for the bugs hitting the glass lamps, the veranda is quiet. The neighbor's house simmers toward a long night's rest. Even the dogs are quiet. From the road comes the occasional toot of a car horn, and from the shrubs a stray croak, the chirps of crickets. Pearline is lengthening her evening and shortening her time to sleep. She's afraid of the dreams that will come and instead sits for a long while in the semidarkness contemplating what she plans to tell Aileen and Hermina in the morning and what she wants to propose to Derek. Josette is the only obstacle.

The phone rings, and it's Hermina asking if she has power. "Brown's Town, too, and Discovery Bay. Might even be the whole island, for all I know. Anyway, lock up good and see you in the morning."

Pearline doesn't lock up. She embraces the night, lets it wrap itself around her.

Derek's gait is slow and heavy. He's coming back from his morning walk. Pearline knows that this is how he begins his days, but, for the first time, she looks at him through Aileen's eyes, sees what Aileen sees—an idle young man content with doing nothing. They're waiting for Hermina to come, and Pearline has laid out everything in the back room—the photo, the newspaper clippings, the birth and land transfer papers.

"He's starting art school," Pearline says. "We starting the application process."

"He have money to pay for that?"

Pearline waves her hand as if to bat the question away. "That's not what I call you here for."

"Don't tell me you paying for it?" Aileen says. Her eyebrows are raised, her nostrils flaring.

"Well . . ."

"Now mi know say you done los' you mind. How his education become your problem? I tell you from long time 'bout this business of letting people take advantage o' you."

"So you want me to give the money to a stranger, some random charity, rather than help mi owna blood? No way Ah can sit here and watch the young man waste his life. That not helping him, and it not helping me."

"Come back here acting like you rich. All that money you save up soon gone. And when you up in age, don't think him coming back here to help you."

Pearline can see the reason for the morning's visit dissipating, replaced now by this more urgent issue.

"All the sacrifice we mek to take care o' Papa, and you come here with you boasty self, flashing money round to pay tuition for a boy you don't even know. Meantime, you wan' hold on to the land and the money me and Hermina could use to ensure we set for our old age."

"What you mean 'boasty self'?"

"No bother wid it. Too early this morning for me to raise mi pressure." Aileen turns away, clomps down the steps, opens and slams the car door shut. She opens the door again, puts one foot on the gravel, eases her head out. "I hope Josette can talk some sense into you."

Pearline, her heart racing, her mind doing cartwheels, walks to the steps and back, trying but failing to tamp her anger down. How dare she, Pearline thinks, counting back to the thousands of dollars she sent home over the years for each medical emergency, a new roof after Hurricane Gilbert, seed money to expand Rupert's cattle-raising endeavors. Aileen knows nothing of the sacrifices she made—how many times she wanted to buy a new pair of winter boots but couldn't, how long she drove with a broken muffler before she could replace it, how many nights, bone tired, she trekked to a second job so the extra money could pay for something back home.

"How dare she," Pearline says out loud. "And to bring Josette into this. As if Josette going beat me."

She imagines Aileen's car rounding the corners, coming out at the clearing at Mount Olivet, winding around yet more corners on the way to Brown's Town. She tries to time the drive, waiting out the minutes till she can call Aileen to let her

know exactly what sacrifice means, to point out what Pearline herself has lost—a husband and a strong relationship with
her daughter—all because she worked so hard to maintain
their life here and not come home a failure. Nothing calms
her—not the breeze under the cherry tree, not the walk to
the clearing where she can look out to sea. She can't let go
of what her sister thinks of her. She repeats Aileen's words,
exaggerating the scorn inherent in the words *boasty self*, whipping her anger with no immediate release. She sees again the
differences between her sisters and herself. She takes chances
and they don't, and she is certain now more than ever that
this difference will widen the chasm between them now. She
comes back to the veranda, checks again how much time has
passed since Aileen left, and raises herself to get the phone.

Pearline feels herself falling, hears the chair scraping the
floor and the patter of little footsteps coming to her. She
knows that Claudia squats, places a sticky hand on her cheek,
and says, "Sister Pearl." Pearline speaks, and even as she does,
she knows her words have no meaning; the order in which
they come makes no sense. Just as quickly as Claudia comes,
she leaves, her footsteps quicker this time, her voice drifting
away like an echo in a tin can. Pearline is aware of every little detail—the floorboards squeaking and dipping, Claudia's
small fingers, Derek's broader hands lifting her body, Derek's
voice passing on an urgent message, the car engine turning
over and the wheels crunching the gravel beneath.

PART II

MESSAGES ON THE WIND AND SEA

Summer 1993

16.

RAIN BEATS ON THE WINDSHIELD AND ROOF LIKE fingertips on a drum. Even through the patter of raindrops, Pearline hears the cascade of voices—a jolt of sound that comes at random times and which she hasn't been able to stop since the stroke. It's no longer dreams that come when she's at rest but a full-on chatter that sometimes sounds like a swarm of birds. Other times, they are distinct voices, primarily her father's, but her mother's breaks through as well. Rupert is no longer coming to her in her dreams but inhabiting her heart, her head, her soul. She's trying to distinguish when the voices come, what she hears when and where. The distinct chatter and individual voices are louder when the car nears the water, softer when the road curves away on a cliffside hidden by dense vegetation.

They're on the north coast highway now. The road curves alongside the coastline, and every now and then, Pearline catches a glimpse of water, the blue hue muted under the clouds, the white froth of waves lashing against itself, curling over and under before spreading out on the shore, or a river gushing and spilling into the sea. When the sound rages, she looks to the mangroves, the natural buffer between the sea and the land, as well as between her and the voices. But even as she seeks a buffer, she knows she wants to hear what the spirits have to say.

Pearline hears the folk song Irene sang through the patter on the windshield. Irene made the song her own, substituting Annie, David, or Gerardo for Liza: *Every time mi memba Liza, waata come a mi y'eye / Wen mi tink pan mi nice gal Liza, waata come a mi y'eye / Come back, Liza, come back, gal, waata come a mi y'eye / Come back, Liza, come back, gal, waata come a mi y'eye.* The song always makes Pearline's eyes water, reinforcing the image of her mother singing and washing and weeping, crying for the children she wouldn't see again in her lifetime.

There's a moment that Pearline remembers: She is seven, maybe eight, scrawny, curious about everything, including why Irene cries when she sings. *Because I gave my children songs.* It makes no sense to the child Pearline was then, but now, older, wiser, she knows that Irene lived Rupert's Cuba dreams, and with no dreams of her own, no plans independent of his, the thing that she could give her children was songs. In Cuba, Irene had no control of the place around her, but she controlled what she could—the language her children spoke, the songs they sang, the culture they soaked. Rupert didn't. Across the sea, over the land covered with forest green, Irene had carried her English songs and English ways. She didn't toss those overboard as she did the memories of the land. She sang the songs in the yard and insisted her children go to English school. She thought of the children as bread dipped in tea— English tea thickened with milk—the white, sturdy bread softening and the stain of the tea spreading. From the beginning, she stubbornly insisted they were not Cuba's own, quashing their attempts to speak Spanish, insisting day after day that her children speak English when at home. She made sure her children understood "home" was another country altogether, a place they would soon be.

Pearline holds on to that little memory, her mother's insistent voice repeating, *I gave my children songs so they could find their way home.* But the feeling, the triumph of finally understanding what Irene meant, is short-lived; except for this folk song that plays in her mind over and over and which she hears from time to time in other venues, she doesn't remember the specific songs Irene taught her.

Pearline shifts her eyes back to the road, the mangroves giving way to open sea, Falmouth's narrow streets built to accommodate horses and carriages rather than trucks, more swamps filled with reeds, the low seawall against which the waves beat, anemic remnants of coconut trees. Aileen times their arrival well. Josette is standing at the curb outside Arrivals with two red suitcases at her feet and a floppy hat shading most of her face. Aileen steps out, and Josette gives a little squeal, hugs and rocks her aunt, then runs back to the passenger side, leans in through the open window, and kisses Pearline's cheek. "How you feeling?" But Josette doesn't wait long to hear her mother's answer. "Let me put the suitcases in the trunk." Inside, breezy, excited, Josette says, "I'm surprised you came, Mom. You're doing much better than I thought."

"What you think?" Pearline asks. "You think you coming to find a cripple?"

"Doctor said she got lucky this time," Aileen says, talking

over Pearline, waving a hand as if to say *Don't mind she at all.* "Just a small stroke. She really lucky 'cause health care out here is a joke."

Pearline waits for Josette to say something about her returning to Brooklyn. But thankfully, she doesn't. Pearline knows now what healthcare here means. She woke in the women's ward to see a row of flimsy cots stretched out beside and in front of her. Thin curtains on shaky rods enclosed some of the cots. Otherwise, they were all exposed, the patient's illnesses and treatment on display to visitors and staff. She'd forgotten what the wards here were like. The doctors made rounds in groups of six, standing at the foot of each bed and talking, one person describing each patient's history and progress. They didn't interact with the patients at all but moved on to the next like patrons in a museum observing the exhibits. She's here now in the car because of Hermina's neighbor, Dr. Malcolm, who took over her care and transferred her to a private facility. She's afraid that without his intervention, she would have lingered in the public hospital, helpless.

"Small stroke, but she still not one hundred percent," Aileen says. "You'll see what I mean."

Pearline turns to the window, pulling her lips tight, blocking out the conversation in the car. She knows what Josette is thinking. Her thoughts are not about Pearline directly but about her father, the helplessness of knowing her father was gone, swallowed by the gaping hole of his sudden, unexpected death. He said good night, sat with Josette as she prayed, pulled the blanket up to her neck as he always did before leaving the darkened bedroom, his shoes swishing on the carpet, to put away the pots and pans and tidy the kitchen. He would have made breakfast in the morning—coffee for himself, hot chocolate for his princess—and the scents of cinnamon and vanilla, onions and garlic, and the tinned mackerel he liked to warm and eat with boiled green bananas would have been filtering through the house. Except that morning, the scents were absent, which is how Pearline, returning from her overnight job, knew something was wrong. She called his name, put the kettle on, peered in Josette's room, and hurried on to theirs. The room was eerie, silent. She called his name again, checked his pulse, and knew. She called the paramedics and hurried Josette out of the house and on to school, which meant Josette spent the day at school not knowing the depth of the hole that had just opened up in her life.

Every day since, Pearline has asked some version of *what if.* What if I hadn't worked that night? What if I had called home overnight? What if I hadn't worked as much as I did? What if I had let Josette stay home from school that day?

Pearline steals glances at Josette, who is leaning back, eyes closed, letting the breeze ruffle her hair. When Aileen points out the location of the glistening waters even though they can't see the water fluorescing in the daytime, she opens her eyes again.

"You know, all my life I live here and I never once go out on boat ride to see it," Aileen says.

"Maybe we can go before I leave," Josette says. "If we have time."

"Maybe." Aileen hunches closer to the steering wheel.

Josette starts humming out loud and Aileen picks up the tune, singing along, jerking her shoulders.

"The folk group at the airport was singing it, right?" Aileen asks.

"Folk group?"

"You know, the folk singers in madras who greet you outside baggage claim?"

"Oh, them. Yes."

Aileen's voice fills up the car, drowning out the tapping rain. When she comes to the end of that one, she picks up another folk song and another, singing to keep from talking. Or so Pearline thinks. If Aileen hadn't been driving, she would be swaying left and right, the rhythm permeating every muscle, every bone. "Come, come," she would say, reaching out her hands to draw someone beside her to build a tiny choir. They drive into St. Ann like that, Aileen singing, Pearline quiet, Josette tapping out the rhythm on her thigh, the voices floating up and around Pearline, drowned out temporarily by Aileen's songs.

The tires crunch on the gravel, and Derek and Claudia come out immediately as if they are attuned to the sound. Since the stroke, Pearline hasn't been speaking much, afraid of how her words come out, and she stands aside as Aileen introduces Derek and Claudia to Josette.

"Cousin?" Josette asks. She looks at Derek and back to her aunt, dipping her chin and letting her eyes ask, *Whose child?*

"Every family have secrets," Aileen says. "Derek's father is our half brother."

"You remember Yvonne? You might not remember her. Anyway, she's Claudia's mother. Yvonne was the one looking after your grandfather."

Josette nods, reaches out to hug her newfound relatives. Pearline braces for Josette's comments about the secrets Pearline has begun to keep—the plans to leave Brooklyn, the newfound cousin, the symptoms that should have signaled to a nurse a stroke was imminent. With Josette, everything comes back to the way her father died, succumbing to a stroke in the middle of the night, alone, while Pearline went off to an overnight shift caring for an elderly man. Josette, never one to miss a chance to point out Pearline's failings as mother and wife and daughter, surprises. She says nothing. Theirs has never been an easy relationship. It's neither contentious nor soft, nor chaotic and dysfunctional, but a seesaw that's never found its balancing point. Josette found that balance with her father, and when he was gone, she accepted that Pearline would never provide it. Pearline is not the one in whom Josette confides.

Pearline takes her time mounting the steps. She's less steady now and walks with a discernible limp, which the doctor assures will disappear soon. It is Aileen who waits to watch Pearline climb the stairs. Josette has gone ahead, and Pearline is not surprised. All these years, Josette has seen her as a stalwart figure, a fighter, and Pearline has never done anything to appear vulnerable or needy. And now that she is, it's not her job to train her adult daughter to see what her mother needs. In time, she thinks.

Derek has made a pot of pumpkin soup, and he ladles some into bowls. Hot liquid splashes, and he snaps his hand quickly to ease the burn. He moves in the kitchen as if it's his own, scooping chunks of watermelon and papaya into plastic containers, wiping down the counter, cleaning up the way Pearline would. He's taken over. The pipes rumble, the sound seeming to come from over and under the house.

"Tank empty," Derek says. He turns off the tap and heads outside to the pump house.

How easily he has fallen into the rhythm of keeping this old house running. Almost nothing works the way it's supposed to, and already he knows the quirks and the house's rhythms, how to push Pearline to rest, welcoming Josette but not giving up the place he has carved for himself. Pearline stands to the side, and, instead of shooing Pearline, he moves around her, stopping every now and then to ask a question to which he already knows the answer.

"I'll bring it out to the veranda." He's buttering bread, laying it on a plate next to the soup bowl. "You go ahead. Take your time."

Pearline takes her soup on the veranda. She watches Josette wander around the house and yard, looking at the remnants of her grandmother that remain everywhere in the house. Pearline watches Josette wander to the grove where her grandfather is buried, to the chair under the guava tree and back. Claudia keeps her distance from Josette, but she sits by Pearline's feet, resting her head on Pearline's leg.

Aileen sits for a while. "Ah leaving before night come down. Can't do the night driving at all."

Josette leans against the railing, her back to the driveway that's now covered in shadows.

"The doctor said her speech may be slow to come back," Aileen says, counting out each reminder. "She still needs a brain scan. All her pills on the nightstand. Derek know where, what she taking, and when."

"Still need a brain scan?" Josette asks.

"Third-world medical system."

"So when?"

"Tomorrow. Hermina set it up already."

Pearline finishes the last of the soup. "I was a nurse. Remember? I know how to take care of myself."

"And yet, still, here we are." Josette holds Pearline's gaze.

So far, Josette's statement is the only hint of what she's thinking—that Pearline is again taking on too much, working so as not to fail, all the while missing things: her husband's death, her daughter's needs, her own body's signals. Pearline knows what's coming next—how much she has put into taking care of Derek, how she has adopted Claudia as a stand-in for her own grandchildren. She knows exactly how Josette will word it: *I see you have Claudia and Derek, your new children.*

Aileen seems to be waiting, too, for whatever Josette will say next. The quiet waiting settles on them, and Pearline purses her lips. "Take this for me," she says to Derek as she leans her neck against the back of the chair. In the midst of the silence, the birds, a flock of parrots, start up again. The caws are loud— the one thing that seems to hold them all.

"Damn birds eat everything," Pearline says.

"Need a slingshot." Derek, back on the veranda, holds his hands up and mimics shooting at the birds.

"What you know 'bout slingshots?" Aileen's face softens when she asks.

"My father," he says. "On summer holiday I used to come here. Me and my cousins had nothing to do but shoot birds and play ball."

"Soccer?" Josette asks.

"Soccer. Cricket. One time we made a pushcart." He shakes

his head, smiles. "Fell out an almond tree and broke my arm. Had it set right there at the hospital in St. Ann's Bay."

"You a real yardie," Josette says and laughs.

Pearline nods. "Night coming."

"Appointment at eleven." Aileen says. "Till tomorrow, then."

As Aileen leaves, a neighbor, the Baptist lay preacher, comes to pray with Pearline. He wears a black shirt with jeans and thick leather sandals.

"Evening, Sister Pearl." He's walking up the steps as he speaks. "Couldn't let another evening pass without coming to pray with you." He nods toward Josette and Derek.

Pearline opens her palm, gesturing toward the chair Josette has vacated. "Thank you for coming."

At another time, Pearline would have offered him a drink, but she fears he will linger. She bows her head, urging him to get on with the prayers. And he obliges, opening a little prayer book before launching into a long prayer not at all inspired by the book he holds. Each time he raises his voice, it sounds like he's scaring God into action. "Heal your child, Sister Pearl. Let her have presence of mind and use of her limbs," he says.

Silently, Pearline corrects his prayer. "If it is your will."

"As you saved Jonah from the whale's belly, save Sister Pearl from this sickness."

Again, Pearline says, "If it is your will." She keeps her eyes closed, not wanting to see Josette's brows raised and eyes waiting to catch hers. She knows Josette is laughing. This prayer only confirms what she thinks of preachers. *Who are they,* Josette always asks, *to tell another man how to live or to tell God what to do? Who are we to tell God how to run His world? Isn't that what prayer is—the pleas of those without faith?*

The pastor prays for God's blessings on the household, halts his words for a long moment. When it seems he's run out of words, he starts again and asks God to "lead His wayward children home. Bring them to your house, Lord. Let them know that they are loved."

It's Derek who brings the prayer to a close. He says a loud "Amen" and pushes his chair back. It scrapes the floor, breaking the preacher's trance. It's Derek who ushers him on, excusing Pearline and leading her from the veranda. The minister's car makes a whirring sound, and Josette laughs. "Sound like a helicopter." Josette breaks the tension, pushing them back to what promises to become their norm—extended periods on the veranda with silence collapsing around them as the nighttime chorus of chirps rise up, the three of them like a family—a mother and her two attentive children.

There's a lot of daylight left—at least another two hours by Pearline's calculation—and she asks Derek to take her for a swim. She feels the pull of the water, an urgency to submerge her body and hear the voices chattering beneath the swish of the waves.

"Now?" Josette asks.

"Therapy." Pearline nods. "All I need is thirty minutes. Night won't even come before we reach back here."

The land's heartbeat, Rupert used to call the sea. She understands it now—how the water's rhythm remains with her body long after she leaves the beach, and she can lie at night lulled by her body's memory of the rocking waves. Rupert had a habit of going down to the seaside early on Sunday mornings. Church was not his thing. But he went to hear the water talk, though he never told his daughters what he heard. "Every time I hear a wave crash against the shore, I hear a voice," he said. "If you hold still, you'll hear what the sea telling you." There, on the shore, looking out at the waves swelling and rolling, is where he made his big decisions.

Like Rupert, water is therapy for Pearline now. Derek takes her for a daily swim so she can regain full strength on her left side where the stroke has made her weak. She has work to do—a house to save, siblings she must find, her father's wish to fulfill—and she won't let up. Not yet. Pearline's early-morning swim is also a version of Rupert's Sunday-morning ritual and trek to the seaside to get consent for whatever he dreamed of doing.

She's stepping and watching the water wrap around her ankles, waiting for a message like the one Rupert heard before his first trip in 1917, waiting for the full-on chatter. It's inescapable, and she's no longer running from it but leaning, welcoming the sound, waiting for the messages the voices bring, whether her mother's raspy voice or Rupert's.

She wades in and lets her body float, welcoming the water enveloping her like a shroud.

With the stroke, Pearline is acknowledging more things now: the messages the wind and seas carry, the whispers in the rooms of the old house, the grief that passes from generation to generation like a mutant gene. What she has long acknowledged is the legacy of failure. That legacy has a shape to it, and she has worked hard to thwart that legacy. Only now is she seeing her mother's and father's pain for what it was: grief. Generation after generation picks it up and carries it forward.

She carries her mother's grief, and Josette will carry hers. Josette's children will carry their mother's. It's as old as time: a mother loses her children, never seeing their faces again. A continent loses its children, young and old, stolen and sold across seas and rivers and mountains. And the new country loses them again, over and over, sometimes brutally, sometimes because the grown children leave for Panama and Cuba and Costa Rica to make up for what wasn't here on this island they made their own. These days, the children, like herself, leave for America, talking to the remaining family over the seas, their voices like the rasp of gravel sliding. And there are the children a mother leaves behind to save some of the others, the babies who don't survive infancy—this grief more recent, more fresh, touching her generation directly. It's too much sometimes, generations of pain and hurt folding and unfolding, wrapped up in every word, every decision.

All Irene wanted was to find her children and stem that flow of grief. And now Rupert has left it for Pearline. His grief, bonded to his memory, is now Pearline's, something she thought she had escaped by leaving for America. It's hers now by default, or so she thinks, because neither Hermina nor Aileen took from Rupert what he asked of them. Pearline is the daughter Rupert could always count on to shape and invest in his dreams. She is the daughter he always said was most like him: fearless and stubborn.

This evening, the sea is silent. She's aware of Derek hovering nearby, watching her the way a parent watches a child. She flips, swims, working her arms, fluttering her feet, waking the voices that have chosen to remain silent. She lets Derek hold her arms while she kicks as forcefully as she can. She makes exaggerated circles with her arms, dips and bobs, until Derek says, "Time. We'll come back early in the morning."

Pearline is reluctant to leave, disappointed, even. And she looks back with longing at the flat, calm sea, the dash of orange deep on the horizon.

Josette is still on the veranda when they get back. She holds Pearline's gaze for a long minute before she looks away, hiding whatever emotion is becoming visible in her eyes. Despite her daughter's unspoken feelings, Pearline feels settled. The reason Josette is here is not the reason Pearline prefers, but it is what Pearline has been waiting for: Josette to come back home. The settled feeling is like a satisfied release of breath after a long wait is over. She wants to thank Josette, to explain it to her, but she can't find the words to describe the feeling.

The spirits are settling too, Pearline thinks. For the moment, they're quiet, calming themselves, temporarily appeased that Josette has come. Josette is not who the spirits ultimately want, but her arrival is a hint of what's to come. As soon as the temporary satisfaction eases, the voices' chorus will rise again as they wait for the arrivals that will truly settle them.

17.

SEAWATER DAMPENS PEARLINE'S COLLAR. SHE FLICKS AT THE droplets, tucks the towel again into the neckline of her shirt. She's back in Mount Pleasant, and while she should be moving faster—showering, eating, and preparing for Aileen and Hermina to arrive and drive her to the radiology center—she lingers in the morning sun, letting the heat dry her hair and neck and the evaporated salt remain on her bare arms and legs. The morning's trip to the beach was again quiet, the air by the water still, the message she's waiting to hear still not forthcoming. She wants to head to the little family cemetery, but she doesn't trust herself to walk that far alone, and she doesn't want company. Since she's come home from the hospital, she hasn't been alone.

Gather the children and keep them close, is what she's thinking. *Anytime they come, I will be here saying, "You come."* This is what she wants to hear again, clearer this time, a confirmation of what she concluded the previous night.

Pearline has often reimagined the scenario of how her family returned to Jamaica originally. She imagines her family of eight—Hermina isn't yet a part of their cohort—in Banes packing and journeying home together. There's a shift in the wind, the early hint of a hurricane swarming toward land, whipping the sea, bending and uprooting trees. It comes two days later, and for two full nights, the wind-whipped rain batters the little yellow house, each howl of wind frightening the children anew. They pass the night telling stories—Irene talking about her father's time in Panama, his wish to see the United States of America that the foreigners he met in Panama described, and Rupert talking about going to the river to catch crayfish.

When the winds die down and rains cease, they find that the massive limbs of the breadfruit tree have smashed through the covering over the outdoor kitchen area, small ponds of water pool in the yard, and the neighbor's house is mostly gone, reduced to half its size. The banana and plantain plants have fallen, and their leaves—some still green, some quailing—flap in a small muddy pond.

"Better we go on home," Irene says.

She imagines that Rupert says "yes," that the family of eight gathers the last of their things and sets sail for Jamaica long before the troubles that came in 1933 led them home. What then? She asks but never answers: What if they had indeed come home before 1933? What if Irene could have lived her life with no regrets, with her family intact and spread out around her?

But what is true is the opposite: A hurricane sent Irene and Rupert and Annie to Cuba. When Pearline closes her eyes, pictures vintage photos of Jamaicans aboard a ship in the early 1900s, she superimposes Irene and Rupert onto the bodies, silhouettes in the early-morning light. And she pictures them in the hours before they arrive at the wharf, Irene holding baby Annie, a curious girl who twists left and right to take in everything around. Behind them is their house partially leveled by a hurricane. The limbs of the breadfruit tree cover the outdoor kitchen area. A pear tree partially covers the bedroom, leaving the interwoven planks of the wattle and daub walls exposed. Small ponds of water pool in the yard, a remnant of the previous night's rain. Banana, plantain, peas, yam hills were all gone. Irene is sheepish, ignorant of how Rupert's first trip ended. But she is also holding on to hope, trusting Rupert with her and Annie's lives, looking forward to better.

Politics sent them home to Jamaica in 1933, without the now grown baby Annie, once again looking for better. Pearline tries to hold on to that last part—her family members moving from one country to another, always looking for something better. She won't let the stroke stop her from imagining that her family members can have better here without venturing to foreign lands to find it.

Before long, Josette comes, remaining in the doorway, standing like a sentinel protecting something precious within. "You have to get ready," she says.

"Coming just now." But Pearline's feet and bottom remain planted. She has no desire to move, no urgent desire to contend with the radiology technicians or any strangers.

"If you not feeling up to it, we can put it off for today. But the sooner we get it done, the better."

"I know all o' that. But look at little you coming to tell me what to do. Is this mi come to?"

"Somebody have to look out for you."

"I thought I would be deep into my old age before it come to this. Deep, deep. Who knew? Thought I would have more time. Not even six months since I come home, and look at me. Can't even take care of myself."

Pearline is not one to pity herself. She's never made time for it. She's worked instead, eliminating with the multiple jobs she worked any opportunity to lament her lot. Josette knows it too, and the way she looks at her mother reminds Pearline that the person she is becoming is not the same one her family knows. Burdening Josette with her thoughts about the frailty of human life is not what Pearline wants. Instead, she longs to feel like her old self, the self-sufficient woman who made plans and took action, facing risk head-on. She longs to be the daughter her father thought she was, the one who takes his dreams and amplifies them. She longs to be the woman she came home to be.

Claudia giggles, her little voice like a bell echoing, breaking the rhythm of Pearline and Josette's conversation, and Pearline leans into the moment. "I feel for some banana porridge," Pearline says, but she doesn't look at Josette, doesn't act as if she's asking Josette to make it. "Ask Derek if we have any green banana back there."

She doesn't want the porridge. She wants to be alone— something that hasn't happened since she's come home from the hospital. Someone is always within reach, hovering near the curio cabinet in the dining room and peeping through the open front door at her, or sitting next to her on the veranda in the matching wooden chair. Her bedroom door stays ajar. It's easier that way for Josette and Derek, or Hermina and Aileen, to peek in to ensure she's breathing or hasn't passed out. She doesn't fear being alone. It is how she hears the spirits that whisper, and she wants to hear the stories again.

"Look at Mama." Aileen stares for a long time at the blurry photo. She's biting her lip, and when she speaks again, there's a tremor in her voice. "My God."

Josette has taken the photo from the dresser, and she waves it around like an archaeologist who's made a significant find. Pearline wishes she had put it away before now, buried it in a dresser drawer under layers of clothing or returned it to the trunk; for this is not the way she wanted it revealed.

Sixty years later, who does a big sister become? What of the older brothers? They age forward to match a perceived image, a mash-up of Irene and Rupert and Hermina and Aileen and Pearline, and they age backward to another time in Aileen's and Pearline's memory when they were teenagers on the verge of becoming adults. Hermina has no such memory. Pearline watches her sisters discover and rediscover their siblings, rediscover their parents six decades earlier and Aileen and Pearline as toddlers. It's another feeling altogether to be a witness to her sisters' discovery, to watch them squint and their eyes grow bigger as recognition blooms on their faces.

Hermina leans in closer, pinches the other end of the small photo. "I never know Papa had this picture all this time. Where you find it?" But she doesn't wait for an answer and neither does Aileen.

Aileen blinks away a tear. "I couldn't remember Annie's face. My own sister and brothers and I don't remember what they look like. I could pass them on the street right now and I wouldn't have a clue. They could walk up in the yard and still I wouldn't know them." She moves a finger from face to face, stopping for a long moment on each, then angles the photo away from the sunlight and moves her fingers again beneath each face. She names them all, her parents and siblings—Annie, David, the twins Arturo and Gerardo, Pearline, herself. "I couldn't have been more than five or six. Pearline was a toddler. Maybe two? Maybe three? I don't remember this day at all. But I remember Mama calling Arturo a photographer."

This might be the only picture of Pearline's early childhood. At least, it's the only one she can think of. In the other one—a studio photo—she is in her late teens, dressed formally in white with matching gloves and a pillbox hat. She barely smiles in that photo either, too nervous or too conscious of the eyes on her and the permanence of the image.

"What happened to Arturo? Nobody ever talks about him." Josette takes the photo, studying every face.

"He gone long time," Aileen says. "Let his soul rest in peace."

"Which one is Arturo?"

"This is Arturo and his twin, Gerardo."

"Mama would cry if somebody said his name." Hermina looks out past the cherry tree. When she sits like that, angles her face, she looks like Irene. "His death hit her hard. Funny how I never knew any of them, but when I look at this picture, I feel like I know them. Feel like is people I siddown wid all the time."

Pearline nods. She's afraid to speak, fears the weight of her tongue and volume of her tears. But she also can imagine them here, sitting on the veranda with coffee or chocolate tea and slices of sweet potato pudding made soft the way Irene liked it.

"One time, Arturo come home with a little girl," Aileen says. "I remember this clear as day. My clearest memory of him. She was a wisp of a girl, not much bigger than Arturo himself, big bulging plaits in her hair make her head look bigger than it was, oversized. Mama and Annie were still there. You won't remember this, Pearline, 'cause you were still little."

"As if you all that much older than me," Pearline says.

"Hush, Pearline. Like I was saying, Annie never leave for Santiago de Cuba yet. Anyway, Arturo run come in the house like rolling calf chasing him. Funny thing, I just remember his feet, brown and dirty on the floor Mama just polish. And he running and shouting, 'They're picking them up. All the Haitians. Everybody.' Papa start to panic, ask him where. He say everywhere. And then Papa say, 'Not a one of you leave this house.' And I know it serious.

"But is Arturo Papa looking at when he talk, 'cause if any of us was going leave, it was him. Mama said that boy wanted to witness everything. Didn't want to hear nutten secondhand. Had to see it for himself. So all of we crouch down inside the house, Rupert in the front room, peeking, snatching glances at what he can't see. But when he tell it afterwards, everybody was outside grabbing their goats and cows, clothes from the line, babies, anything.

"All of that happening and the little girl get left and Arturo bring her home. She couldn't speak a word of English. But she know little Spanish, and we find out that she went to buy coconut oil and come back to find her mother and father gone. When everything die down and the truck gone, we ask and we ask until we find some aunty of hers."

"What happened after that?" Josette asks.

"You looking for a Hollywood version," Aileen says. "But nothing happen. Or that's all I remember. You talking 'bout sixty years."

Aileen's story matches Pearline's dreams except that Aileen's details are clearer, and Aileen places Arturo in the house when she doesn't. When Aileen stops, it feels that everything around them pauses. The birds still. The breeze stills. The buzz of traffic on the road dies down to an imperceptible hum.

"Arturo would have been somebody big," Hermina says. "That's how Mama used to put it. He was going to be somebody, but life take him when he was just a boy."

The morning sobers and nobody rushes to leave for Pearline's appointment. Instead, Aileen and Hermina bend toward the photo again, transfixed by this memento of the past, its unexpected resurgence into their present day.

"I tell you that you look like him." Aileen looks up at Derek. "Nuh true?"

"I can see it," Josette says. "It's the eyes. You have Papa's eyes."

"Is the mouth I see," Hermina says. "Same way Papa used to set his mouth."

Derek glances at Pearline, and she can't tell whether he feels fully welcomed now or whether he is embarrassed by the scrutiny. But she nods slowly, and when she does, he smiles.

"So where you find the picture, Mom? Any more?"

"In the trunk."

"That trunk still there?" Josette asks. "Grandpa used to tell me a body was inside it. Said there was no more room in the yard, so he buried his father inside the trunk. You couldn't get me near that room or that trunk after that. Even now, I wouldn't even sleep in there."

Derek chuckles softly. "That's like my father and clowns. Big man like that still scared of clowns. Won't even stay in a room with one."

"What's the story with the clown?" Josette asks.

"I don't even remember."

"Funny how fear works."

"What else in the trunk, Mom?"

Pearline hesitates. Again, this is not the revelation that she envisioned. "Come," she says.

Pearline leads. She walks toward the back bedroom with Rupert's knobby walking stick—painted cerulean years earlier to match the color of the outdoor chairs—tapping out a rhythm on the floor. She rocks as she walks, her gait thrown off by the lingering weakness in her right leg. The procession behind her is quiet, their movement almost ceremonial. Pearline fumbles with the door's lock, which she has taken to locking as her father had, then steps aside to let Derek push the door open. He does so with a flourish, leaning forward and ushering them into the sparse room in a way that mimics the antics of a cartoon butler.

"Open up the windows." Pearline lifts the stick to point, unnecessary as it is.

"Put down the stick and min' you fall," Aileen says.

"Bossy, sah." Pearline eases to the bed, points again with the knobby stick to the trunks pushed up against the wall. "I can only bend so much." Pearline taps either side of her. "Sit down. No sense for unu to break unu back. We don't need no more cripple."

"You an' your dramatic ways," Aileen says, but she sits beside Pearline.

One by one, Derek pulls out the papers Pearline has organized. He lines up the letters first, and Aileen, Hermina, and Josette lean forward to read them, reading out of order, and trying to pull the details together. Josette doubles back, reorders them by date, and rereads them.

"What happened?" Josette asks. "Who double-crossed who?"

"You watch too much movie," Aileen says, slapping lightly at Josette's shoulder.

"She could be right," Pearline says. "Something happen." She lifts the stick again, taps another pile of papers that she wants Derek to lay out. "Birth papers."

"Look at that," Hermina says. She's pointing at nothing in particular, just marveling at everything all at once.

Aileen holds up the dress. "Annie was a seamstress," she says, and as she speaks, Pearline thinks the morning is beginning to sound like a long-delayed wake, not for individual family members but for the family as a whole. "Just like Mama. Things were rough. Papa wasn't working in the fields then. Maybe the harvest was over. I don't remember now. But we didn't have much. Mama was pregnant or sick. One or the other. But it was Annie who brought us food. Annie who looked after Pearline." Aileen has a faraway look in her eyes. She rubs her hands against the material of the dress, feeling the boning, opening and closing her mouth as if she wants to say something more.

When they've gone through everything—the official correspondence, travel documents, trinkets—Pearline points to a place beyond the door. "Look in my room and bring the big brown envelope in the top dresser drawer."

Josette moves this time, and inside the room, everyone is quiet, waiting for Pearline, who sits like a queen at court. They're mesmerized, subdued even, by what has emerged from the trunks.

"This?" Josette holds up a brown envelope.

"Put it right here." Pearline takes her time unfolding the papers. She doesn't lay them out but holds them in her lap. "Remember when we went to the attorney's office and he read the will, he said Annie Headlam owned a piece and we couldn't sell?"

Aileen and Hermina both nod.

"Sell?" Josette asks. "Who want to sell the land?"

"Never mind that," Pearline says. She wants to tell Josette to be quiet. But she holds her tongue. "This is why." Pearline holds the copy of the deed and Annie's birth records together. "I went to the Registrar General's office. See here?"

Pearline taps her finger against the space on the birth paper where *Annie Headlam* is written. She moves her hand slowly across to the deed, resting her finger again on the name *Annie Headlam*. "Now look at the date."

"How?" Hermina asks. "That can't be possible. Annie name Headlam? How so?"

"Better yet, how come her name on the papers?" Aileen's brow is knitted, her lips curling.

Hermina waves. "Besides, Mama and Papa bought this land when they came back from Cuba in '33. If not '33, then '34 or '35. How her name on it?"

Pearline is enjoying the slow release of information, the way she holds her sisters. "That's what they led us to believe. Truth is, all those years, they were squatting. We were squatters."

"Squatters?" Aileen says it so scornfully that Pearline wants to laugh.

"Yes, ma'am. Squatters. And if you look at the date the house was built, you will see that what Papa and Mama said all these years about building the house when they got back was a blatant lie. They didn't build a thing. Fixed up, yes. But build, no."

"Squatters." Aileen is fixated with the word.

"The Headlams didn't come back to claim it. And we kept on living here. And how we come to own it is simple. There was a time when the government was giving away land, redistributing land and wealth, regularizing people who had been taking care of property without papers. Mama and Papa could show how long we were living here, and that's how come we even have papers for the property."

"Where you getting all this?" Aileen straightens her back.

"Research. I have my ways." Pearline wants to hold on to something. There's too much history to navigate in that single relationship, more than she wants to explain to Derek or Josette.

"So what now?" Josette speaks first. She points to the letters stacked together on the bed. "What's the secret that Grandpa wouldn't forgive?"

"Papa was a hard man," Pearline says. "He didn't forgive easy. So whatever he did, he had his reasons."

"Stubborn and selfish," Hermina says. Then, defensively, she adds, "I not going lie. He was selfish and he was stubborn."

A quiet comes over the room. There's truth in what Hermina says, but Pearline acts as if her words are blasphemous. She huffs, pulling up her shoulders, sitting taller, tightening so much it seems as if she shrinks and elongates at the same time. Aileen clicks her teeth, but she, too, doesn't say anything.

"So you have to find Annie and her children?" Josette asks, breaking the silence.

"Yes," Pearline says. "Nothing we can do without her."

"Now I can see what Papa meant," Hermina says. "Ages ago when we first told him to sell some of the land, all he said v as, 'You have to find the other owners first,' and point to Mama grave. Wouldn't say nothing more. So was a big surprise when the lawyer say Annie Headlam name on the deed. Now it make sense."

Pearline taps the trunk with the walking stick, the sound like worn-out shoes tapping on the ground.

"He never come straight out and say it. But my mind tell me something wasn't right. Took him some days to tell me a little more. Not all of it. Not all of this that you find here. All the same, you have to go doctor, Pearline, and none o' this matter now."

"It matters," Pearline says. "He won't rest fully until we find them." She resists the urge to look at Derek, to confirm what she has suspected—that Aileen and Hermina know more than they have let on.

They're all standing, quiet and contemplative, when Pearline says, "Wait," and sits back down. "Open that again." She leans forward and takes out the pile of yellowed newspapers. "Spanish," she says. "Aileen, you used to teach Spanish. You can tell us what this say."

"Tomorrow."

18.

PEARLINE IS MEASURING TIME. SHE CAN'T SLEEP AND instead watches the shadows moving against the wall, tree limbs dipping, leaves fluttering and showing another level of wakefulness she would rather not see. She's aware, too, of a presence, not in the room itself, and she thinks her father has returned to sit in his favorite chair. She closes her eyes and waits for what will come, another telling dream, a disembodied voice calling, a hand brushing against hers. She's not sure how long she waits, but when she finally gets up, the sky is still dark but lightening ever so slightly. Now she can't move around as quietly as she once did, but she tries, taking small steps, pressing her hand against the wall instead of tapping the cane against the floor. The front door creaks, and she stops to look back, hopeful neither Derek nor Josette have gotten up to mother her.

The air is chilled, and she leans against the railing looking up at the lightening sky. It's too early to read the clouds, so she steps back and turns away, startling herself as she does, dropping the walking stick and stumbling back against the rail. The stick clatters, wood against wood, and Hermina, asleep in the chair, jumps up.

"What you doing here so early in the morning?" Then Pearline sees the chalk mark again on the door. "Don't tell me you out here all night."

"I just want to sleep one good night sleep." Hermina is leaning forward, lacing her hands together, rocking. "Every night I go to sleep and I dream the same thing over and over. Every night since Papa died. You know what I dream?"

Pearline knows that what Hermina carries is heavy. It is a beast that burns inside her, simultaneously eating away at her soft insides and hardening her heart against stubborn men with dogged determination. It is her father, the repercussions of his stubbornness. Pearline nods, sensing her sister's need to unburden herself layer by layer.

"Where to begin," she says, only it's not a question but rather Hermina reorganizing her thoughts. "After looking at that photo yesterday, it's like the picture wake up every spirit. Can't sleep since Papa die, and now it even worse."

Pearline is quiet, afraid to make a move, afraid to wake the spirits at that very moment and miss what Hermina says. She's picturing her father in the chair, hearing Hermina speak and also hearing his voice, picturing his hands moving, him tapping the back of one hand against the open palm of the other, reaching up and wiping his brow, adjusting his invisible hat.

"It begins with a new law in 1933, *La Ley de Cinquenta Porciento*, the Fifty Percent Law," Hermina says. "The law say that half of all employees at any Cuban business had to be Cuban."

And so begin the dismissals. Rupert isn't spared and neither is Irene. "There is little food, mostly what they can reap from the little plot of land Rupert farms. Maybe the law wasn't first," Hermina says. "Maybe it was the forced repatriation of anyone who wasn't working. Maybe it was the deportation of all migrants. Mostly Haitians. Maybe it was the trucks coming at random to round up migrant laborers. Maybe it was the talk of the holding cells at the wharf where the guards took the migrants before they shipped them off to another island. And you know how that kind of thing go. Some people went to their rightful country, and some end up in another country altogether."

Hermina refuses to look at Pearline and instead stares out at nothing.

"Perhaps it was the song that start it," Hermina says. "*Arriba con la ley de San Martin.* Up with the law of San Martin. *Arriba con la ley de San Martin. Arriba con la ley de San Martin.* San Martin enacted a law that we should carry out. Round up all the Haitians and send them to their country yoked like oxen. Up with the law of San Martin. Yoked like oxen to their country."

"Who is San Martin?" Pearline asks.

"That don't matter now. It was the law. That's what matter. *Cuba for Cubans.* That's what they said when they made the law. Why stay?"

Pearline tries to ask another question, but Hermina waves her off, pressing on to the end of what she has to say.

"It was hard for Papa to see his own people come down to nothing. But he couldn't return home with nothing. He left home with a dream and sixteen years later had nothing. The house and the plot of land to farm were still a dream, would

remain a dream when he returned. And there was Mama saying over and over, 'Ah ready to go home and be somebody
again.'

"It hurt him to see his family like that, splintered, splinter-
ing. *Wait it out,*' Rupert said, for he had already lived through
so much—the tedious labor of cane harvesting; the dead season that made men into all kinds of things they never imagined: beggars dependent on the kindness of strangers; La
Chambelona revolt of 1917; the massacres in Jobabo; the sugar
crises of 1920 and 1921; numerous attempts to repatriate all
migrant workers. *Everything that go wrong in that country they
try to blame on us. It hard to live in a country like that when all the
people show you day after day that they don't want you there.* And
still Rupert said, *Stay. It can't stay like this forever. Cane still here
to cut, and when the harvest start, things going to get better.*

"It didn't get better. There was no work, no food. The law
turned them into paupers. Because of the children, they were
hanging on. Annie found a job in Santiago de Cuba. Arturo
was a photographer's apprentice. Gerardo picked tobacco.
Then Arturo died."

This is the part that Pearline remembers too. But she isn't
sure if it is her full memory or a memory filled out with images
from the dreams in which she remembered being in the front
room of the little yellow house, tucked in a ball on the floor.
She replays it now, as if it were happening all over again: Her
family has split in two. Irene and Annie have gone to Santiago de Cuba in search of work. Her father—left in charge
of David, Arturo, Gerardo, Aileen, and Pearline—is frantic.
Outside the house is mayhem. The rural guards have come

for Haitian immigrants and any immigrant who may be out of work. Screams bounce like raindrops on the roof. Horses' hooves and footsteps and engines add to the rhythm. There's too much sound, but even with the noise, she can hear Rupert calling for Arturo and Gerardo and David. She remembers David crawling in, hiding with her and Aileen, and a sling-shot falling from his front pocket. Gerardo and Arturo are supposed to be at work, one picking tobacco leaves and the other at the photographer's studio. Still Rupert calls. And she worries that he, too, might not return. Pearline doesn't yet have a word for this fear of rural guards and forced repatriation that stamps across her body like quick footsteps in the dirt. But she hears a truck in the distance, the engine rumbling, the rural guards shouting in Spanish and broken English, a chorus of voices swelling up and around the harsh commands, and she cries because she thinks that he has gone.

But she hears his voice again and Gerardo's.

"Where's Arturo?"

"He went to get the camera."

"For what?"

"To take pictures. Get it in the newspaper."

"How long he gone?"

"Few minutes."

"Go on inside. You shouldn't be out here. Listen to me, bwoy. They will tek you too. David in the house. Go stay with him and your sisters, and don't you leave."

They wait for long moments. The evening turns cloudy. The shades of blue and gray and white deceptive in the waning sun. When the sun sets, the clouds gush, the rain so heavy it stings.

Near midnight, the weather eases and Rupert gets up again, looks out in the drizzle for the rain-soaked boy. Two days pass before Arturo is found.

Pearline is listening to Hermina again, only she imagines it's her mother speaking. She reframes everything Hermina says in Irene's voice, as if she's there in the room, explaining everything that happened and transporting Pearline back to the little yellow house. *All now, Ah don't know who kill him or how he die. What it matter? He dead and gone.* The last of the visitors have gone, but the scent of the fried plantains, fried chicken, and rice and peas the visitors brought lingers as if the guests had only just come. There is a hint of ginger and cinnamon a neighbor had brought for tea. Grief hangs in the air like rolling balls of fog. *This country won't take another one of my children. I have sacrificed enough.*

Irene won't hear Rupert's protests and instead starts looking for a way to bring her children home.

"Monday morning I go to look 'bout the papers. When I reach, they tell me something wrong with the documents for Annie, Arturo, and Gerardo. That's how Rupert fin' out I register Annie with her rightful name. Headlam. Not Greaves. Register her as Annie Headlam out of spite 'cause those days I was still bitter 'bout the way Rupert sneak off and leave me. It burn me so till all I could do was find some way to spite him. After all that time, it come back to bite me."

The house hushes for a brief moment. "Annie's name was one thing. The other was his children turned against him," Hermina continues. "When Rupert find out that Annie write letter to the Emigrants Protection Program seeking assistance with our passage home, all hell break loose," Hermina explains.

Pearline imagines the letter, Annie's slanted scrawl mirroring the letters in the trunk. *We're in a bad way. If you can find it in your heart to help a family of seven.* She pictures Irene throwing up her hands and saying "Praise God" when she learns the Emigrants Protection Program will help. She pictures Irene telling Rupert, "We have passage on a ship. Next week Tuesday. Only problem is, we can't take all the children at once. Annie and the three boys will stay. No, two boys now. Two boys."

Rupert, the stern, grumpy version she remembers from the last day on the wharf in Santiago de Cuba, is watching his family splinter, has witnessed his children plotting against him, set him to return to his island like a pauper. Everything builds and magnifies his failure, outlines the family legacy like chalk on concrete. He felt small. There was nothing triumphant in his return, at least not the way he imagined when he first stood on a beach in Montego Bay listening for a voice from the sea to tell him what to do. There was no silk shirt, no pocket watch, just a few pounds he and Irene had sent home over the years waiting for their return.

It's so clear now. Rupert's sixty years of pretending these children of his did not exist all came down to this one humiliating moment: the children on the wharf, gleeful and excited and hopeful, and Rupert mindful of his failure exposed and magnified by the way he was returning home. And there was Irene, forced to leave her three children because her plan to punish Rupert by giving Annie the Headlam surname had backfired.

How long Irene waited for Rupert's anger to ease so she could fulfill her promise and bring her three oldest children home. How lost they must have felt, two boys who were not fully men and a young woman newly married. Pearline aches for them, and she aches for Josette too, for whom the news of her mother's planned departure from Brooklyn to Jamaica was a surprise.

"What he said," Hermina says, "what haunt me every night is this: *It is time that I tell them I forgive them.*"

"So you let a dying man go to his grave without even promising him his one wish?"

"He never get the chance to ask. I know what he wanted, and I was so angry with him, with how he made Mama suffer, that I never gave him a chance to ask. And every night now he come and make sure I regret it."

It's hard for Pearline to hold her anger inside, to not let it bubble uncontrollably and spill out. She has to be careful of living too boldly, too loud and unrestrained, lest the stress push her blood pressure to uncontrollable heights. So she walks the length of the driveway and back, leaving a distraught Hermina on the veranda, and taps out a rhythm on the gravel pathway. The rhythm soothes, and, feeling closer to her old self, she pushes herself to take another turn and another. She watches the sun gradually light the leaves, the little flames of sunlight filtering on the ground, and the birds that swoop low flutter their wings and glide away.

When she looks up, there's a flurry of movement—Josette and Derek talking animatedly and both looking out at her on the driveway. Josette comes toward her and she senses trouble. "What?" Pearline asks.

"Uncle Paul called looking for Aunt Hermina. Then we couldn't find you and we didn't know what to think."

"You young people worry too much. I wake up and see her out here. Say duppy haunting her. But duppy right to haunt her."

"Why you say that?"

"If only you knew." Pearline looks up at Hermina, slumped in defeat, sleeplessness winning again. "Make her some tea. Nothing too strong. Make something that will calm her." Before Josette turns to head inside, she adds, "You call Aileen too?"

"Yes, we didn't know what to think."

"Then make a big pot. 'Cause before you know it, she reach here too. Now we have one bag o' excitement. I can't take it. Can't take it at all."

Hermina is turning the furniture around inside, sprinkling rum in the corners to appease Rupert's spirit. Pearline, too weak to move the furniture back in place, says, "Better you leave the rum by his grave. Leave him rum and food out there." And when Hermina steps outside with a saucer and a plastic cup of rum, Pearline nods to Derek. "Put it back how it was."

One side of Paul's shirt hangs from his belt. It's crushed, something he pulled from the hamper or the clothesline, with little care for how he looked. "What happen?" he asks as he stoops before Hermina. "Wake up and don't see you. Car gone. What happen?"

"I just want a good night's sleep." Hermina repeats it as if it explains everything. "Just a good night's sleep."

The morning is more than Pearline wants to bear. She simply

wants to go for her morning swim, to feel the water wrapping around her body, to feel weightless. She is thankful when Aileen shows up. "Maybe you can talk some sense into her."

"Me?" But Aileen sits next to Hermina, urging her to drink the tea. "It will make you feel better." And to Josette she says, "Put a little drop o' rum in there."

Already, Pearline is tired of the ruckus. She's been holding back since the morning, and she simply wants to ask her question again, this time asking both Aileen and Hermina, together, "So you let a dying man go to his grave without even promising him his one wish?" She thinks about the question, twirls it around her mind, then as calmly as she can, she says it.

"If only you know how it hurt Mama day after day to not be able to talk about her children," Hermina says. "To not be able to call their names. To not go and find them. After all that time, now he wan' come act like he sorry. No. I wouldn't give him the satisfaction."

"And you say Papa was a hard man," Pearline says. She senses Josette moving to stand behind her chair, feels the weight of her daughter's palm and wants to brush it aside.

"He was," Aileen says. "He was."

"You too, Aileen?" Pearline asks. "You feel the same way?"

"When you in America, is me and Hermina here. Me and she listen to Mama cry." Aileen stirs the tea, tastes a spoonful. "When you come and acting like you know everything, it hurt. All the same, you have one stroke already and no reason for you to get a next one over this."

"No, tell me," Pearline says. "Everything out in the open now."

Aileen repeats what Hermina said: There was no money, not enough for a family of seven to travel home. Most of those who wanted to leave walked hundreds of miles and days or weeks to find their way to Santiago de Cuba. Irene was pregnant then with Hermina. Walking was impossible with young children, impossible, too, for a pregnant woman. The plan came to Irene quickly, like pieces of jagged rocks, tumbling and slicing the earth, marking the loose dirt before resting with the jagged edges pointed up. Irene stumbled over each piece of the plan brought to her, her legs wavering unbalanced and arms too limp to break her fall. Each bit of the plan was its own sharp-edged rock, slicing and cutting at her core because she knew with certainty that she would have to leave a part of her family behind and work against Rupert, who was determined to remain in Cuba rather than return home at the government's expense. Irene did what Rupert couldn't and wouldn't. She saved the family with the help of her daughter, and Rupert never forgave them. Not until the very end.

More cars come. Phillip and Dominique, Eric and Sammy, everyone taking tentative steps, then spreading out on the veranda and spilling into the living room. Pearline sits with the blue walking stick she doesn't need, too deflated to move and mingle. Before long, the scents change. The house smells like Sunday, and Pearline sniffs out the aromas—red beans boiling in coconut milk, thyme and scallion and pimento, salt fish that's just come to a boil, fried plantains. The distinct odors bring her no comfort. What she wants is to be alone, to hear the spirits Hermina has tried to chase away.

Out of nowhere, Claudia says, *"Jagüé."* She says it the way

Rupert used to say it. Claudia walks to the railing, mimics Rupert's stance, and says, *"Casa del jagüe."* She glances around as if surveying the family members and the land, then she runs off toward Derek, wrapping her arms around his leg as if he's been gone for a prolonged time.

19.

IN THE DISTANCE, THE MAN WHO LEASES THE LAND MOVES the cattle from one pasture to another. He's thinning the herd, separating the animals that are ready for slaughter from the ones that aren't, preparing for the coming end to his lease. This is another of the changes Hermina and Aileen engineered when Pearline was hospitalized. As Pearline looks out now, she is of a mind to walk out there and undo what her sisters did. It's not a long walk, not a trek she would have thought twice about before. Now she considers the uneven grass, her unsteady gait. It's only a matter of time before she regains her full strength and sets in motion her plan to convert the land into the farm her father dreamed it could be.

"Rain," she says, and steps back to the rocking chair.

Josette is sitting in the opposite chair, and she looks up, bends her back, and peers up at the sky, trying to read the clouds. Pearline knows when the rain is coming. Josette doesn't. The morning breeze is still cool, and to the northeast, thick clouds bank and build upon themselves, thickening and deepening in color.

"Tea ready."

Without speaking, Pearline holds out her hand as if to take

the cup, and Josette steps back inside to pour it. Waiting, Pearl-ine presses her back into the chair and lets it rock.

"You know," Josette says before she even crosses the thresh-old, "you really should think about coming back to New York and doing speech and physical therapy, the angiogram the doctors want to do . . . all of that."

"I going to do all of that right here. Which one of your aunts tell you to tell me that?"

"Neither."

"Hmm. They trying to get me to leave, sell this place."

"Even after yesterday?"

"I don't know what change. See?" Pearline points to the pas-ture. "Few days in the hospital, and they chase the man off the land. End his lease and push him off so they can get ready to sell."

"But you said that they can't sell it."

"True. But you don't know them. That Hermina is a sneaky one. She know 'bout business and things. I know 'bout nursing. And if I'm not careful, she will sell the land from under me."

"She's your sister."

Pearline looks up quickly and then back at the cup, the steam curling toward her face. "Blood don't always matter." But what she is speaking of is something else. She's thinking of the difficulties between her and Josette.

Claudia is next to wake. She comes out on the veranda in an oversized T-shirt, rubbing sleep from her eyes. She stands at the railing like Pearline normally does, eyes to the sky. She looks left to right at the hint of a cloud forming, then pulls up the footstool next to the rocking chair, sits at Pearline's feet.

Pearline strokes Claudia's hair, smoothing the short strands above her ears that have curled up. Claudia is learning what Josette hasn't—that the sway of the trees and the sky teach what she needs to know.

Pearline is measuring time. She knows that having one stroke increases the chances she'll have another. She knows she will not rest easy until she fulfills her father's request. She has to move quicker and, with the stroke, she can't go alone, at least not now, and it's only a matter of time before Derek gets his bearings and she loses him. What of Josette? She's seen Josette's jealousy, how she hunches her shoulders and draws into herself when Claudia sits by Pearline's foot, how she watches Derek as if this young man can and will take her place. Whatever she asks of Derek has to include Josette. She's easing back to what she started to ask of Derek when she took him to the museum and held up his artwork as a view of what is possible. The task Rupert set out for her looms.

Pearline is making up for the past, engineering a trip that mirrors her father's, engineering Josette's and Derek's futures, and drafting a map to find lost lives. At Derek's and Josette's age, Rupert—robust and full of dreams—had already taken risks, lived a whole life in Cuba. Not that they have to follow his path, but they are already behind, playing catch-up to meet the bar Rupert set on that first journey he took to Cuba. She reminds herself that what she's doing is snapping the generational grief. She's making room for herself and the generation after to not carry Rupert's and Irene's grief forward.

When Pearline finally sips the tea, it is cold and tasteless and not the cocoa that she wants and which Derek has learned to make. But she doesn't tell Josette. "Warm this up for me," she says instead.

Now that Josette is here, Pearline takes her to town to see about her affairs. She doesn't want to dwell on death or the possibility of it, but she knows it is inevitable and it's better to be prepared. The suddenness of her husband's death was hard. Sometimes she thinks sudden death is the hardest, and other times she thinks the process of dying is harder. Not death itself. The person is gone, the light in the eyes and the warmth in the body gone. Sudden or not, unexpected or not, the person is gone. You cover the casket with dirt and you move on, sometimes quickly, sometimes slowly. Sometimes the loss is a wide swath of sea. Sometimes it's a river; it flows away from you. But the long, drawn-out process of dying—the sickness, the wait, the anxiety of thinking you may have missed that last moment—that's the hardest. Pearline wants to ease one portion of it for Josette and line up her affairs for the inevitable.

The congestion of Flatbush and Nostrand Avenues, double-parked cars and a stream of taxis carrying passengers from the mall to the produce and discount shops along the streets, hasn't prepared Josette for driving around the deep corners. Pearline braces the way she would on an amusement park ride. Josette slows and stops, braking so suddenly Pearline expects a collision from behind. She's forgotten it's a market day, and the town—a mix of old and new buildings seemingly built without a town plan—is congested too. One packed minivan after another go in either direction, music so loud she wonders how the driver hears the passengers calling for their stop. Produce, discount underwear, plastic shoes, and kitchen tools spill out onto the sidewalk. Josette and Pearline inch slowly through the town.

The air inside the bank is much too cold—so cold it burns. Pearline's hand shakes when she hands over the bank book, and her voice also quivers. She knows that what she's doing is tying Josette to the island in a way she's never done. For the longest while, Jamaica was for Josette synonymous with her grandparents; the entirety of their existence was wrapped up in the country's name. Now, with her name on the accounts, her name tied to Pearline's share of the family land, Pearline is ensuring that Jamaica is becoming something else. It's no longer just a place Josette will come to visit. Pearline's existence—her life and her death—are now wrapped up in this land. And Josette's as well.

When they return, there's the smell of pumpkin soup and curried chicken. The smells wrap around Pearline, but they bring her little comfort. Instead, each distinct scent, the pumpkin soup especially, begins to remind her of sickness and death, the house filling with pots and pans of food family and friends prepared. Derek is again in the kitchen, solidifying his place, protecting the house. His presence reminds her of what she has to do. She's winding down her life when she shouldn't be, when she still has work to do—a house to save, siblings to find, her father's wish to fulfill.

Outside, Pearline stands at the railing, back bent and face turned up to the evening sky. The sun colors the wispy clouds orange. There's a small pan of water, and the sun hits it, the flame reflecting from it too. In that moment, she is her father, except she isn't surveying what she has grown. She wants to regain some semblance of her former life, get back to her habits, finish her task before she runs out of time.

They're not back for long before Aileen and Hermina come to measure Pearline's progress. There's no mention of Hermina's meltdown. They speak primarily to Josette.

"Tell her no stress. All this business 'bout the house have to stop." And, turning toward Pearline, "You worrying yourself too much 'bout it. If we can sell it, we should. Get rid of this headache and find something small and manageable. I mean, you could come live with me. All that space I have . . ."

Josette raises her brows, leans forward to look at Pearline's face, and Pearline is momentarily strengthened by Josette's reaction.

"We have to," Hermina says. "See how it killing your mother? Taxes, upkeep, and whatnot. You don't know the half of it, Josette."

Pearline bides her time, watching Josette, waiting.

"Plus, we could all use the money," Aileen says.

"Grandpa wouldn't like it." Josette sounds like a child. "Grandma either."

Hermina is quiet for a while, working her mouth from side to side. Then she says, "You 'fraid fi eye, you never nyam head." She glances at Pearline, then says in perfect English, "If you are afraid of the eye, you will never eat the head. You never heard that?" She's looking at Josette, silently challenging Pearline.

"Not at all."

"Your mother never teach you nutten. If you spend too much time looking for the good opinion of someone, you will never prosper. You can't spend your life trying to please your grandparents or live their lives. They dead and gone long time."

Pearline closes her eyes, begins humming as if the conversation around has nothing to do with her.

"If you don't want to be haunted you do," Josette says.

"Thought you progressive, first-world Americans didn't believe in duppy and spirit life. Leave that for us country folk. All the same, there will come a time when my children and grandchildren don't want to have a thing to do with this piece of land. Then what? It sit there until squatters take it over? No way. Better to sell it now."

Hermina has forgotten her meltdown, her own attempt to shake herself loose of Rupert's haunting.

"Well," Josette says, "you still need Mom's permission. And she still have her faculties, so you talking to the wrong person. Puss no business in a dawg fight." She glances at Pearline. "See, my mother taught me something." Josette laughs long and loud, and her voice carries, filling up the space like an oversized balloon inflated to fit every crevice of the veranda.

Long after Hermina and Aileen leave, Pearline remains on the veranda, watching the night insects gather around the bulb and spread out along the wall. She's waiting for the croaking lizards to come, creeping up to grab at an unsuspecting moth. If she stays long enough, Josette and Derek will join her, one to sit with her, the other to cajole her to turn out the light and lock up. Josette was always afraid of the night and its sounds, especially the sounds she can't match to a specific thing.

Claudia comes to say good night. She smells like roses and peppermint. The scent lingers when she leaves. As she expects, Josette and Derek come. Josette sits in the chair next to Pearline, and Derek leans against the rail, his back to the night.

"I want to ask you something." Pearline speaks before either of them do. She is looking at them both, shifting her head, reading their faces.

Sitting out on the veranda late into the evening reminds Pearline of her childhood days, her parents sitting like town griots telling stories around a candle's light. The electricity is off as well, another one of the frequent power cuts plaguing the island. Derek and Josette switch places. He takes a chair and Josette leans against the rail, throwing her head back to the night dew and looking up to the moon and the specks of starlight. Deep in the dark, the crickets chirp, and the night-time sounds that would have been blunted in New York close around them. There's a quick yellow flash of a peenie-wallie's light and another and another. Just as quickly as Josette moved to the railing, she pulls back to the door.

"Come." Pearline leads them inside. Behind her, Derek holds a flashlight and Josette the oil lamp, both angling and arcing the light so Pearline sees what's ahead. She stops near the telephone table, where she tacked maps to the wall and taps the plastic. "I want you to find them for me." Pearline moves her finger to the northernmost tip, taps *Havana*, and traces a line southeast to Camagüey and Santiago de Cuba on the opposite end of the island.

"Who?" Josette asks.

"You know who." Pearline taps her finger again near Camagüey. "I was born in a little house in La Güira, Banes. Me and Aileen. And if we had stayed, Hermina would have been born there too. The house was yellow, and the floor as red as that you see out there. Every Saturday, Mama polished it with a little coconut brush. When you find the house, look for the coconut trees lined up one beside the other. Mama bury the navel string of every baby born in that house. And over the spot, she planted a coconut tree. A tree for every baby born in the house. If the trees not dead, every one of the navel string tree should still be there."

Josette and Derek are quiet, and without the hum of the refrigerator or radio or Claudia laughing, the quiet seems eerie.

"Mama used to say all the time that it rained like Noah's flood the day Arturo and Gerardo were born. Flood come and Noah line up the animals two by two. And just like the Bible say, two babies come. Only one live past his teenage years. Only one live." Pearline pauses and taps the map again. "I would go myself. But look at me here. Almost cripple."

"You not cripple, Mom. All you need is therapy. Come back to New York, do your therapy, and then you can go to find them."

"No, no. I don't have that kind of time. Who knows if my body will hold up. I might not have another stroke, but the way your aunts moving, the day I leave is the day they sell off this place." She lifts up the knobby walking stick, brings it down heavy on the floor. "And I not going to let Papa spirit haunt me all my life. And don't tell me nothing 'bout spirit can't do me anything."

"I wasn't going to say a thing," Josette says.

"You think I don't know you." Pearline turns away from the map, faces Derek and Josette. Water pools in her eyes, slides down her face. She doesn't move to wipe the tears away. "Two things Papa whisper before he die: 'Find them for me' and 'You are my memory now.' Even if it kill me, I going to do what he ask. Without Aileen. Without Hermina. Without you if I have to. I will find them. The dead must rest, and this is the only way how."

20.

"Take me to the beach," Pearline tells Derek. She is again standing at the railing, back bent and face turned up to the morning sky. It's early, not yet six, and the sun coming up colors the wispy clouds orange. The horizon looks like a flaming fire, and even the trees themselves look like they are lit, look like a representation of the biblical burning bush that Moses finds. There's a small pan of water, and the sun hits it, the flame reflecting from it too. She's trying to regain some semblance of her former life, slowly getting back to her habits.

Claudia, awake much too early, overhears Pearline's request, and it becomes a family outing, with Derek driving them, rounding the corners like he was born to drive these roads. Pearline looks out across the overrun valley at the wide swath of blue seas and imagines the possibilities. She feels the breeze on her skin, and even before she gets to the water and hears the waves crash against the shore, she begins to listen for the voice. Like her father, she's listening for confirmation, waiting to look out at the waves swelling and rolling, to make her big decision.

Pearline picks her way across the sand with her father's walking stick in one hand and Josette holding the other. She's stronger now but doesn't feel that she's back to her full strength. She walks up to the wet line on the sand, looks down at the water rippling over her toes, hands Josette the cane, and totters in. She isn't much of a swimmer, but she slips her head under and moves, coming back up for air, then pushing her body again against the current. Buoyant, she forgets the effects of the stroke. She arcs her arms and moves the water, flutters her toes, and propels her body forward. She will win no medals, will win no praise for her grace, but she's determined to regain full strength and carry out the tasks her father left for her.

She's like a child here, and the fishermen off to the left look at her, this old woman out of place among the nets and small boats turned down in the sand. After she swims, she stills herself, listens to the waves breaking and sweeping the sand.

Instead of listening for the voice, she does something she hadn't previously thought of doing. She sends her own message, sends her own story across the sea. She lets her story float on waves that break against the sand. "It's time," she says. "You wait too long already, and now even me might go home. Papa and Mama never forget you, and I'm going to find you."

It takes a moment for Claudia to accept—or remember—that Yvonne, the woman on the veranda, is her mother. Claudia looks at her shyly from a distance, measuring her mother—the silken hair extensions bobbing against her exposed back, glossy lips, eyebrows waxed to a thin line—against her own memory of the mother who left nearly six months ago now.

"I hear you take sick," Yvonne says to Pearline. "You me come back come look after."

"Bless you," Pearline says.

"Watch here," Yvonne says. "You forget me already? Six months and she forget me."

Perhaps it's the voice or Yvonne's innate scent, but Claudia takes a step forward, gingerly puts her arm around her mother's waist, and leans into the hug, then allows herself to be lifted off the ground. She pats Yvonne's face, presses her palms against both cheeks, runs her hand down the length of hair.

When Claudia says "Mommy," she says it with a question, a quiet one. Yvonne, on the other hand, is loud, effusive with her hugs and physical touch. She measures Claudia's growth, her weight, shifting the girl from one arm to another. "What a way you grow big."

On her own feet again, Claudia doesn't want to let go or move out of sight. She's waiting for something else. She's uncertain of what comes next, uncertain whether her mother's return is temporary, uncertain whether she is the one who will be leaving next, and her face shows it. She eases away, inching slowly toward the footstool by Pearline's foot.

"See what I bring for you." Yvonne eases a doll from an oversized tote. It's still in its packaging, tied to a cardboard box.

Claudia sprints toward the doll, eyes the shiny hair and skin as brown as her own.

"Let me open it for you," Josette says.

Introductions done, pleasantries exchanged, Yvonne sets to work, taking over as if she never left. She fills a pot with water, puts red beans on to boil, and sets to sweeping, raising up a cloud of dust in each room, then leaves the little mounds of dust—dead bugs and flies, dirt particles that blew in through the windows.

"Glad you come," Pearline says to Yvonne. But what she means is that she can think about her second plan if Josette and Derek won't take up her first.

Yvonne comes in time for the Independence celebrations, which feel like Rupert's wake all over again. Paul brings goat meat and sets up two coal stoves outside to boil mannish water soup and make curried goat. Aileen, Hermina, and Yvonne set up in the kitchen, chopping vegetables and herbs for the soup, steaming rice, shredding cabbage for a salad, flouring and frying chicken parts. The celebration seems premature, but nobody stops it. Pearline sits quietly, almost doll-like on the veranda, watching her family dribble in with pots and covered dishes and drinks. She is like a shadow without a voice, preferring not to speak, answering with one or two words and pretending to be in worse shape than she is.

Pearline doesn't want the family here, doesn't want the celebration at all. Ronnie's family comes too, and for a moment it's like it was when Ronnie was alive and Josette still a child here for a summer or Christmas vacation and Pearline and Ronnie sponsored a family get-together to see everyone at once—story after story, ska and lovers' rock playing from the transistor radio or stereo, dominoes clinking, Ludo players racing to the finish on an oversized board, the smells of curry and mannish water and boiling coconut milk and Red Stripe beer mingling in the air. The sun is relentless, the clouds scarce.

Pearline reaches for Claudia though, brushes the child's plaits with her fingers, and encourages her to read. Pearline nods when Claudia gets a word right, says "ah" in a short, quick breath when she gets a word wrong. She is patient throughout as Claudia puts the sounds together.

Cousin Jackie pushes her son, Christian, toward Josette. "Ask her," she says.

Josette reaches for his hand, pats the seat cushions. He looks back at his mother, raises his brow.

"He wants to know what Brooklyn is like. His father send for him, and he going up next week." Jackie smiles, but her smile doesn't touch her eyes. Neither of them seems to want this opportunity.

"Well," Josette says. "It's a little bit like Kingston, only bigger."

Surprisingly, Pearline no longer knows how she would answer either.

"You know what, ask your cousin Derek over there," Josette says instead.

Christian runs off.

"How old?" Josette asks.

"Eleven." Jackie watches him running off. "Eleven years old and still can't get him to walk and not run."

"You don't seem ready to let him leave."

"That's mi one son. But they say things better for him over

there. More opportunities. Everybody say me selfish to want to keep him here. Me one son."

Pearline knows what Jackie means, remembers her mother's longing for her adult children and grandchildren she'd never meet. What she says is inconsequential. "So it is with us. We're a family of nomads, moving for opportunities, putting down roots where we land but always coming back right here."

"Not always," Jackie says. "Since his father leave here, him foot never touch Jamaica again. And I warn him not to take mi son and make him forget where him born and grow."

When evening comes and everybody leaves, Pearline, Yvonne, Claudia, Derek, and Josette sit outside in the cool night air, all of them quiet and seeming to be waiting for something definite. Time moves slowly. Even the things of the night seem to have taken an early rest. No frogs croak. No crickets chirp. There's no quick yellow flash of a peenie-wallie's light, no May bug turned on its back and buzzing as it tries to flip itself over. Their watchful wait feels like an impromptu wake, the moments after a funeral has ended and the family is drifting slowly away.

"Mi glad mi come back," Yvonne says. "Miss everybody."

Pearline nods. Even though she didn't want the gathering, she feels the same, feels the stories floating over her like waves.

"Mi hear say you going to Cuba," Yvonne says.

"Have to." Pearline doesn't look at Yvonne. "It's time."

"I know what you mean," Yvonne says. "The whole time mi gone, me thinking 'bout Claudia. What if mi couldn't come back? What if something happen to me over there? And mi think 'bout my grandmother and the children who leave and never come back. Winsome leave. Nobody ever see her again. Not even come to her mother funeral. It hard."

"It hard, yes. Can't tell you how much time I see Mama cry."

Quiet creeps over them again, the only sound that of the bugs hitting the lightbulbs and flying blindly into the wall.

Derek leans forward, touches Pearline's hand, and says, "Yes. But no way I'm going without you."

Pearline is thankful for the dim light and the murky shadows. Neither Derek nor Josette can see how much her eyes water. What she is thinking of is two things: the baby boy who died too early and Derek, the young man who fits neatly in the space into which the boy should have grown. In the dark, Pearline watches the shadow of a tree sweep across the walls, trying not to think she has found the son she always wanted.

When Pearline turns in, it is Yvonne who helps. She no longer needs an escort, but she doesn't turn Yvonne away. Sleep doesn't come readily. Time passing feels like a tangible object, a wooden cross that sinners bear. It's the weight of things unknown. Josette and Derek remain on the veranda, silhouettes in the partial light. "Of course you have to go," Derek says. "If she dies now, you'll never forgive yourself for not going."

"I know." Josette is trying to keep her voice low and failing. "I feel like she's trying to give me back something she took away from me."

"How so?"

"I wanted to make films. Documentaries. She told me to look for something else that could pay the bills. And I did."

"You hate it?"

"I don't love it."

"Maybe this is your story," Derek says. "Maybe, just maybe, this is it."

"It would make a great story, wouldn't it?"

Josette hasn't yet said what Pearline wants to hear, but she knows it's coming. This is the gift she has wanted, to be able to say *You come* and mean something other than Josette's physical presence. And she does indeed want to give something in return: a story to tell, a map to find the lost lives.

In the morning, Derek walks into the room, sits on Pearline's bed slowly so as not to make it creak. But it does. He looks around the room, strokes his chin, the stubble of beard. Sometimes the quiet way he sits in contemplation, waiting for the right moment to speak, surprises her. Then Pearline sees what he has done: He's cut his locks from the root, evened out his hair as best he could, then combed it out in a low Afro.

"Your hair."

"Thought I would change it up," he says.

He's still quiet, contemplative.

"Suits you."

He takes a long breath, holds his shoulders up a bit longer than the usual rhythm of breathing. "Longman dead."

"Longman?"

"From our little gang," he says, and Pearline knows he is telling her something he won't tell anyone else. "He was the friend I've known the longest. Fifteen years." Derek weeps and Pearline lets him fall against her shoulder, tilts her head to touch his.

21.

MORNING RAIN DRENCHES THE GROUND, CLEANSING THE air. Poinciana petals stick to the grass as if they belong that low. Everything moves slowly, waterlogged by the morning's rain. When the sun starts emerging, it comes and goes, flickering behind the clouds, hesitant, it seems, to light the day.

Pearline carries the stories Irene wanted to tell her children all these years. Josette carries Annie's letters. Derek carries Rupert's hat. They're in the car with Aileen and Hermina, but they're mostly quiet. Hermina drives. She's a less timid driver than Aileen, but she prefers not to talk when she's behind the wheel.

Pearline feels a calmness that she hasn't felt in a long time. She looks out at the water and hears nothing—no stories, no partial dreams, not her father's voice nor that of her mother. She thinks of nothing other than how the shades of blue vary from turquoise to blue-black, how the white froth of waves looks like a splash of milk-white paint. The waves have a rhythm of their own, impossible to catch and time.

"I wish . . ." Aileen begins to say.

"Never mind." Pearline pats Aileen's thigh. "Next time."

"You really think you going to find them?"

"If not this time, another trip. I won't stop looking. Papa won't let me sleep, and you know I like my sleep."

"You telling me," Hermina says.

Derek takes a quick look back, catching Pearline's eye. But neither says anything, and Pearline quickly looks away, ignoring Josette's raised eyebrows questioning what secret her mother and cousin hold.

They're already near Montego Bay, the airport runway visible now, when Aileen asks Josette, "What about your job?"

"We work that out," Josette says. Her tone is almost dismissive.

"She know better than to let her old mother go alone," Pearline says. She's only half joking, because what she really means is that her sisters would have let her go alone, and telling Aileen "next time" was purely superficial. But she's also protecting Josette from Aileen's scrutiny, the teacher's urge to probe and redirect.

Pearline hasn't worked out exactly why Josette chose to come, except perhaps that she's afraid Derek will replace her. But she knows why she wanted her there. The way Pearline looks at it, this trip is a map for lost lives—Josette's and Derek's and her siblings in Cuba—and a way for Josette to find her way back to the visual stories she wants to tell. She wants it to be similar for Derek, for him to pick up where Arturo left off.

She comes back to one thing: With all the trouble, Rupert never talked of regret. Irene did, but Rupert believed in himself to the very end. He could have died of malaria or the Spanish flu, could have been killed by rural guards in 1917. Still he held on, digging in tightly to prove to himself and Irene and his family that he would not fail. And still he failed.

The more Pearline thinks, the clearer her sisters' fears become. This dream of Rupert's that she is chasing isn't his dream necessarily, but someone else's, something he was taught to believe. Rupert's dream emerged in the shadow of wanderers who sought their fortunes in other lands, destroying what they found, remaking cultures and peoples. The longer she looks, the more she sees it, this albatross that could spell her death. And yet, there's something life-affirming and hopeful in her quest and in the possibility that Derek and Josette could break with Rupert's legacy of failure and still carry on the idea of his dream.

"And your girls?"

"They have a father too," Josette says. She hesitates for a moment, then adds, "And their grandmother and aunties helping him. They're all right." Then, more forcefully, she says, "They will be all right for another week without me."

Soon they're at the airport, a gaggle of arms hugging and waving and patting.

"Walk good," Aileen says, and Hermina nods and whispers the same.

Pearline is a few steps away from the security guard when she turns around and walks back toward Hermina and Aileen.

"This trip meant a lot to Papa. And you can imagine what Mama would do if she got the chance to do this. And the house meant just as much. Just imagine, coming back from Cuba and owning a little piece of the property that your ancestors used to work on. Imagine owning a piece of the property your ancestors said wasn't yours, couldn't be yours 'cause you didn't look like them. Just imagine it." Pearline looks down, blinking away tears. She wants to say more, to implore her sisters not to do anything with the house in her absence. She doesn't know what else to say.

"Mine you miss you' plane," Aileen says.

Hermina leans in to Pearline, whispers, "Hurry up and come back and tell Papa so he can stop haunting me."

Pearline nods. What she has said is enough. She doesn't look back at her sisters, but she imagines them staring at her as she makes her way through security, looking long after she's no longer visible, both of them sober and pensive.

On the plane, Pearline looks down at the island below her dwindling to nothing, the buildings that become mere specks of color, the vegetation that merges into a single blob of green, the blue-green sea that shimmers and ripples. She's more nervous than she expected, and she closes her eyes, leans back, imagining her mother or father on this trip, going back to the island they left so long ago on a schooner called *Rapido*.

The plane touches down with a single jolt, and someone in the back claps tentatively. People stir again, their movement like the sudden release of pent-up breath. It's fitting, Pearline thinks, that they arrive at night; for this is a trip that will put some ghosts to rest and awaken others. Havana is struggling and drowning in its crumbling memories. Cuba has held on to its network of sixty-year-old American cars. The cars belch black fumes in utter defiance of the end of life, while cars of a similar age in other countries are rusting on concrete blocks within forests of overgrown grass. Fortresses and castles, some three hundred or more years old, look down upon the city as if still prepared for battle. Pearline wants to believe that the old and the new coexisting means her siblings' lives have been preserved, whether all three or one or two. Sixty years later, who have her long-lost sister and brothers become?

The desk clerk says, "Jamaica, no?"

"*Sí,*" Pearline says and looks to Josette, for she's still hesitant about speaking in public.

The clerk pauses, then says his grandparents were Jamaicans too.

"Really. Do you know where in Jamaica they were from?"

"*No sé,*" he says. "Long time . . ." He falters, unable to complete his sentence in English. "My mother was baby." He cradles his arms, looks up, and smiles. "*Mi madre no sabe.*"

Pearline wants to tell him something comforting, but they're in the same position, both of them with unknown family separated by a sea. She taps Josette's arm. "Tell him," she says. When Josette doesn't, Pearline says, "I was born in Banes. I left when I was a baby." She too cradles her arms.

But the clerk shakes his head. He doesn't understand what Pearline says. Pearline uses her fingers, taps her chest, mimics rocking a baby, then says, "Cuba." The man smiles. Perhaps he understands, Pearline thinks. She wants to say more but finds she doesn't know how to mime parents or siblings, how to say what brings her here, and gives up trying to translate her family's story to a stranger.

"This is what Papa was waiting for," Pearline says as they walk away. "We can't waste time."

Pearline steps out on the balcony and looks across the city lit up at night. She holds up her father's photo. He squints at the camera, his chin up and his glasses askew. Pearline is standing behind him. She is youthful and fresh-faced, a version of herself she barely remembers. Although she holds Rupert's photo, it is Arturo she thinks about—the boy destined to live an extraordinary life. The last time she saw him, she was three, and perhaps because of it, the anxiety, the tension, the fear, the frantic footsteps are all tattooed in her memory. It's the memory she has been holding at bay, pausing it and replaying the moments around it on repeat, the moment that made Irene say, "Not another one. This country will not take another one of my children."

In the morning, the desk clerk points the way to the seawall, Old Havana, and the ports. Derek and Josette get ready to move on to Banes to find the little yellow house, but Pearline says, "No, I want to see every bit of this city. Even if it take me all day or all week, I'm going to see everything."

They walk around the narrow streets of Old Havana, circling and circling to find the Havana address that at one time belonged to Annie. A truck backs onto a narrow street, its wheels crunching on cobblestones and the sides of the tanker threatening to brush the walls of the buildings. One after another, people come carrying plastic jugs in their hands or strapped on bicycles, and others haul water up to rooms above the ground with makeshift pulleys. The buildings are mostly old and crumbling, except, of course, in the sections of Old Havana where tourists sleep and eat and wander and where the courtyards are like any true Spanish village—the horses' hooves clop on the cobblestones, and the elegant mansions that once belonged to the city's wealthy now house museums.

This is where Annie came, this city on the other end of the island, far away from Banes. Perhaps she, too, wanted to shed generational burdens, start fresh without the trappings of parents and their history weighing her down. They don't find the address, and when the sun gets too hot and Pearline tires, they head back to the hotel. Derek points to the desk clerk they met the previous night.

"Excusame," Josette says. *"Puedes ayudarme?"* She slides the paper across the counter.

The clerk nods and draws out a map that shows the address in the opposite direction in which they had gone.

"Gracias."

"Tomorrow," Derek says.

But Pearline won't wait. She points to the seawall. She wants to look out to sea. She misses the voices, and she wants to catch them. The seawall is old and crumbling in places, the rocks behind it jagged and dangerous, and the sea beyond the rocks looks black rather than the Caribbean blue Pearline knows. In the distance, a castle overlooks the sea, and it is there she thinks the canons blast each night at nine.

Again the voices come, carried above the writhing waves. It is a single voice, stronger now, and she thinks of it as Arturo's, the pitch permanently caught in the range between a boy's high pitch and man's deep bass. Something wet, thicker than water, circles her hand, oozes between her palm and the *malecón*'s aging concrete wall. Blood? Mud? Wet sand? But there is nothing except for the solid concrete wall and her imagination. Night is coming quickly. The voice still comes. It doesn't pause, and then she thinks the voice is waiting for her to tell it something. She throws her voice to the sea to let the wind pick it up and carry it where it will. "Papa remembered you at the very end."

This is the first thing she tells Arturo, accepting fully and completely her role as the one who holds the family's memory. There is a moment of stillness, and the voice rests. A breeze stirs the water, causes the waves to lap against the rock, and the voice rises again. This is the story all his children wanted to hear, that they were remembered at the very end. There's more to tell, but how do you condense sixty years?

On the second day, they follow the desk clerk's map to a building Pearline thinks could have been the one where Annie lived. On the way, they cut through La Colina, the home of the Universidad de la Habana. There's a tour guide with a group of tourists. He says Rupert's word *jagüe* and points to a line of trees. "The *jagüe* tree is also known as the tree of a thousand feet or the tree that walks," he says in halting English.

Pearline pauses, steps closer to hear what more the tour guide has to say. Up close, the tree looks like it has countless feet branching out from the trunk and boring down into the ground.

"The trees," the guide says, "begin as a parasite on another tree. The parasite sends shoots to the ground. The new roots grow and eventually choke the parent tree." He brings his hands up, circles his neck, mimes a choke. "The new tree is now composed of numerous stems and vines."

When Rupert said *la casa del jagüé*, he may have been referring to his children solidly at home in the land of their birth, the country he tried to but couldn't adopt. Or he may have meant these trees are rooted, steadfast, and strong. The trees borrow and burrow to make their own roots. And this makes Pearline think Annie and David and Gerardo may not have strayed far from Banes and its community of people transplanted from the English-speaking Caribbean or the little house with the red floor she remembers. She tells herself that like the tree, Annie and David and Gerardo have made Banes their own and waited there to be found. She wants that to be true. She wants to be on her way to Banes.

They walk along the *malecón*, circling back to the old address for Annie. Josette practices what she'll say, perfecting the question. The building, massive, no longer a bright white, stands tall—a testament to its once glorious past. Three floors up, there's a woman hanging out of a window. She waves a little and pulls back, aware now that she mistook the three for someone else.

"*Hola,*" Josette calls.

She leans a little farther out, squinting in the sun. The woman could be Josette's age, maybe a few years older. Her skin is as richly brown as Pearline's, and her hair a mop of soft, unruly curls.

"*Una pregunta. Hablas inglés?*"

"*Un poco.*"

"*Por favor.*" Pearline holds up the old picture of her family and a more recent picture of her sisters. "*Una pregunta, por favor.*"

"*Un momento. Espere.*"

It takes Pearline a moment to realize the woman said *wait.* Her heart beats a little faster. She imagines marble stairs, the stranger running to greet them, her slippers clomping on the floor, the words she wants to hear pouring out of the woman's mouth. She's ready to go to Banes to see the little yellow house that has not left her memory, the children who did not leave her father's memory. And she knows now that her father wants her to right his wrongs.

As Pearline waits for the woman to emerge in the doorway, she turns in the direction of the sea and whispers the beginning of their story to Rupert and Irene. She's speaking mostly to Rupert. Six months have passed since she buried him, but this moment feels like she's putting him in the ground again and giving him permission to rest.

The photo of this moment doesn't exist yet. Josette will document it with the camera she carries like a crutch. Derek will paint it, both the house from Pearline's memory with the red floor and the house as it is now with cracks in the foundation, wet sheets thwacking as the wind blows them up and about, and an old man standing on the steps looking out with his hand above his brow. He will paint another of the man walking down the steps. Josette will photograph the man with his hands stretched out and his mouth open to say, "Long time."

And she will capture his arms shaking as he embraces Pearline, his hand pointing in the direction where Annie and David live. Pearline will bury it all in her memory, grateful that her siblings haven't strayed far from Banes.

"I am your memory," Pearline tells her father. "Gerardo keeps watch over the little house in Banes. He's named it *La Casa del Jagüé*, after the tree with a thousand feet. I am your memory. Go on and take your rest."

ACKNOWLEDGMENTS

The House of Plain Truth would not be possible without the support of many.

Thanks to the entire Zibby Books team: Zibby Owens and Leigh Newman for believing in the manuscript and taking it on; Jeanne McCulloch for guiding me through thoughtful edits; Kathleen Harris for shepherding the book through the final stages; and Graça Tito for bringing the cover to life. Though I can't name everyone, cheers to the entire team.

Thanks to my agent, Sha-Shana Crichton, for finding a home for the book.

A big thank-you to the organizations that supported my work through fellowships and space and time to write, especially Black Mountain Institute at the University of Nevada, Las Vegas, which awarded me a fellowship to write the novel. The first draft I completed during that year in the desert is the foundation upon which this current book sits. Thanks to Hedgebrook and the Virginia Center for the Creative Arts for providing space and time to write and revise.

I owe many thanks to the writer friends who read drafts of the manuscript in the early stages: Stephanie Allen, Karen Outen, Doreen Baingana, and Angel Threatt. Your encouragement and thoughtful critiques paved the way for the book you're holding today. Thanks also to Carole Burns, who read a later draft.

And as always, thanks to my family—my sisters, Calaine and Judy; my father, Charles; and late mom, Norma—and the friends who answer random questions about culture and their experiences and memories without always knowing why.

ABOUT THE AUTHOR

Donna Hemans is the author of two previous novels, *River Woman* and *Tea by the Sea*, which won the Lignum Vitae Una Marson Award. Her short fiction and essays have appeared in *Electric Literature, Ms. Magazine,* and *Crab Orchard Review*, among others. She is also the owner of DC Writers Room, a coworking studio for writers based in Washington, DC. Born in Jamaica, she lives in Maryland and received her undergraduate degree in English and Media Studies from Fordham University and an MFA from American University.

@donna_hemans
www.donnahemans.com